KAITLYN LANSING

A Man of Action

First published by Lansing Press 2022

First edition

ISBN: 979-8-9866719-5-6

This book was professionally typeset on Reedsy.
Find out more at reedsy.com

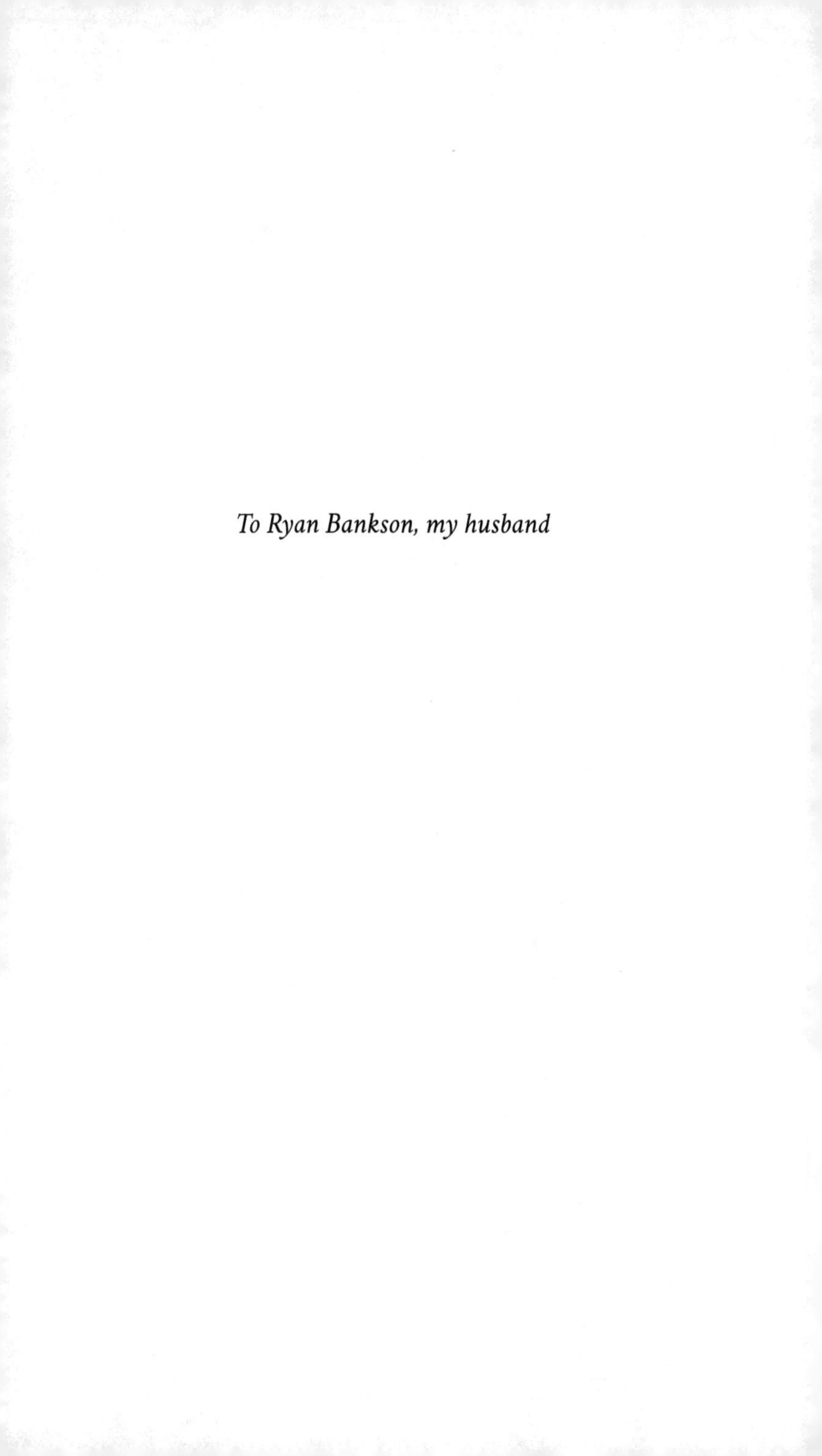

To Ryan Bankson, my husband

Contents

I

PART ONE

CHAPTER I

"Congratulations! Family and friends, it is my honor to introduce to you: Mr. and Mrs. Fleischer."

And that was it: the rings were exchanged, the kisses were given, the husband eternally intertwined with the wife. A new chapter began for the happy couple, Conrad and Elizabeth Fleischer, who both now bore the unfortunate last name of "butcher" in German.

Perhaps the name though was apt, thought Elizabeth, as she had butchered her relationship with her last husband and Conrad was a butcher of people—criminals, to be more precise.

Sitting around the dining room table enjoying the bits and bobs going around after their wedding, she could not help dwelling on how much harder it was to worship a man than it was a god. A god, she thought, says nothing in return and remains ever-present in your mind but never physically close. A man is a fleeting creature who gets as physically close to you as possible and then leaves—whether it is to work, play, or abandon ship.

Exactly three years ago, Elizabeth woke up one morning in her house to find that her love had gone. The rooms were bereft of his things and she figured he had discovered her inventory of male things: boxers, kissing pictures, promise rings, just stuff belonging to dead times and might-as-well-be-dead people. Still, he was not her first.

It appeared that life was too long, according to Elizabeth. If Romeo and Juliet had lived longer rather than died with their pure love, then they probably would have ended up in divorce court. Life was long enough to fall in and out of love—to be overwhelmed with new love, only to fall out of love within the same season. Living was all about movement and change, and certainly, nothing in her life stayed static.

Needless to say, Elizabeth had a cynical view of love by the time her first husband got away in the summer, which gave her the entire gloomy winter to think about what was next for her. She often fell upon bad news when people could be the most mobile. The warmer months were real times of change, not the New Year. She always felt apprehensive around June, July, and August for that reason. People moved, picked up, left, switched, carried on during those months.

But all she wanted was stability. Elizabeth, with her black hair and blacker eyes against her ghostly skin, wanted a hole to crawl in and never leave again. The term homebody was made for her.

When she slept in her bed at night, the only way she could fall asleep was curled up into a tiny, skeletal ball, just big enough to fill the hole she wished to hibernate in.

She had dreams about one day living in a castle, which gave her enough unique spaces to hide in, but they were all completely under her control. The area she was left in had plenty of Queen Anne-styled houses that were built in the late nineteenth into the early twentieth century in America.

However, her next romantic prey was not seen living in such

a lovely house. She spotted him leaving his small, modern house one morning to go for a jog. Elizabeth was walking on her way to work when she spotted him closing his front gate. It had black spikes as high as a six-foot-tall man, much like himself. They were imposing and the front of the gate bore his surname: Fleischer.

At the time, she never knew the meaning of his last name. All that drew her in was this handsome man with his brown hair and browner eyes and his frightening gate. She turned around once more after she had passed him on the sidewalk and glanced at the muscles working underneath his tanned flesh. They moved underneath like pulleys in a factory.

In her agitation, Elizabeth desired to catch this new man and became determined to keep him at all costs.

***

Their wedding came shortly thereafter and today was meant to be the happiest day of her life...again. But determined to make this one last, she stopped any and all connection to her previous boyfriends and other play things, threw away all her boxes of things, mementos of earlier times and sexier moments, in order to come to him as clean as the day she was born.

In this day and age, it was not difficult to wash yourself clean of past wrongdoings. All a person had to do was audit their paper trails and digital accounts for any and all moments of ecstasy, for nothing made a person more jealous than a stranger who is only seeing a part of the whole. Everybody was out to get Elizabeth for her beauty and scandalous behavior. The best thing for her to do was to hide, hide in this Queen Anne house, and wait for the apocalypse.

In fact, that is something that brought this powder keg of a couple together. They were both rather misanthropic types with a desire to maintain their hypochondriac ways. They loathed most people—not those that were morally good, but certainly those that were bad or felt that they were somewhere in between.

In the Fleischers' utopia, everyone would behave toward each other with the utmost respect and formality. Etiquette would be taught in all schools, and children would be treated like little adults in many ways. The only violence to break out was when someone violated another Man's rights. The justice would come in swiftly and all peace restored. Otherwise, to each his own and money was earned with an honest day's worth of work. Society would run on civility and honesty, with little help needed from the courts, the police, or the military.

Unfortunately, the Fleischers knew they were surrounded by people who did not act civilly or earn their money fairly, while the corrective action was marred by red tape and bureaucratic rules that put an end to swift justice.

Governments grew larger as justice grew scarcer and the Fleischers watched the world crumble before them both. Having no power within society, the two joined forces and essentially barricaded themselves inside their own Queen Anne-style house, which they lovingly referred to as "the manor." The house, to them, felt like another person, one who did not lack the refinement and good taste that their neighbors' houses did. It stood tall, built in 1885, acting just as haughty as if it was built yesterday, though some of the shingles had rotted away and the paint in the attic was peeling and the animals had had several generations come and go from its drafty crevices.

The style of the house was named after Queen Anne's reign

on the English throne from 1837 until 1901, the end of the Victorian era in Europe and abroad. It included all the "gingerbread" trimmings and pinnacles and bits and pieces of stained glass windows with serial balconies and peaked gables and dormers and rococo traceries that caught outsiders' eyes as they passed by. All these parts came together to create an intricately imposing outside, which at the same time promised just as sophisticated and elegant an inside.

The style originally was meant to echo the medieval English homes and the spikiness of the manor did reflect the macabre. The architects of the time to bring this style to America were seeking to defy the industrialized world and bring back the detailed, handcrafted work of the medieval era. The house exuded a kind of romantic and gothic feel, though Elizabeth and Conrad believed it to be much too close to other houses.

Over time, and as the town grew, the suburban portion of the area was filled up with more and more houses, so many, in fact, that they nearly looked built on top of each other. The best ones overlooked the town's bluffs and had enough space in between to forget one even lived next to other human beings. But this was not where the Fleischers' residence was. They found themselves in this decade surrounded by neighbors with hardly *any* room to walk outside at all, save for a little side yard that Elizabeth planned to grow vegetables and flowers in next spring.

The asymmetrical form of the manor led most people to believe that the small family inside of it was as strange in their behaviors and tastes—which was not wrong. The newly married couple planned to have children eventually. They even went out to purchase a small wooden rocking horse to put in one of the guest rooms that would later become a nursery for their first child.

However, children were not on their minds at the moment. Currently, they desired to see the world crumble already so that they could start anew. Oftentimes at night, they lay beside each other and talked of ways to burn down the neighbors' houses without getting caught or mailing their drug-addicted teenagers more illicit drugs before calling the police on them or scaring them all into leaving by robbing their houses in the middle of the night. There were so many ways to get rid of those they did not want around.

The house itself inspired ideas between them too, for it had little hidden rooms and outdated servants' quarters throughout the house. The basement, built out of limestone and black as pitch, easily resembled a dungeon in a medieval setting. Many times Elizabeth found Conrad down in the bowels of the house, inspecting parts of the stone and feeling around the dirt for various chains and ashes from old fires of long ago. The chimney had since been left cold until they bought the house about a month earlier. Conrad cleaned it out and warmed the hearth once again. His tasks were mostly house repairs, trash disposal, and all things financial.

The woman's work around the house involved cleaning, cooking, and sewing. Elizabeth did such things with rigor and grace. Though since her previous role as wife, she had been trying to learn how to be one all over again with a different spouse. One day as she was dusting away the ever-present cobwebs, she said to Conrad: "Look at this spider! He must be the 'crazy uncle' of the bunch, sitting out here vulnerable, visible to every passerby." She looked up at Conrad, who was watching behind her, hoping to elicit a reaction like her previous husband did when she said such things, but he said nothing. Elizabeth was devastated.

She had no inner jokes yet, like lovers usually do, and it was so difficult to make Conrad smile. But at the same time, she was surprised that the "crazy uncle" joke even erupted out of her, as if she expected him to read her mind! She thought herself a silly fool for testing him in such an unfair manner and she focused her hurt on the spider who produced nothing but pain in her soul. Taking a tissue that lay beside her, she grabbed the lone spider and made sure to squish the life out of it in her hand. The black blob, which subsequently soaked through the tissue, was visible to them both. Conrad only nodded his approval and turned to leave.

Elizabeth was alone then with her anger, still feeling unsatisfied with smiting the tiny life given to her. So, she rose and put the anger into her cleaning. She dusted without a light touch, nearly knocking over every precious porcelain vase they owned in the process. And then she vacuumed while humming sea shanties about dead lovers and cold bones that were masked by the roar of the machine. She made sure to suck up every living thing in that house that she considered uninvited.

Their aggressive behavior defined their property. Neither of them wanted gawkers or people investigating for themselves in the old, haunted-looking manor, especially when Halloween was about to come round again. The Fleischers swiftly annihilated anything that got inside.

The bugs and the bats and the rats were all executed, stomped on, and generally exterminated by poisons and other manners of brute force. The manner of her cleaning could only be termed cruel. As Elizabeth finished off her victims, she cleaned the mottled-looking, artificial plants that were strewn around the rooms: some were long vines of English ivy while others were black roses or real dried flowers that might as well have been fake. The dust fell to the floor, rendering her vacuuming somewhat pointless. She promised herself to get to it next month if their socks did not already pick it all up.

***

The couple got married right at the beginning of October when the leaves were on fire. The Queen Anne-styled house mimicked the autumnal world outside with its use of only golden yellows and reds and oranges and browns and greens. None of the exterior paint included blues or grays or anything too vibrant. They were the colors of fire. Their house looked the best in the sunset hours of the fall, as the leaves fell silently to the ground.

There was some terra-cotta ornamentation done right under the front roof and many of the bricks and their mortars were of the same dark red hue. Burgundy was used as a highlight color for many of the accent pieces on the house. Needless to say, the couple's favorite color was burgundy, dark red, crimson, anything akin to blood.

The interior was filled with tiles on the floor in the kitchen and bathrooms and along the edges of the fireplace, while old wooden boards stretched alongside the entire first, second, and attic floors. However, the basement was all made of limestone. Every room included a unique, usually floral-patterned wallpaper, the bathtubs featured claws, and the stairwells were etched with acanthus leaves. The manor could occupy a man for days with all of its details. And that is what made the Fleischers never want to leave.

Rather ironically, the first architects of the Queen Anne style who had wanted to go back to the handcrafted days before industrialization in their designs were actually brought to their golden years by industrialization itself. For the decorative tiles became industrialized, and they became much cheaper to use to create more beautiful Queen Anne homes in America. The woodwork, too, was created by machines and that made it much faster to put up houses with balloon framing. Better ways to create larger panes of glass with fewer impurities led to the creation of larger windows, allowing much more light inside the often dark living quarters of the manor. New innovations like the gas stove and cold and hot water faucets and central heating and cooling and improved hardware all contributed to the more modern home that needed less maintenance and overall work and provided more comfort to its owners.

The manor was beloved for all those reasons by the new couple. They could have the historical beauty with the modern appliances. To their surprise, on the rare occasion that they did invite guests over, there were still people who complained of not having a fan installed in the bathrooms to hide their vulgar sounds and odors. Or there were others who wanted the wallpaper ripped off and some "brighter" paint colors used on the walls. Needless to say, those guests were never invited back again. For Conrad and Elizabeth, nothing needed changing in their manor. Everything was absolutely perfect.

The fact that the house had character and offended some modernist types made it even lovelier to them. Other people could just avoid the manor entirely, and they could not care less. Of course, there were always tittering, fat, old women walking in gaggles and chatting about inane things while their husbands all walked quietly behind them, quietly observing the world. The old women would shriek and squeal upon seeing such a frightening house, while the men would scratch their heads and think up various explanations about the state it was in. Silly women ramble through life without truly worshiping and tending to their husbands in a noble, respectful, and caring way, thought Elizabeth, as she peered out of the upstairs window. She held the lace curtain open to observe their husbands walk behind their women silently and, perhaps, stoically—though having chosen such women was a mistake.

Elizabeth let the curtain fall and turned back toward her husband. He always provided her with the next domestic task, which she was craving right now…or maybe she just wanted an excuse to stop thinking about those detestable women. If only she could cuckold them, using their husbands for her pleasure while she forced their wives to watch…then maybe they would finally go silent. Elizabeth smiled.

Meanwhile, she found Conrad holding out the yellow measuring tape against one of the basement walls.

"What are you up to?" she asked.

"Just measuring these walls for some new furniture I ordered today," he said, continuing to measure and record his numbers down on a scrap of paper.

"Furniture for down here?"

"Yes, darling. Why do you have to ask so many questions?" By his tone, Elizabeth knew to back off. She shook her head and waited for his next move. "Did you finish dusting and vacuuming?"

"Of course, dear."

"Then be of some use and grab me a new pen from upstairs. This one has seemed to have run out."

Conrad stood there shaking the life out of the pen and then

licking the tip, as if trying to excite it into releasing just a bit more ink for his benefit. But none of his tricks worked, and his swearing increased the longer she took. Covering her giggle, Elizabeth took her time approaching her husband with his much-needed pen. He waited until she got near and then snatched at her arm.

"Oh! That's not fair! Stop it!" She struggled to get out of his grasp. Their play fighting happened frequently, and it only served to tie them closer together. For, you see, Elizabeth never really wanted to get away.

Conrad nipped at her ear as he grabbed the pen and wrote down what he had been trying to retain in his mind for the last several minutes that she had been gone, puttering around upstairs.

She waited until he told her to go away, which she took to mean that all the chores for the day were done. Feeling a bit disappointed, Elizabeth decided to try and relax by stepping out onto the porch veranda and sitting on their swing. The porch swing creaked with its rusty chains and dirty cushions, and the icy chill of fall closed in around her throat, causing her to clench her teeth, but she still loved the manor's swing.

The swing gave her something to do with her feet as she rocked herself into a kind of forced relaxation. Elizabeth could *never* relax; she was simply not that type. Relaxation was surely a pathway straight to living the rest of her life attached to the couch and the television that inevitably sat in front of it. No, she refused to become fat and lazy like those tittering old women. Her body must be treated as a temple, and so she acted as such, propelling herself forward on the swing while daydreaming about the apocalypse.

The view from her swing was miserable, however, for there

were houses across the central road and houses to the left and right of her. She was trapped on all sides with a view of what her neighbors were up to constantly, though she would rather not know of their very existence. But there went her neighbor directly across from her with his socks in his sandals and his shorts too high up and his glasses much too prominent on his face, watering his flowers before they died at the first frost. And to her right, those neighbors comprised an entire family—from the youngest to the oldest—all taking a smoke break on their front porch.

The previous owner of the house said that the houses built so close to ours used to be the servants' quarters and, as they were small and less opulent than their own home, it seemed fitting that a group of criminals lived there now. Elizabeth turned her attention to the left of her, where the neighbors were all morbidly obese and would surely never starve for the winter as they could hide extra nuts beneath their double chins and solely live off their fat for a good season or two.

In her sudden distaste for "the outdoors," Elizabeth made her way back inside, slipping in as quietly as a phantom in the night. Conrad was nowhere to be seen yet again, and the daylight was quickly fading away earlier and earlier as the fall grew older and older. She turned the candelabra on, which was wired through the main post of the stairwell. Each bulb was shaped like a flame, reminiscent of the ordeal the previous owners had to contend with by burning beeswax candles that they typically hand-poured to make their own sticks. The ancestors of this manor also lived on the old iron furnaces with a coal area in the basement used to provide heat all over the house. The woman of the house and her servants always had to clean up the coal and make the candles for the house to keep running smoothly…and Elizabeth did not even want to consider dealing with chamber pots. All in all, her duties were mild and relatively clean tasks, unless the mice or bats decided to make a home for themselves in the manor.

There was one night a bat squeezed itself in between the ceiling trim and the water pipe fixture going up through the wall. In horror, Elizabeth watched as the bat made itself smaller and smaller in order to get into the house. There was a terrible storm outside, which must have scared it. Without sparing her a moment to think, the bat flew in disoriented and crashed into one of the walls, only to fly right over Elizabeth's tucked-under head, her screams reaching Conrad's ears just in time for him to see the bat flying around in terror.

Grabbing a beater for clothing and rugs off the wall, wrapping his shirt around the outer rims, thereby creating a sort of net, he swung after the bat. He missed the first few times until he caught it on its way up to the trim of the parlor, where it wanted to hang for the night. But the bat got caught in Conrad's net and as he brought the net down to the ground he yelled, "Get my machete from the wall!" Elizabeth was too frightened not to obey, though she felt awful already for what he was about to do next.

With the bat still trapped underneath the net against the floor and Conrad's other hand wielding the machete, he began hacking the bat to pieces. Elizabeth had never heard a bat scream before, but it rang in her ears long after the screams had ceased to exist. In the dark glow of the sunset, the room cast in red, the couple could both see Conrad's shirt soaking up the stain that was growing rapidly.

Lifting up the makeshift net, Conrad carried the deceased bat out to the trash and threw the corpse away without a second thought. The threat had been eliminated. Wiping his hands clean and the floor that was now stained red, Conrad lay back down on the couch to enjoy the rest of his evening in peace, while Elizabeth tried to drown out the screams with a bit of liquor from the dining room cabinet.

By the next morning, the red stains on the wood were still there. Elizabeth knew her task was to find a way to get them out of the wood. She poured salt down over them to allow the blood to get soaked up from the grain. This helped tremendously, but she still felt like a splotchy shadow was there. Though asking Conrad about it, he disagreed. "The stains are gone!" he declared. "Well done, wife." And with a tap on the behind, he went off to go do what men are called to do—work on their "personal projects" in their own self-declared caves.

CHAPTER II

The floor stains never disappeared for Elizabeth, but like many things in the manor, they stopped attracting her attention after a while. After all, a Queen Anne-styled house was made to distract and attract its owners and guests. The entire interior had intricate wallpaper and stained glass and China and pictures hanging everywhere and turned wood and more elaborate engraving all over the place. It was a house stuffed to the roof with handcrafted beauty in any and all forms.

The manor had its own literary flair as well, with motifs spaced out around the entire interior. Upon first moving in, Elizabeth took note of the three dominant images that kept cropping up.

The carved shell motif was on many of the faceplates behind the doorknobs or in the metalwork of tiny shelves or on the staircase posts or other chairs scattered around the place. The history of the shell dates all the way back to the Greco-Roman times as a representative of the goddess Aphrodite, who ruled over beauty and love. The shell itself signified fertility. When Elizabeth discovered this tidbit in a book she found in their library, she smiled a crooked sort of smile. For children were not wished for just yet in this place, though she was happy to have the sentiment and reminder labeled all over the house.

The ball and claw design on the bottom of each of the bathtubs were all transformed from a dragon's claw to a lion's paw. Meaning that the idea originally came from the Chinese image of a dragon guarding its treasure—a crystal ball or a pearl or some sort of precious jewel. But when the English furniture makers caught on to the idea, they changed the dragon into a lion to represent England more easily. Still, the overall idea represents the guarding of treasure or even wisdom or purity from outside forces. This manor was certainly guarded furiously by its new owners. The couple would flay anyone who trespassed alive and feed their own flesh back to them.

The final motif here was the acanthus leaf and the scrolls carved around it. They were also found on the doorknobs and their faceplates, in metalwork around many of the mirrors, on the posts of the stairwell, and on several pieces of furniture too. The motif also dates back to the ancient Greeks since it was a plant found in the Mediterranean. It was a thistle-like type of plant, which the ancients used on their columns for many of their important public buildings. Throughout the ages, the acanthus leaf motif symbolized immortality, or at least the immortality of the soul. Elizabeth chose to see these plants as symbolic of her and Conrad never leaving this manor since they would be immortal in both body and spirit as long as modern medicine kept up with them. They both had decided that this was their home forever and there would be no new owners "after them." This symbol was truly her favorite as well as Conrad's for its meaning was one they would sign a deal with the devil for—anything to keep what they had gained.

The Queen Anne-styled house was truly representative

though of the Fleischers. Their desires for fertility and guarding what was theirs and immortality itself were palpable in the way they interacted with the outside world. It was certainly the life of two people who had a deeply personal, private domestic sphere and a skeptical, reluctant public sphere. They only ventured out into the outside sphere out of necessity, like for new identification cards or vital records or groceries or banking.

Both the lord and lady of the manor looked in confusion at people who would invite them on camping trips or out to the movies or travel to a place that was not their own stately home. For why on earth would they want to be anywhere other than their paradise? Where all the amenities are taken care of and what they found beautiful was already inside their own four walls?

People would always push back with "Oh, but what about making memories" and all the "experiences" you can get from going out. By then, they were both in their thirties and set in their ways. The Fleischers had seen enough of the outside world by now to know that no place was like home—their *own* home.

What could be better than a manor full of symbols they valued and ancient trinkets that they had each collected over their lives? What place could ring more true to their souls than a manor full of their own skin particles and fallen hair and dirt carried in from their yard?

No, thought the couple, there was nowhere else they would rather be than in their own home. Sure, they could view images of other manors and castles and cathedrals from around the world. They enjoyed knowing *about* them, but they had absolutely no desire to cram their way through crowds of putrid strangers, all making the same trip to see the same guarded images, to take the same sloppy pictures with them in front of the same places. All so then they could cram themselves in a boat or a plane or a train or a car or whatever mode of transportation was necessary to get them to that select destination. They found there were simply too many people in this world all breathing the same air and running the same race.

But they were different, and they demanded what was different. And if they could not eliminate people from the face of the earth in droves, then they were forced to stay within their property lines and keep everyone else *out*. Their lifestyle mantra was simple—no one else in, no one else out, like a blood-brain barrier. Was the organism still alive? No, but they desired the manor to look dead anyway in order to deter the outside away from the putrid corpse that inside was like the sacred garden.

Elizabeth and Conrad were a team. In this sense, they united together to protect their house. This was their first baby. They did not desire to own a pet together like most newlywed couples, no; they wanted to care for an old manor together. And the manor, though filled with more modern contraptions, still required an exorbitant amount of maintenance. And nowadays, without the common use of servants, Elizabeth was the main cooker, cleaner, and sewer of the entire place.

It was for this reason that her full-time job was at home, while Conrad worked as a contractor of sorts who often brought work home.

***

The two met while Conrad was running about doing his errands—buying various home repair items, like duct tape and trash bags and gallon buckets and other random sharp tools. Elizabeth worked in a library before domestic life called to her. So, on that fateful day, she was walking to work, knowing he would be around, and just happened to walk by him. They both had looked each other up and down, giving one another a pat down with their eyes. They both kept walking but slower, and after being several feet away, they each turned around to stare at the other, nearly missing each other's backward glance.

The next day, Conrad was prepared. He waited in the same spot by his car with a single rose in his hand for the mysterious woman who wore such strange clothes for the modern day. The day before when she passed him, she had on black Chelsea boots that covered up her tiny ankles, her legs were covered by navy blue leggings to keep her warm, and on top was a beautiful jewel-green dress that cinched in at the waist, almost like she was wearing a corset under her clothes. She also wore a royal blue peacoat over the top of her dress to keep her warm, while her black hair draped down her back and swayed in the wind. Whoever she was, she exuded the Gothic and Romantic periods of a time long ago lost to the taste of the modern world.

There she was, walking in the same exact way she did yesterday, and she was hoping to run into him again by the way she smiled upon approaching him.

"Hello, I was hoping you would be in my way again."

"In your way?" He loved a feisty woman.

"That's right. I was just minding my own, walking to work, and there you were utterly distracting."

"I do apologize, but you had much the same effect on me. Your attire is quite...different."

"Old? Outdated? Utterly feminine? Yes, I've heard it all before. Personally, I think it is fitting for a librarian to be in what I wear. Doesn't it exude feminine and educated to you?"

"Well, I'm not sure what to call it, but it certainly got my attention. Here, I thought this would be the right gesture for such an outfit." He handed her the single rose, which was nearly black in its color.

"We're off to a darkly romantic start, aren't we?" she smiled.

"Yes, I suppose we are," he said. "Would you like to join me for a meal tonight?"

"Of course. I get out of work at five. Pick me up?"

"With pleasure."

The two went on about their day until five o'clock when the group of librarians exited the building after all the patrons had gone, and Elizabeth found Conrad standing there beside his vehicle.

"Where are we going to eat?" she asked.

"At my home."

Both stayed quiet with lumps in their throats until he pulled into his garage.

The garage was small and cramped. He had tools strewn all over the place, and there were odd stains on them. Nearly running away from the get-go, Elizabeth took a deep breath and hoped that the inside of the house would not look the same.

The garage door led straight into the house, which was nearly as small as the garage but extremely tidy. For a man living alone, it seemed to do him well enough. He hunted around for all the lamplights he could turn on to fend off the darkness and the two sat down at the dinner table, where he had already prepared a meal of chicken and mashed potatoes and peas, a hearty meal for two.

"This is very good, thank you," she said as she covered her still-chewing mouth. Her manners struck Conrad at once. She looked like a doll who belonged in his domain. She fit the esthetic so well, though a less cramped house would make her appear grander. He knew how grand she was.

"You make this house look much better," he said.

Elizabeth looked up, her eyes ablaze with desire. For she saw a man's space devoid of a woman's touch. The garage, especially, gave her thoughts of invading a wounded animal's space. He might enjoy dominion over his entire property, but *she* knew how to make him happy in it. So she said, "I think you should hunt me and stick me up on the wall like a taxidermic animal."

And in that single sentence, Conrad wanted her.

They spent the rest of the meal chewing in silence, focusing on the chicken breast that lay before them and exactly how taxidermy would work on such a creature. Wiping her mouth gently with a napkin and setting her fork and knife in an X-shape on her plate to signify her being finished, Conrad removed the dishes to the kitchen sink.

She offered to help, and the two stood next to each other, close enough to feel the heat emanating off one another's skin. The water cooled them both down as they played with the bubbles, and Elizabeth giggled in ecstasy.

Cleaning dishes had never been so enjoyable to Conrad, and he wanted an eternity of nights like these where he had a partner doing the grunt work alongside him. Standing there at the sink, his body loomed perfectly over top of hers. She seemed to come straight from his limbs. She was meant to live in the space between his arm and his side. There was no way, he vowed to himself, that she was allowed to escape now.

Meanwhile, she felt his heat, and he was tall, but without being overbearing or enormous compared to her. He held a strength over her that was immensely attractive. All she wanted to do at that moment was to serve him, and well.

They bumped their arms while handing plates to each other and each time felt like a zap to both of their bodies. Neither of them had ever felt so sensitive before this moment. Rather quickly, Elizabeth lost the ability to lift another plate. She had grown weak, zapped of all her electricity, it seemed, as Conrad paused to observe the effect he had over her.

Her knees wobbled and her stomach tightened as much as her breathing. Conrad knew that if he did not act now, then he would lose her interest. Without drying his hands, he caught her before she lost her ability to even stand, and the two of them melded into the other. While Elizabeth grew weaker, Conrad grew strangely stronger. Lifting her up, he threw her over his back like a child and carried her to his bedroom.

***

They never engaged in a kind of soft, sweet lovemaking. Conrad believed that that kind of love only came at the end of a lifetime of being married. No, their sex was crude and loud and rough. Elizabeth was no stranger to sex, but she had never before felt so feminine. She had never melted before and felt complete trust for a man. Nothing in the world could strengthen her at this moment. Not only was she pinned down under his body, but she could not contain the painful pleasure she had to endure, and so she *had* to scream. There was no other option than *to* scream.

Conrad, on the other hand, was also no stranger to the fair lady and her wiles. But he had never before imagined being utterly consumed by her smell and filled with a rageful lust. He felt a need to punish her strongly, punish her for making him feel so much when he did not want to feel so riled up. She deserved to be beaten down with his power, *all of it*. Down, down, *down* he pressed her into the bed, though at times he had images flash in his mind of it being a hard street or, at least, a wooden floor. He thought she deserved no more pleasure for making him so crazy.

They were both combative and dangerous, like feral animals. When he had finished, both lie there breathing in the odor of their own sweat and secretions. Conrad had proven to Elizabeth that they were not nice to each other—that they did not have any desire to be "nice" to each other. They *loved* being cruel, defiant, proving to themselves and each other that they were made of metal and not of soft flesh.

Though Elizabeth loved nothing more than hiding her face away under Conrad's arm. She was strong, but at certain times, she felt weak and utterly dependent on him. His warmth and firm physique made her mad, as she trembled when he got near. Oftentimes, he cornered her and frightened her in the small house, like this entire relationship was a game. In a way, they mated as animals did—often confusedly and instinctually. The female would innocently lay there, looking around, until the male came over and had his way with her and she would bite and fight a bit, but the mating still occurred until they both rolled around in satisfaction by the end.

That was how it was between them, a game of hide and seek. They played this game for months. There were even times when Conrad would appear in the stacks where Elizabeth was reshelving books. Of course, there were too many eyes watching for them to be romantic, but she knew he was there for her and waiting until he could mount her again.

They were mean in their games too. Conrad often came to pick her up, but sometimes the door would be locked or he would drive away when he saw her. There were times when Elizabeth hid behind a tree and made him wait on her at the library for several minutes or she would claw at his back when he had her trapped. Maybe outsiders would call them strange or awful or toxic people, but they were perfectly happy pushing the other one over like a pair of bickering siblings.

Their shenanigans continued for a year until Conrad proposed. He did not get on his knees like the old-fashioned men did, for he thought it looked weak. And he was not a weak man. After all, he chose Elizabeth, and she chose him. They were equals in that respect. Instead, he opened the box in front of her as she sat down to eat dinner with him.

There were no crying tears of joy or screaming from her, just a pure smile that made her eyes nearly close. She beamed. In her quiet joy, she knew she would be kept in his domain, in his sphere, for as long as she lived. She said, "I knew you would do it from the moment you said I looked good in this house."

"You caught me," he said, smiling. "I bought this ring shortly after that night. It has been sitting in my closet collecting dust."

"You are naughty for waiting so long."

"Oh really? Wanting to get married so soon? Do you want my life insurance? My retirement? I'm sorry to tell you it is not enough to last you a lifetime, honey."

Both of them laughed.

And so the couple were engaged that week and moved into the manor within the next month. Having few family or friends, they agreed to have the wedding in the formal parlor of their new home to "christen" it as theirs in this very special manner. They said their "I dos" shortly after moving in.

***

So, the life of the Fleischers began. Elizabeth played the role of the perfect domestic housewife, while Conrad played the role of the perfect masculine provider. Their lives together were new and fresh and everything was exciting. They were like children again, learning about this new sphere of life and living. She read books on the subject, while he worked later hours. The two saw each other for breakfast and dinner, even though Conrad was often in and out of the house all day.

She frequently found him carrying tools in and out, like he was building something in the basement. She ventured down there one day, and Conrad was stacking bricks against the limestone walls.

"What are you doing? You're making the basement smaller by adding all of those bricks!" she whined.

"I need them for work, honey. Now go back upstairs and be a good girl," he said, already covered in brick dust and the soot from the floor.

Elizabeth glowered at him before turning her back and wagging her behind in his face. She slammed the door to the basement for good measure. What on earth was he building down there all day? she wondered. At his previous home, it seemed that most of his work was done in that gross and cramped garage. Shivers ran down her spine as she thought about their new basement looking like his garage did. She thought she must put a stop to this bad habit of working in cramped quarters.

The next day she got the crazy idea to slip into the basement while he was out getting whatever other tools he needed for his job. Waiting until she heard the back door lock, she took out a broom in case he came back and caught her down there. Then she launched down the stairwell and into the gloomy basement.

There were two tiny windows at the top part of the basement, which let in a pitiful amount of light. Thankfully, she also carried a flashlight down with her and she shined it on his bricks. They were all stacked up neatly but not sealed together in any fashion. Perhaps that would come later. Bumping into a cheap, plastic table as she backed away from the bricks, she turned and saw the glint of a sharp object laying on top. It was a set of surgical instruments: the glint of light bounced off a series of scalpels and next to it were forceps and scissors and bone cutters. Elizabeth swallowed hard.

What could he need these materials for if he was building with bricks? It just made no sense. Turning around, back toward the brick wall, she saw on the floor the duct tape she watched him carry in on a previous day. There was a shopping bag on the floor next to that. Gently lifting the drooping bag, she peered into what the bag held and it looked like some kind of vice, rather medieval in its spiky design.

This was truly turning into a house of horrors, she thought, as she took in the room as a whole for a minute, which was covered in cobwebs and was so utterly lacking in light. Plus, due to the manor's size, there were many rooms in the basement, dark corners of which she had never even really seen. She cautiously walked forward, and in the middle of one such room was a single chair. Not a plastic, flimsy chair akin to the table he had his tools on, no, this chair was made of wood and could have been pretty if it had been allowed to live a life upstairs. But for some strange reason, it was placed down here.

It even included the marvelous Queen Anne-styled turned pillars for the arms and the back of the chair was decorated as well with scrollwork. The cushion, though, was thin and worn down from who knows how many hundreds of people sitting on it over the years. The legs ended in a bird's talon clutching hold of another ball. The talons looked sharp and even more threatening than the lion's paws that were on the furniture upstairs. The entire chair looked as strong and rooted as the tree it came from.

Elizabeth wondered where the chair was originally in the house since no one would have left it here to rot in the dark. Conrad must have carried it down here without her noticing when they first moved in. Why would he be keeping secrets from me? she wondered, biting her lip in dismay.

Upon closer inspection of the grand chair, she leaped back and gasped, slapping her own hand over her mouth. There were holes drilled into the gorgeous woodwork of the arms. It was a travesty to ruin such a luxurious item, she thought. But what would he do with holes in the arms? There were two equally large holes in each side of the arm, as if he were going to weave something through them like the back of a corset.

Looking around to and fro, her eyes landed on a pile of thin rope. She reached down for an end piece that was uncoiled and tried sticking it through one of the holes, and it was a perfect fit.

Elizabeth placed the rope back down and backed away. Her head shot up when she heard the garage door open and she fled the scene with her broom and flashlight in hand. Racing upstairs, she managed to close the door just as she heard him jostling the knob. Nothing was more frightening than hearing the doorknob rattle, she thought, as she ran toward the front door.

She could explain her hoarse breath better if she was sweeping up the front porch. After all, the leaves were falling all over it and the squirrels kept hiding nuts in the cushions of the porch chairs. It needed to be cleaned anyway, and after those discoveries, she required some fresh air, as chill as it was.

CHAPTER III

Conrad entered the house with a case of beer and some bags from the hardware store filled with the mortar needed to hold the bricks he had purchased together. He looked around and noticed that the door draft stopper that was usually snug up against the basement door was now slightly slanted. Conrad had gained his keen sense of observation from his mother. Growing up, she always knew when he had moved something in the house. It used to drive him nuts. Because shortly following her observation would come, "Where were you today? How come you threw your math homework in the trash? Why is the toothpaste not where it normally is?" All of these questions paraded around him and forced his hand several times into telling white lies.

Eventually, he became a rather good liar and his mother—though observant—could not imagine that her boy was anything other than an angel. She would do anything for him.

However, when he became an adult and moved out of his childhood home, he thanked his mother for teaching him the skill of observation. For he used it in his work. He honed his skill so well that he could even tell when others were lying by a twitch of the nose or the way the wrinkles around their eyes contracted.

Conrad could smell out a liar and a cheat and a criminal and he used all of his skills to serve as a kind of agent of the law. For his work, his clients paid him handsomely. This money served to pay for their lifestyle and he even had time to pursue his own cases of interest.

However, he required the proper working conditions to do his job so that was his principal task for each day until he could get another contractor. So, carrying his mortar and other items, his eyes moved from the slanted door draft stopper to where he heard the sweeping sounds of his wife outside on the porch. Without questioning her straight away, he descended the steps down to the basement.

She had moved the rope, which means she noticed the chair. She had probably peeked into the bag. Of course, she had seen the bricks and probably his tools on the table. What must she think of me? he wondered. His heart would not allow him to question that right then. He only had so much money saved and time was slipping away. So, he got to slapping the mortar together and on his bricks, building up his wall higher and higher, all around the main part of the basement with a singular path leading to the room segmented off containing the chair. He even constructed a kind of crude vaulted ceiling with cheap wooden planks to help hold up bricks on top of the entire thing. The wood was to help keep the structure from caving in. There was wiggle room between his brick creation and the rest of the rooms of the basement, but Conrad's "office" portion filled up much of it.

It took him a few days straight of working on his brick office. When it was complete, he had added a single door to the front of his creation, which had a deadbolt and normal lock to secure fully the office. However, it was now pitch black, so the next task by the end of the week was to run an electrical cord up to some crude light fixtures that he had placed in the middle of the main basement floor and the segmented-off section.

Finally, he brought all of his tools inside the office: the tape, the rope, the chair, the table, the surgical implements, the bag, and anything else he could think of at the time. Conrad's office was complete by the end of the week.

That weekend, he probed Elizabeth a bit about how she was feeling. He stopped her one night in the kitchen as she was mixing dough for fresh bread.

"Hello, dear," he said, gripping onto her hips. He pulled her near. "How are you this evening?"

She could feel his smile on the back of her neck. But she always hated being bothered while she was cooking, so she shook him off and told him, "Oh, not right now, dear."

Conrad stood staring at the floor, dejected. He could feel her pulling away for the first time, and it enraged him.

He moved back closer behind her. "Just ignore me then. I'll just stand here like a kitchen ghost watching you. For, you see, I was killed by a mean, old wretch in the kitchen when I was a young man and must stay trapped in this very room for all eternity."

"That's very romantic, love."

He screwed up his face, as if truly shocked that what she garnered from that tale was anything like romance. But inside, he had his answer.

"Can you pass me the salt at least, Romeo?" she asked.

"Of course, my Juliet." He picked up the salt more delicately than he had ever touched her and handed it over, careful not to spill any onto the countertop.

So there the couple stood, newly married and already set

in their own ways within the home. Could either of them imagine being in the same exact way forever? Would the fire between Romeo and Juliet ever have lasted once they were married and put in a home together? Or would they suck each other dry of joy or require newer and stranger ways of maintaining their lustful passions? Unfortunately, there was no play about that, and the two had to tread into uncharted waters.

Conrad gritted his teeth, as he controlled a barrage of images flashing before his mind's eye of taking a chef's knife right out of the holder and chopping off her dainty little fingers. He loved her so much. Such evil thoughts should never penetrate his mind, he thought, as he moved away from her and scurried down into the depths of the basement "office."

***

Smacking his head, he had learned as a child that his mother had given him another delightful gift, a disease of the mind. Yes, her side of the family was filled with mentally sick individuals from descendant to descendant. Conrad was given the same sick mind that functioned perhaps too well since it gave him images he did not want to see and thoughts he did not want to have…at least not about the ones he loved the most.

He remembered walking home from school one day and envisioning opening the door to his house, as he always did, to find his mother hanging there, lifeless. He had this frightening thought for days and days on end, but he told no one until one afternoon his mother was in the kitchen and she caught him looking so pale as he walked in that she inquired as to what was wrong.

"Nothing, I'm fine," he said, starting to scrunch up his face in sorrow.

"My goodness, boy, what's wrong?" she pleaded.

"I...I...please don't send me away, Mama!" he said, clinging to her apron and vowing to never let go.

She guessed it from that sentence. He had thoughts that were so horrible they could never be said aloud. Otherwise, he must think doctors would take him away to study. His mother had her bouts of it and she had seen her family ravaged by the thoughts and images too.

She bent down slightly and held her boy's head hard. She kissed him and said, "You are not alone, my dear. Your whole family has the disease. It's a disease of the mind, but you will live and, eventually, learn to live with it just like mommy."

Conrad would never forget feeling normal again for just one moment when he realized he was not the first nor the last person to have dreadful thoughts of things that were dark and scary. He gulped down his tears and for a while, he even stopped having those horrible thoughts about his mother.

Today, though, they were still as present as ever. As he grew up, he learned to ignore them—to cope with them. But he knew that his character and personality and the decisions he kept making were irrevocably intertwined with the way his mind worked, the images that kept him up at night. There were several ways that he learned to cope with the violent thoughts; for one, he tried to double-check the doors at night, and he kept baseball bats by each, and guns in his bedroom, which he locked before going to sleep. He was always armed on his errands outside. Because he knew that if he could have this violent imagination, then there were others who would act on them.

You see, Conrad made it his job to stop those who acted on

their bad thoughts in order to make himself feel better. The line between good and evil had become murky as he grew up since he never believed in God and he, himself, was having such horrible, intrusive thoughts and images. He figured after a while that those who were good must be the ones who actively chose not to harm others, even when their free-floating thoughts provided the worst outcomes.

He believed that there was free will, but sometimes it felt threatened when his thoughts became pushier or louder. A therapist that his mother had sent him to once told him that free will was all about action—he always had the choice to use his mind to think or not, so even when thoughts entered his head, he always had the ability to choose whether or not to pay attention to them—to hold on to them or let them float past and out of his mind once again. Conrad had read books on the "banality of evil" and what exactly makes people "evil" as opposed to "good." And it often frightened him because evil people were always cast in this murky shadow, as if evil was this phantom of madness, like an incurable disease, that gripped its victim and forced him to do awful things.

Conrad often looked at his thoughts as a gauge of when the devil would come and take over. On the days when images constantly kept popping up, then he felt like the devil was near to taking over, and on the days when they were slow or completely gone, the devil was at bay. He would not become evil today. Eventually, the more literature he read, the more he realized that what makes a person "pure evil" is the person who *chooses* to commit violent acts against others. This was the rarest kind of person, but one who could devastate the lives of so many. While most people were a mixed bag of actions, those either had to add up to an overall morally good person or a bad person. A lot of the "bad people" were those who did not think at all or who were appeasers of everyone, no matter what. The "good people" learned from their mistakes and always strove to do better next time in their behaviors, which were used to prolong their own happy and long lives.

It seemed to Conrad that most people today were these morally bad types who were a mix of good and bad actions. Their hypocritical behavior made him ill and their mealy-mouthed way of getting by in life made him irate. He wanted a world filled with morally upstanding people. He wished that morality was not such a muddled and confusing science. The principals should all be laid out neatly in a book like those on etiquette found in many Queen Anne-styled homes of the time.

That way he could read the book to his future children and hope that they abided by those principles, and if they did not, he would have less mercy on them than nowadays when people seem to lack any moral value system at all. It was all muddled with pagan and religious beliefs and old proverbs and confusing examples.

Just the other day, Conrad was at the cash register of the hardware store and he saw the magazine rack beside the checkout conveyor belt. The magazine covers were splashed with "Meet the Infamous Serial Killer in this Week's Interview!" "The Most Evil Man in the World?" "Pure Evil Walks Among Us!" But what made them "evil" exactly? What was "evil"? The articles threw the words "kidnapping" and "rape" and "murder" around as if regular people were supposed to know how to feel or *what* to feel about something so foreign to them. At the same time, the friends and family members of the criminals always said, "I had no idea!" "He looked like a completely normal guy!" "Who knew that this guy next door could do something so heinous?" And that is what made Conrad fearful. People talked about evil like the plague had touched someone's house in the night just because they had not lathered the blood of an animal over their door. Or, worse, evil was this ghost of absence and made the killer into its victim as if the killer's body or soul had been sucked out by something otherworldly. It took years of thought and reading and experiencing life and actively thinking about it and reflecting before Conrad declared himself good and made a more distinctive picture of the bad or, more so, evil person.

He had watched interviews when he was just a lonely bachelor of sadistic psychopaths who described faking empathy and offering help only to get to a parent's child. He got a glimpse of how sharp and aware these people were in obtaining their goals just because they wanted it. They looked no different from him or other people out there. They spoke clearly and persuasively, just like other people. There was no significant moment where the evil took over or a ghost slipped in through the mouth. The difference was that they could feel nothing toward others, which helped facilitate putting their fantasies into action. Because they felt so little that only indulging in fantasies allowed them to at least feel something, some tiny glimpse of what genuine pleasure was like.

And while Conrad, in his manly sort of way, drank to facilitate his ease of expressing his feelings, on a day-to-day basis, he was an emotionally level man. Perhaps, he may get a stranger calling him "cold" but he did feel, and he still had images flashing through his head on a daily basis that those strangers would probably never be able to handle for a minute, let alone a lifetime.

So, yes, Conrad confirmed to himself once again that he was good and his goodness could be proven over and over again in his work. He grabbed those who had been caught doing evil things by him and taught them a lesson. His good clients tended to be families who knew of his services and offered up a family member who was misbehaving and deserved what came next. You see, Conrad did not believe in heaven or hell, but he knew men could live like gods or devils, and the society they lived in controlled them—they were a part of the human race.

Before Conrad had met Elizabeth, he had only met women for one thing—sex. He never asked them to come back home with him. He never wanted to know their families. Heck, he did not even care to know their names. He was waiting for a spark to emerge that would tell him she was the one and only and that never came...until Elizabeth. She looked at him with the same depth of knowledge. She could comprehend more about his soul than perhaps even he realized. Their marriage was inevitable, only now his work would become more complicated with a woman around the house. Someday, she would know.

He ruminated for a long time, before bringing his first job to the home, about how to tell her. Conrad thought over the problem for days, weeks even. He sat down in the intricate wooden chair in the dark basement, just staring at the floor. If she knew his soul, then she would not run away...or would she? She is a woman, after all, he thought. She is delicate in certain ways and, yet, so strong in others. Her spirit is ferocious. But what would she think about this? All of this? He glimpsed over at the rope and the hole he had drilled earlier that month in the chair. There was still wood dust covering the basement floor, which she probably hadn't even noticed. But they were legally married now. It would take time to undo all that they had just committed to. Perhaps that would be long enough to subdue her, to soothe her concern, to make her consider what I was doing, he thought. Right, he committed to telling her over dinner that evening. He could recreate their first date and make it romantic. Women loved that kind of stuff, he thought.

Kicking up some of the soot from the basement floor, Conrad watched it fall back down all over his own shoe. A streak of gray covered his nice brown shoes, the leather ones that he bought to talk to clients in. His clients expected him to continue offering his services. Hate blinded many of them, and they thought that the legal system never did enough to right the wrongs committed by others. He always heard from his clients that there is no "eye for an eye" anymore; they will not even allow the death penalty! Some people got solace from knowing that the criminal may suffer under the hands of other inmates once in prison or perhaps some inkling of remorse may creep into their hearts, though, as Conrad reminded them, psychopaths feel no real emotions. They only get off from the tingling sensations of their groins. Those sick perverts! Conrad smacked his knee in a rage. There was so much evil out there. Monsters who act on those thoughts that even he knew were horrific. He was good, and they were bad.

***

Hoisting himself up off the chair and shaking the soot off his shoe, Conrad felt more prepared and calm. He was a man of feeling, though he did not show it unless he had a good amount of truth serum in him. But right now he was as sober as ever and he had to go out shopping for the items needed to recreate a romantic evening dinner. So, out he went, while Elizabeth was busy folding laundry.

She watched him leave the house yet again in a rush. In and out and in and out! she thought, shaking her head as violently as she shook out the wrinkles from the sheet she was folding. The one chore she did not mind doing was the laundry because the clothes all smelled so good and warm, and afterward, the smell of fresh fabric still lingered in the room.

This last month, settling into the new house, Elizabeth had noticed and heard all the construction going on in the basement. And as the brick walls grew higher, so did her concerns. Perhaps she had married him too hastily. But she had never felt this kind of chemistry with a man before—he seemed perfect for her. Whatever he was up to, she trusted she would come to no harm. He had never beat her, though he playfully threatened to, yet he showed respect to her always. She knew that usually once a man had a woman tied up in a legal marriage, then his behavior could start to disintegrate, but nothing like that had happened with Conrad. In fact, she wanted to punish herself for even questioning such things.

But being alone in her own head so often these days, she could not help but wonder what he was up to. Folding the final bits of laundry, she finally put them all back into their designated drawers and chests and closets. By the time she had finished with that, Conrad could be heard opening the door again. Deciding to run down to meet him for a quick catch-up, Elizabeth scurried down the stairs and ran right into him.

"Hello, dear! My, what do you have here?" Elizabeth saw his arms covered with bags of groceries. "Here, let me help you," she lifted off some bags from his marked arms.

"I wanted to recreate our first special dinner together," he said.

"What is it for?" Elizabeth wanted to get right down to the heart of his sudden act of affection. "There's no anniversary or holiday today. I always check." Her heart rate spiked.

"You got me. I do have something rather important to talk to you about, but won't you just let me cook you dinner first?"

"Oh no, you know I'm no good at surprises, dear. Please, just spare me and tell me now. Are you seeing someone? Do you not love me anymore? Are you a serial killer? A rapist? What?!" Her mind was reeling now with ideas about his past and what was possibly in store for her. She had trusted him so completely that his leaving was never considered an option, especially since they were just starting their life together. She felt like shedding her mortal coil right there in the kitchen.

Conrad always knew how to get Elizabeth out of her own head. He quickly gripped her shoulders and shook her gently, looking straight into her eyes and pleading, "Absolutely not! I am a good man who married a good woman. I want to talk to you about my job because it is unusual. Maybe I can just start telling you as we cook the meal together. How does that sound? Okay?"

Elizabeth could not think of eating now or ever again, depending on the news. "Sure, that's fine. I'm not sure I'm hungry now, but maybe after you finish, I will be."

Conrad cleared his throat and opened the bags with the chicken in them. Of course, the meal was a simple one of chicken, mashed potatoes, and peas. The peas were in a can and simply needed warming, the chicken could just be stuffed in the oven for thirty minutes, and the mashed potatoes could be made while the others were heating up. He handed

Elizabeth the potatoes to wash and peel while he basted the chicken and prepared the oven.

"Let's see, where do I begin? I suppose I'll just tell you what it is and you can ask questions. Yes, I think that's what I'll do," said Conrad, peeking over at Elizabeth to see how she was doing. She stayed silent and looked as pale as the inside of the potato she was peeling with trembling hands.

"People, usually families, even sometimes the police, use me as a sort of extrajudicial agent of the law. I mete out justice where it needs to be served as a kind of contractor."

Elizabeth remained quiet, with only the sound of the peeler running down the potato in her hand being audible.

"My clients ask for me when they do not want to go through the legal system. I find the criminal, apprehend him or her, and bring them to a secured location…which was a garage before and will now be our basement…"

"Are you mad? Why would I want a criminal inside our house?!" Elizabeth shouted. "For how long? How exactly do you serve justice?" Her face went even whiter than the potato innards.

"Honey, the door inside the brick office I built will secure them. Many of them do not even require being held overnight. They just need a little roughing up and acknowledgment of what they have done before I let them go."

"Do they see your face? What if they come after you later?" Elizabeth asked.

"I usually wear a mask of some sort and they do not come to until they are inside my office."

"Do you change your voice?"

"Not really, I doubt they could pick my voice out of any lineup of men around here. It's nothing special."

Elizabeth gripped the edge of the countertop in front of her stripped potatoes.

CHAPTER IV

There was a long pause between what Conrad had just shared and the whir of thoughts buzzing around in Elizabeth's head about it. At least he still loves me, she thought. But he himself could be a criminal...but then he said it is only done to criminals, which makes him the good guy. But is not that what the law is for? Why circumvent it? Finally, she asked: "But why avoid the law?"

"Because they do not always serve justice properly, and my clients all believe that. There is a need for people like me out there. I get the job done."

"But how do you know who's an actual criminal without creating a full case?"

"Elizabeth, I fell in love with you, not just for your beauty, but for your attention to detail. You and I are a lot alike in that way... When you look at people on the street, say when we are taking a walk around the block, you are seeing the same things as me. You notice the grimace of certain creatures; you overhear conversations that only a narcissist would have; you can tell when the jewelry a woman is wearing was stolen."

She blushed as she stared down in between her feet. It was true that they need not even look at each other anymore to know that they both noticed the same flaws in people. That was why they both preferred to stay away from them. In their home alone, they could control what good people could come in and made sure that all the rest stayed out.

"But what…what exactly do you do to them?" she asked.

Conrad did not want to look up into his angel's face; he did not want to witness any disappointment or disgust for his actions. So, he sat there quietly for a while, lifting his gaze to take in her face before he opened his mouth. Fear still contorted it, but her lack of understanding was better than her knowing. Still, it was only fair to tell her the truth.

"I torture them," he said.

Elizabeth's face went green, and she dry heaved into the kitchen sink before she could control herself. He thought that she could have fainted, which may have been worse. He could control himself when it came to watching his wife bear a little nausea, but not much more. He hated seeing her suffer.

"You…you tor-…you tor-…," she tried to get the word out, but her lips grew numb and her tongue tied.

"Yes. Now, I promise that outside of my thick brick office I just built that you will not be able to hear a thing," he said.

"Are you sure? And how am I supposed to sleep at night knowing that there is some tortured criminal down in our basement who would love to get a chance at revenge? What about our future children, Conrad?" Her eyes watered and she began to weep violently.

Conrad rose from the kitchen table where he sat while they waited for their food to cook. He went into the bathroom to grab his wife a tissue. "Please don't cry, darling. I love you, but this is what I do. Maybe perhaps one day I can even show you my work. In no time, you could become accustomed to it!"

"How could I ever become accustomed to torture?! You

sound psychopathic!" she yelled.

Conrad needed to calm her down somehow.

"Why do you have to do this for a living? Can't you just leave it behind and get yourself a normal job?" she cried.

"But I'm good at what I do. In fact, I *like* it."

"But...but why?"

"It reminds me of who the good guys are and who the bad guys are. It allows me to contribute to society in the best way that I know how with my skill set. I want to right the wrongs of people who think that a lifelong prison sentence—with food and shelter and water and even television sets and video games and exercise time outside—is the only punishment they will get. But many of the people I deal with, rapists, pedophiles, kidnappers, murderers, do not even deserve the *gift* of another free breath. They should be maimed, forced to suck for dear life to get the next breath, and unable to experience any more happiness whatsoever for the crimes they have committed. Do you understand now, even a tiny bit?"

Elizabeth had never known there were still people like hit men or "agents of the law" or whatever way he described himself, let alone that she would find out that her *husband* was one of them. Yet, something was happening in the back of her mind. She did not know what was going on, but she knew she would *never* leave Conrad over this discovery. She would remain by his side, no matter what. After all, he even declared it himself that he was the good guy. Right?

"But you are on the side of justice? Is that how your...clients speak about you?" she asked.

"Yes. I am good, Elizabeth. I truly hope you believe that." He gripped her shoulders again and stared at her. "I am good at rooting out evil from this world. I want it to be a *safe* place for our children to grow up in and their children afterward, and so on."

Elizabeth nodded her head, but it was melancholy. She knew that she would have to get used to being around a man with a violent profession. He was not only her protector, but the protector of hundreds of others out there who had or could have been affected by a criminal's actions. Through the tears and sorrow, she was proud of him.

"You don't have to decide anything tonight, love. Just think about it. It is a lot to understand," he said, avoiding her eyes.

"Well, I don't know how I already know, but I'm not leaving you over this, Conrad. I wish I had known sooner, but at least I know now and not years later after we have already had children or something. I love you, dear."

They squeezed each other tightly, exhaling only when they released one another.

***

A new feeling crept over the Fleischer residence after that evening. Conrad and Elizabeth ate their chicken, mashed potatoes, and peas, mostly in silence as they both thought about how to involve the other in his line of work.

How could I possibly become okay with Conrad hurting other people? Elizabeth thought, chewing slowly on the soft meat. Did people taste like chicken? What did cannibals think? What is wrong with me? she wondered, switching over to the peas quickly to get the taste of chicken out of her mouth.

Meanwhile, Conrad wondered about how he could show her his work. How can I introduce her to my world? A world that I know and find meaning in? Eventually, she will need to understand the images that flood my mind daily. What if our children become monsters? What if they do not use their gifted minds for good? He sat there horrified at the thought that his own kin could betray him. Before Elizabeth had mentioned children, he had never considered how he would carry out his job around them. He shifted uncomfortably in his chair, scooting it up closer to the table, and making an awful scratching sound on the floor.

"Oh! Don't scratch the wood up, dear," said Elizabeth, hiding the fact that he startled her out of her *own* horrible spiral of thoughts.

Once they had finished, the two of them set their silverware down and stared. Elizabeth could only tear up as he looked at her with pleading eyes. They both knew that this job may tear them apart, or else it would seal them together for good due to the illicit nature of his work.

Elizabeth felt like the many housewives she had read about who were attached forever in the history books to their mobster husbands. Suddenly, her role as accomplice became nauseatingly clear—either she leaves him tonight before witnessing anything or she stays and commits herself to him regardless of his crimes, even if they were for the good of society. For in the eyes of the law, his "job" was certainly illegal.

However, Elizabeth did not know how he could have gotten away for so long with his deeds. Perhaps the police looked away from his crimes?

Elizabeth had to know: "Dear, how have you not gotten caught yet?"

Conrad kept looking straight at her teary eyes and said: "All good people want justice." And that was it. He said nothing more, and the two headed off for bed.

But neither could sleep: one thought about all manners

of torture found in books, while the other thought about all manners of protecting loved ones from harm. Elizabeth tossed back and forth, while Conrad laid straight on his back with his arms over his chest like he was already a dead man.

Elizabeth wanted it all to be a dream. She wanted to have that white picket fence and those babies who yelled with glee. She wanted to always feel light and free from guilt. But she also wanted Conrad. They made such a strong team, such a wonderful pair of lovers, and children only formed in her mind when he was also in the picture. Her heart was bound to his—to serve him. Maybe, she thought, there was a way to stay with him and all that he was and learn to feel light again *with* the darkness. The notion of another way out of this mess kept Elizabeth from doing anything rash. Rather, she stayed in bed and kept trying to fall asleep, eventually succeeding.

Conrad wanted Elizabeth to stay with him. He loved her, but he would not change his career for her either. Both would bring him happiness, but if he lost one, he would only be half the man he could be. He knew that the only way to console her was to show her exactly how much pressure he put on criminals, how much blood he expelled, how much pain he inflicted. If she remained in the realm of the unknown, who knows what more awful things she might come up with in her own mind? He resolved to teach her, whether or not she wanted to, in order to keep her by his side. All Conrad wanted was to protect and defend what was his and what was good in this world from the bad. Elizabeth fell asleep first, and he glanced over to see her breathing finally slow down and her face look like a baby's.

When they arose the next morning, they set out to begin yet another new chapter in their lives. They were a pair who knew what they were doing. They knew it was an "extreme lifestyle," but overnight, each had committed to it. Conrad was going to teach Elizabeth and Elizabeth was going to learn to help Conrad.

Walking downstairs to the smell of bacon sizzling on the pan, Conrad smiled. "Ah, still being the good wife, I suppose, even after last night's revealing news? Good."

"Yes, I decided to learn about what you do and help if need be. I know it will be hard, but I trust you."

Hearing "I trust you" come from her mouth made Conrad love her all the more. He put down his fork and rose to hold her in his arms. Even as a newly married couple, they had already started growing into the perfect match of those who had been married for decades. This was probably the largest step on that long road.

Holding each other for several minutes, Elizabeth said: "Oh, I have to flip the bacon now or it will burn." She turned away from him and flipped them, while they both watched the sizzling fat bubbles burst and pop. Absorbed in the sound of miniature explosions, Conrad sat back down to enjoy his first pancake and strip of bacon of the morning.

"I have a client lined up that I know you have seen. I will be getting them today," said Conrad.

Elizabeth turned off the burner suddenly and turned around, the bacon fat still exploding behind her, covering her back and hair with grease.

She stood there, already trembling at the possibilities of what she might witness.

Conrad arose once again and gripped her quivering arms. "I know you are scared, but part of learning from me means you will discover how measured I am in my punishment. I am not the bad guy. Just remember that, my love."

She nodded weakly. "Yes, love," she said. But her body betrayed her as she continued to shake and the spatula she was holding kept tapping the insides of the pan. Trying to steady herself, she held onto her arm with her other hand for support, looking ridiculous and possessed. "Sorry, I can't believe how nervous I am!"

"Would it help you if I told you who I was getting today?" he asked.

"Yes, tell me."

"Do you remember our fat oaf of a neighbor with the equally fat, tittering wife?"

"Which one?"

Conrad laughed. "Well, the one with the stolen jewelry, the showoff wife's husband is writing bad checks. That is a less severe crime when held up against something like murder, so his punishment will be less severe. Some cousin ratted him out to me and wants to see him pay. I suppose he's had enough of his relative's showy, unearned wealth at every holiday party. I don't blame him. So, my job now is to grab him, take him to my office, and remind him that morality is the *only* way to get by when you live amongst other human beings."

Elizabeth grew less afraid the more she thought about what an awful man he was going to be dealing with. She saw her husband in a new light, like that of a knight. He was chivalrous and the way he described his work was noble. The law could never scare their criminal into morality. They treated them with professional aloofness, even kindness that no criminal deserved. She even became enraged at the thought that murderers could be given a break during a trial or given water when they asked for it while their victims lay buried under sticks and leaves somewhere out in the elements. And she loved Conrad even more for starting her off lightly with a less severe crime. She sat down at the breakfast table with him, put her hand over his, and ate everything on her plate.

So, out Conrad went, while Elizabeth tended to some cleaning that needed to be done around the house. They both already knew the time and path that their neighbor tended to walk around the block, but they were never too sure who it would be with. On some days, he was on the phone doing business; on others, he was with his male friends and their wives; and still, on other days, he was just walking with his wife. Each time was different, with no particular pattern. But Conrad knew he passed their house every day at exactly six o'clock in the morning before he had to go into the office.

The neighbor's doctor probably recommended walking as his form of exercise because he was too fat to run efficiently, or it might very well kill him. So, he had committed to walking every day. Well, Conrad hid behind one of the bushes that concealed their mansion before the neighbor walked by at a brisk-ish pace. Luckily, for Conrad, he was alone and jabbering away on his phone for all the world to hear.

Conrad waited for a moment to see if he would hang up, but it looked like he was going to have to hang up the conversation for him. Cutting through the bushes, Conrad stepped out right behind the neighbor's back as he passed and wrapped his arm around him to reach his face with his hand. In his hand was a rag soaked in chloroform and, with the rest of his arm, he choked the neighbor into unconsciousness.

The world went black for the fat man and, being rather early in the morning, no one was out on the block. But a vehicle or a runner could pass by soon, so Conrad hoisted the man up under the arms and dragged him back through the bushes. He had brought with him a dolly and dragged the limp body onto it and wheeled him easily down the side yard path and up a couple of steps into the kitchen. From the kitchen, he called out to Elizabeth.

She showed up white with fear. "H-…how did you grab him?"

"I waited behind the bushes, allowed him to pass, and then I got him from behind with a choke hold and some chloroform. One knocks him out quickly, and the other keeps him out for longer. Now, would you like to help me carry this fat slob down into the basement?"

Elizabeth felt ill but found herself nodding her head up and then down.

"All right, grab his ankles and walk backward carefully. I've got the brunt of him right here," Conrad said.

They both hoisted the heavy man down the stairs and then dropped him to the limestone floor, not all too carefully, as Conrad fished around in his pocket for the keys to his new brick office. Finding them, he opened the lock and dragged the man inside.

"It will be at least another ten minutes before he wakes up. Quick, go fetch my rope and tape, darling."

Elizabeth went to get it off of the plastic table that was now inside the brick office. Handing it to him, he dragged the body further to the segmented room with the chair. He propped the neighbor up into the chair and bound his hands to the arms of the wood. The holes allowed him to make them nice and tight, probably close to the point of cutting off circulation to his pudgy fingers.

She watched him as he then duct-taped over the neighbor's

mouth. And he went back to jiggle the doorknob to make sure that it was locked and the only light that allowed them to see were the two tiny bulbs hanging from the ceiling of the office: one in the entrance area with the table and one in the segmented area apart from the front with the chair.

Elizabeth almost screamed when she saw the neighbor move his groggy head back and forth against the back of the chair. Instead, the scream froze in her throat, as did the rest of her body.

Conrad took over from here. He threw a mask at Elizabeth so that she could cover her face while he covered his own. Then, in a bit of a lower register from his usual voice, he barked: "Do you know why you're here?"

The large neighbor dazedly looked around and began gagging. He was trying to speak…or scream…but the duct tape around his mouth was keeping him muffled. The couple watched the tape slowly rip out some of his mustache hairs individually. Elizabeth winced.

"Hey," Conrad kicked his shin, "I asked you a question."

The neighbor again tried to respond without success. Conrad did not want the criminal to have a chance to explain. He was going to dictate their wrongdoings for them before meting out the just punishment.

Conrad slapped the rounded cheek hard. A red blotch from where his hand had been grew angry as the seconds passed. "You have been caught knowingly writing bad checks, which is an act of fraud. You have used that money to spend on the jewelry and other items that your wife receives. She is decked out in stolen property. Everyone in this town has seen her and knows it. You and I both know that your job doesn't pay enough to buy such things. And now," Conrad slapped him on the other cheek, "you must pay for your crime."

Both of his cheeks now were red from the release of histamine that dilated the tiny blood vessels beneath his skin. Elizabeth watched as his cheeks gave off the impression that he had put on too much blush for his morning walk. Lost in her thoughts, she almost laughed. But she caught herself, horrified that she could find anything funny at this moment.

Meanwhile, Conrad had walked out to the plastic table to find his surgical tools. He picked up tweezer-like forceps with sharp points at the end. They shined in the dim light and Conrad wanted his swindler to see it. Part of the torture was taking time. It gave the criminal the time to recognize the wrongs they committed and to prepare himself for the hell that he would endure for however long his punishment was for.

Conrad stepped up to him with this singular tool in his hand. It looked somewhat less intimidating than the various scalpels and scissors that remained on the table behind him, thought Elizabeth, but she did not foresee what he was about to do with such a device.

"All right, Mister Fraudster, my client said that you have been doing this at least the last year without having gotten caught yet. So, the law failed the good people of this town and now we are getting our rightful revenge for the pain that you caused to the others around you," said Conrad, who was squatting right in front of the neighbor's midsection, twirling the sharp forceps between his fingers, staring at his next job.

"Do you know your fingernails take at least six months to grow back and nearly eighteen for toenails?"

All of a sudden, the fat man went limp in his chair.

"The cowardly swine!" shouted Conrad, smacking him again

across the face until he awoke.

Without a chance to protest, Conrad shoved the edge of one of the forceps' tines up into his right index finger.

Elizabeth covered her mouth in shock while the neighbor began his muffled wail of pain.

Conrad shoved the point in deeper, making his way down the fingernail bed. "I'm thinking that for each month you committed fraud, you should lose a fingernail. I suppose I will be generous and only smash two of your toenails to make up for a full year of crime. How does that sound?"

The man continued to wail in pain.

Conrad dug further and began slicing from left to right until he could use the forceps to tug at the fingernail and tear it right off the bed. The fraudster wept. There was blood coming out of his index finger where all the minuscule blood vessels were broken.

The nails were made of keratin protein, which began at the nail root where the cells would die and be pushed out to form the hardened substance to shield and protect the fingertips. Scientists believe nails were made for evolutionary reasons in order for us to grip objects, groom ourselves, and defend ourselves. Nails only grow at about three-and-a-half millimeters per month, and they are actually connected to the bones through ligaments in our skin. His nails looked pink due to the capillaries under each.

Elizabeth watched as Conrad ripped one after another off, a whole six months' worth of growth and a whole host of brutally damaged capillaries. It would take this man a *long* time to regrow them and during that time he would think over his crimes, each and every one.

"Here goes the thumbnail," said Conrad. He dug in with the

same method as before, only this was a much larger surface area to cover and the neighbor was sweating profusely. He lost consciousness again, probably to his great relief.

But Conrad would not proceed any further until he woke up again. "Elizabeth," he ordered, "go get a bucket of cold water for this pig."

Elizabeth found her legs were stuck in the same spot. She felt as if her mind was marching up the basement stairs and into the kitchen, but her body stayed put.

"Elizabeth, *please*," he urged.

She smacked her thigh, as if it was asleep, and managed to place one foot in front of the other, teetering up the stairs and toward the kitchen sink, where she filled up a large bowl. There was no bucket immediately in sight, and her mind was too preoccupied to care.

CHAPTER V

Somehow, Elizabeth fumbled back down the stairs and Conrad dumped the bowl of water on their criminal. He jolted up and looked down at his bleeding fingers. He looked as if had never seen his own hands before. Trapped in his awe, Conrad dug in to work on the other hand and then he removed the man's shoes.

"Okay, so now we have to get to twelve months and we've run out of fingers, so it's onto the feet," said Conrad. "But I also want you to remember me and the time we've had together, so I'm only going to bruise them and they will fall off later. Let's do the big toe on your right foot and the smaller toe next to that."

Conrad grabbed one of the extra bricks that he did not use on the walls of his office. Hoisting the brick above his head, he released his entire body in the swing and all of his weight landed on that man's toe.

In a newfound panic, Elizabeth worried that someone may have heard him, not only outside of the basement but from outside of the house itself. The cry was so loud. The nail was already discolored.

A bruise arises when blood vessels are damaged and blood leaks out into the skin tissue, causing a red-colored bruise, which as it breaks down the body cleans up the blood causing a variety of colors, such as blue, purple, green, and yellow before the bruise is completely healed. The blood underneath this man's toe was pooling up below his skin, putting so much pressure on the inside that a clear bubble formed full of his own blood. Conrad looked tempted to pop it, but his eyes moved on to the other toe instead. Perhaps it was to allow for the pressure to cause more pain.

Broken blood vessels take two weeks to heal normally and the toenails require several months to push out new cells. In a matter of seconds, the work of months was utterly destroyed. This man's body was under attack, and it could do nothing with speed to fix him.

His heart rate was elevated and all of his chemicals told him to run, to hide, to lick at his wounds while the body pumped blood to all the damaged places and slowly worked to rebuild. His body was like an invaded territory, where its soldiers required time to rest before continuing the fight.

The criminal was no longer wailing or weeping. He was now resting. The pain was washed over by numbness. In his shock, he found he could feel nothing. Yet, there he was, sitting in various pools of his own blood around the chair that he was tightly strapped to. The circulation was missing from where the ropes began down to the tips of his fingers.

Conrad was done. Elizabeth was silent. The Fleischers were forever bound by this dark point in time.

Cleanup was simple. Conrad turned away from the criminal and soaked his sharp forceps in an antibacterial solution. He poured out a blue solution that savagely bubbled all over the instrument. Wiping off the blood with a towel, Conrad set the tool back on the plastic table. Next, he inspected the brick for blood and gave that a good wipe with the towel. And finally, he asked Elizabeth to mop up the floor, newly christened with blood.

At first, she grew sick. Her face turned green once again as she watched it slosh and soak into the mop head. She could not look at the poor man's fingers or she would surely vomit. By the time it had all been soaked up, her bowl, once filled with water, was now filled with blood.

"Where should I dispose of this?" asked Elizabeth.

"In the toilet upstairs."

"But won't that be searched?"

Conrad shook his head, looking disappointed. "Remember what I said, dearie? We are the good guys. This is not a crime scene, and law enforcement always looks the other way. There will be no searching of our house—ever."

Elizabeth did as she was told, still feeling like she was cleaning up after a terrible crime. Pouring down the blood, it mixed with the water and became a faint pink color, which she thought was actually quite pretty. But then she shivered as the thought of going downstairs again dawned on her.

Walking down, Elizabeth saw Conrad beginning to cut his job free from the ropes. He said: "You are to tell your wife that you were punished for your crimes today, and you will never write bad checks again…or do anything else illegal, for that matter. You are a changed man now. And if you do not change your ways, just know that we are all watching," said Conrad, as he grabbed the chloroform rag and placed it over his mouth and then choked him as he had before.

"Help me drag this fat oaf up the stairs," said Conrad.

"Where are we going to put him without getting into trouble?" asked Elizabeth, trembling at the thought of letting him go free after what they had done.

Conrad was having trouble now maintaining his patience. He thought she would understand more quickly than this that they were not the bad guys. "He will probably go to the cops if his wife doesn't first, and I am telling you, they will do nothing. They know how I work and they can tell when I have finished a job. Get it?"

Elizabeth nodded. So, he had done this fingernail ripping before, she thought, gulping. Still, she grabbed the man's ankles and helped Conrad move the neighbor out the side door of their home. He was trailing blood everywhere.

On passing the kitchen clock, Elizabeth saw that a total of only thirty minutes had passed. It seemed like eons down in the basement. But, as she had come to realize, Conrad destroyed slow-growing life in a matter of seconds.

Being that it was now only six thirty in the morning, there still were not many people out. The couple placed the neighbor back on the dolly, covered him with an opaque sheet, and wheeled him back to his house. They dumped him right at the front door and left the way they came, making sure to rinse off any blood that remained on the sidewalk leading back to their mansion.

They did it—together.

"How did you manage to drag people around without me?" asked Elizabeth, feeling a bit better now that the burden was gone from her sight.

"I just managed. I guess I hurt my back a few times, but I haven't had many jobs that obese before either," he chuckled.

Upon reaching home, Elizabeth set to removing all the blood from the floors. However, Conrad advised that cleaning up the basement all the time was not worth it. He had another client job tomorrow.

And that was it. Conrad had completed his job for the day and was already paid for it. He sat on the couch counting his money and even offered Elizabeth a cut.

"No, thank you, dear. I only ask for you to support my lifestyle at home. I don't need anything extra." She kissed him on the cheek as she continued to scrub the floor beside him. Her mind was still whirling with the images of fresh blood and the wails, with no end to that night. She woke up with an aching conscience and shook Conrad to wake him up.

"Conrad. Conrad! Oh, wake up," she pleaded.

He rolled over and stared at her. Realizing what was going on, he did not get mad. Rather, he sat up and held her to him. She wept for hours. But by the time the sun was rising, they had both fallen asleep once again.

With a late start to their morning, Conrad seemed out of sorts. He could not find his pants until he spied them tucked away in the back of his drawer. He forgot to add the butter to his pan, and the eggs stuck. He nearly fell on Elizabeth's buffed-out floors. Nothing was going right, and he was concerned that this would make him miss his appointment with his next job.

In his haste, he kissed his wife and ran out the door, heading for his car without a single look backward. Meanwhile, Elizabeth's heart was in her throat. She struggled to watch him leave. Separation from him now felt impossible, like the moment he left, she ceased to exist.

Elizabeth hummed to herself and kept constantly busy, to avoid thinking about being irrelevant. After all, she wanted to be alone in her house forevermore. There was no one she needed to impress or appease besides Conrad. She enjoyed being independent, but as she scrubbed away at the stains which were not disappearing, she grew overwhelmed.

In her discomfort, she imagined Conrad with his fingernails torn off and dripping blood. Then she saw the bludgeoned bat flying around, all maimed and screeching. Closing her eyes tight, she backed away from the stain she was cleaning and folded her arms around her face—forcing herself into a state of blindness so that at least the monsters could not reach her there. Elizabeth continued to hug herself wildly, humming some silly lullaby to avoid any more brutal encounters with her own imagination.

The most terrible thing about being alone was the chance for the imagination to create crazy scenarios. Elizabeth stood there in her self-created darkness, fighting to create images of the falling autumnal leaves instead of the frightening bat who came back from the dead. But, instead, her mind meshed the two scenes together to create a haunting vision of the bat collapsing in a bed of fiery leaves and exhaling away its final breath.

"Oh! What have I witnessed? Am I not a criminal myself for allowing it all to happen?" she said to no one in the manor.

Her attention turned to the wallpapered ceiling of the dining room as she lay down over one of the many bloodstains. Staring up at the ceiling, with a death-like pallor, Elizabeth cried: "What am I to do?" But the floral wallpaper did not move or answer her. Rather, in its silence, she felt even more alone than before.

The feeling of fainting went away by the very fact that she was already prone on the ground, but then the heat came, followed by nausea. She rolled over onto her side and vomited onto the stain. Now the stain adorned other bodily fluids, and it made her even more ill looking at it.

Elizabeth moved herself onto the couch and lay there trembling until Conrad arrived back home.

He stepped in, dragging another job home. "Honey, come help me! Honey?" He stepped further into the home and caught the smell of her sickness. Conrad grew worried, though he did not have time to fix her problems with a woman who was bound to wake up soon. "Please, darling. We can talk about this later."

Elizabeth trudged from the couch to the kitchen and held the woman by the ankles. "May I ask who this is?"

"Why, of course. This is another of the gaggle, only this time it is one of our neighbor's wives. She was caught shoplifting some expensive dresses and apparently this is not new behavior, according to her own daughter, who she was encouraging to follow suit before she called me."

"Even children use your services?" asked Elizabeth, astounded at the thought.

"They sure do, and I turn no one away," said Conrad. "But I sure hope the next person is not as heavy as these last two." He began sweating as they carried her to the ignominious chair in the basement.

Conrad tied up her chubby wrists to the chair, although he seemed to treat her a bit more delicately and Elizabeth was not sure if this was due to the fact that she was a woman or if the crime was less severe.

Elizabeth was about to go back upstairs, but Conrad grabbed her by the arm. "Stay," he ordered. "You need to become accustomed to this if you are to be my wife." She swallowed with the lingering taste of her own vomit still reeking in her mouth.

At least this time, she did not scream when the job's head began to loll about. The couple placed their masks on, concealing their faces once more, and Elizabeth recognized that this woman was certainly one of the gaggle of tittering women who had so annoyed her the other day.

Elizabeth found it interesting to watch this woman react differently to her capture from the man. After the daze wore off, instead of looking angry, she looked genuinely afraid. I suppose there are many more ways to harm a woman, thought Elizabeth. Women had to fear rape before murder in these kidnapping situations. She watched the whites of this woman's eyes flail back and forth over the entire room. There was not much to see, but she stared intensely at Elizabeth, who put her head down before she could feel anything like pity.

Conrad said: "Please go get my surgical scissors."

Elizabeth obeyed.

As if they were in the operating room, Elizabeth handed off the scissors, which made the woman start to cry and scream. But the duct tape kept most of it muffled.

"You, madam, have been caught shoplifting multiple times now. Stealing is a crime and if you are to live in a civil society with the rest of us, then you must amend your behavior. Don't you ever think that you can get away with a crime. Got it?" said Conrad, poking the scissors into her face.

"Now, my client told me you have probably been doing this for several years but is unsure of how long exactly. Since that is the case, I think it is only fair to take every hair off your head—one for every single day that you have been alive and then some. I will also take this." Conrad tried to pull off her wedding ring but after so many years it was stuck on.

"Hey," he barked, "go get some butter!" He kept pulling and

chafing her skin as she bellowed like an old sow from the pain he was causing.

Elizabeth did as was ordered, bringing down some of the butter that was spreadable since it also had oil in it. She figured that would be easier to use. Even so, the tight golden ring would not budge.

"I guess this punishment just became a bit more severe," said Conrad. Using the scissors, he cut off chunks of the woman's skin around her finger until the ring fit over her knuckle and slid off.

Again, Elizabeth watched as the skin cells, which were flourishing and very much alive, were butchered and hacked off, falling to the floor with a sickening splat. Blood gushed everywhere, and much like the day before, Elizabeth had to sit down. She sat in the corner, hiding her head between her legs. This was too much for her to bear. She knew how slowly the skin grew back. It would be weeks before this woman regained some of the flesh she had lost and her finger would forever be disfigured.

"Got it!" Conrad said. He pocketed the ring to give to his client later as a bonus. "Now, we need to remind you that you are *not* above the law of society. You will be cast out as a leper after I am finished with you."

Taking the surgical scissors back up in his dominant hand, still covered in blood and her skin cells, he began hacking away at her hair. "Did you know that hair is made up of keratin, like nails, and grows only half a centimeter per month? It will take a mighty long time for you to grow your long hair back." He hacked away at every strand, not caring about the symmetry of it all. In fact, he seemed to want it to look as asymmetrical as possible.

The hair fell in bloody clumps to the floor. At some points, she howled when he nicked her scalp. Drops of blood dripped down into her eyes. She kept them closed until he had finished.

"Well, now those dead strands are really dead, laying on my floor like this. It should take at least half a year for everything to start growing back and looking somewhat normal again," he said. "I hope that this has taught you a lesson. It is *never* okay to steal from people who have earned a right to profit. You are *always* being watched, so behave."

The woman only whimpered in acknowledgment as she kept her eyes closed. Her ring finger was swelling up and there was blood still emerging.

Taking the chloroform rag and his arm, he used the same method to put her out. The Fleischers hauled her back upstairs, onto the dolly, and right back onto her own porch.

By the time they entered the house, Elizabeth felt better. It was a strange, dissociated kind of better. Perhaps she was just happy to have him back home. He kept her safe from harm. The world felt safer in general with Conrad around.

"Do you need to talk now, darling?" Conrad asked. The vomit was still covering the floor in the dining room. Elizabeth had forgotten about it and, in her embarrassment, she flew to the spot with a towel to clean it up. But Conrad held her by the waist before she could run off. He spun her around and kissed her tenderly on the lips.

Now Elizabeth was feeling very safe, almost to the point of giddiness...or jitteriness. It was hard to tell, but her veins pulsed strongly as she noticed them beating against Conrad's muscular arms. He was looking at her hungrily. There was too much testosterone in this man, she thought. But she knew that that look meant she could not run away and hide. He wanted her.

Conrad grabbed his wife and carried her upstairs over his shoulder to the bedroom, far away from the blood and vomit downstairs. He used her so violently that all thoughts disappeared like magic from her mind. It was like he physically shook all the worry out of her system. She was not only feeling better; she was elated. And her subsequent screams of pleasure proved that she had utterly forgotten about the horrors of the last two days. She was free.

***

If only her sense of freedom lasted longer, for as soon as Conrad satisfied his hunger, the sinking feeling came back. Her fears of him leaving once more left her cold and frightened. She shivered in his arms.

"Conrad...," she trailed off.

"Hmmm?" he asked.

"Dear, how is it you can be so in control of your emotions when doing work like that?"

"I'm not a woman," he smiled, rolling over to look at her.

"Yes, but how do I become as in control as you?"

"That's why I had you down in the basement again with me today. You will become used to the sights and sounds of this line of work, like a surgeon in an operating room. Get it? You'll become desensitized over time."

Elizabeth had not really considered that such desensitizing measures could work. It had never been done to her before. She was sensitive to everything. When she was little, her mother once brought home an injured bird to help, and Elizabeth remembered crying over it for weeks. She felt so sorry for the bird being unable to fly. Eventually, the bird was able to recover from its broken wing, and she cried again too once she watched it fly away. Elizabeth had grown attached to the bird, even over those few short weeks, and it was hard to say goodbye.

Life had always seemed much too stressful for Elizabeth. It was another reason for her to hide away in the manor. The world and all of its ups and downs could stay outside her domain, as she controlled what went on inside. But now her husband was bringing the outside vermin in, and her stomach turned.

"Conrad, why don't we have children now?"

She heard him audibly suck in his breath before exhaling slowly and saying, "Not yet."

"Would you stop doing this if I were pregnant right now?"

He gave her a sidelong glance. "No."

It was hopeless. She had married a stubborn man. Conrad enjoyed his work and nothing would stop him, so *she* had to learn to adapt—not him.

Elizabeth hid her head in his chest one more time before they decided to get up. They lay there in silence for a while. He stroked her hair and she could have convinced herself from his gentle touches that he was not capable of such violence.

But deep down, she was learning that people have a range of emotions, many that have never even been revealed. What emotions was I capable of feeling that I had never experienced before? Elizabeth wondered. Her thoughts followed this line of thinking as she cleaned up the mess she had made downstairs and into the evening.

When the moon came out that night, Conrad suggested a walk.

Elizabeth hesitated. "Aren't you ever worried that a neighbor might recognize you or someone may try to attack you in an act of revenge—or me?"

"That's why I always carry a firearm," said Conrad, touching his side as proof. "And you, missy, should always have me or a knife or, even better, a gun for yourself on you."

"But I don't want to always live with 'one eye open,' do you know what I mean?" she asked.

"Well, you have things to lose now. That's just how it goes. Human beings have free will. So, it is better for you to be safe than dead."

He was so blunt, she thought. "Yes, dear."

They walked together, without holding hands, through the crisp air. Conrad filled his lungs with it and found a well of energy he had lost after spending it all on Elizabeth. He felt light and springy. His veins pumped hard and his muscles cried out to be used. Circling Elizabeth like a wolf, Conrad ran around her on the sidewalk.

She giggled, "Oh, stop that!"

He howled and sniffed at her.

"Stop it!" she chuckled. Elizabeth was too focused on Conrad's silly antics to notice that she began crossing the street with a car approaching.

Within a split second, Conrad used his arm as a bar to stop Elizabeth from making another step forward as the car passed. He was always aware of his surroundings. It was the second time today that she felt embarrassed. Sometimes, her sensitivity and lack of awareness made her feel like a child and not like an adult.

In her fear, holding onto his shirt, Elizabeth hid herself in his chest outside and cried. He told her to stay on the inside of the sidewalk to him. He would remain closer to the streets from now on. She wished to thank him for keeping her safe and caring so much. His grip on her was made just that much deeper for it.

Together, the couple made their way back to the manor. The sound of crunching leaves was loud amidst the backdrop of such quietude. They felt like the only ones out on that particular autumn night. The moon shone brightly down on their heads.

"Hey, can you see into that home right there?" asked Conrad.

Elizabeth saw the orange glow of the lights coming from inside a home they were passing. The darkness combined with the time of year made seeing into the house so clear. A family was sitting at the dinner table chatting and laughing and eating their fill. A chandelier hung richly over the entire affair. She spoke up softly as if the family could hear them talk: "Yes, I see the entire family eating dinner together."

"That goes to show you how easy it is to become a victim. Anyone just passing by can see what you are doing, where you are located within the house, and who you are with. They need curtains. They need weapons for defense. They need to know that they are not protected by a god."

Elizabeth began to feel awful knowing that this happy, smiling family could ever be hurt. People were so trusting, she thought; people were so foolish, he thought, as they both left the family to their meal. Meanwhile, the night grew even darker and colder before they arrived back at their own home to rest and contemplate the nature of safety.

CHAPTER VI

The next morning, Elizabeth felt more paranoid than ever. She awoke looking at each corner of the ceiling for any maimed bats hanging around. Then she checked the hardwood floor before placing her feet down from off of the bed. Afterward, she put on a dress. Elizabeth made Conrad unlock the room and exit first, as she hid behind him like a baby duck to its mother.

"What are you doing following me around for today?" Conrad asked, scrutinizing her desire to stay close to him.

"Did you lock all the doors last night?" she asked.

"Of course. I always lock the doors I go in and out of automatically. Don't you?"

"Of course," she said, still looking wildly around her. "I guess I'm just afraid that those jobs you have will come back to us and harm us."

"Nonsense," he waved off her worries as if he never considered it himself. But he had, and that was why he was always so diligent and purposeful in his movements. He empathized with Elizabeth's newfound fears, but he believed she needed to learn how to live with them. "You will get used to the feeling after a while."

Elizabeth grew silent since she could find no reciprocated

words of care in Conrad. Sometimes he was so hard, even for her taste. She wished he would open up without the need for booze first. Then again, he was her only rock now. He was her stability and protection. She clung to him until he left the house to collect his next job.

She stayed there in the house, all full of dread. How long could she maintain this level of calm about the situation? One day, she was sure to explode with emotions that she kept shoved deep down, never allowing them to bubble up or loom forward in her consciousness.

To keep herself preoccupied until she would inevitably be called on to help carry the latest body downstairs, Elizabeth traveled up to the attic. The attic is structured completely differently from the basement, with its pointy tops and timbered beams running across the top. But it was just as dusty and damaged as the basement.

The attic looked abandoned. The floral wallpaper was covered in dirt so that the beautiful blue looked smeared and dirty. It was also peeling all over and several chunks were missing entirely. Three little windows lit up the entire floor. In that way, it differed greatly from the dark basement, especially since Conrad had covered the few small windows from the ground level.

As she walked around the attic, her steps made a crunching sound, but she could not tell what was squished beneath. It could have been dirt, dust, bug carcasses, mouse droppings, or all of the above. Her adventure reminded her of why she had never gone up there in the first place. Still, there seemed to be an element of wonder and discovery in the air. The previous owners had left some items behind and the Fleischers had never had time to explore them. In the basement, there were old paint buckets for the house and curtains that were removed and wooden shingles. But in the attic were some baby items made of wood, like a rattle and a rocking chair meant for a nursing mother.

Elizabeth kept poking around, pushing through a half-broken door that separated the attic into individual parts. When she looked up and found a hole in the ceiling, her first reaction was to stick her hand inside to see if anything was left behind or forgotten, and lo and behold, she felt a box. It was smaller than any of the ones lying around.

Withdrawing her clawed hand, she pulled out a beautiful wooden box lined with metal details and swirled hinges. The clasp on the front was, thankfully, without a lock and goosebumps tickled the back of her neck. Her baby hair stood at attention as she unlatched the clasp and opened the box to find a sea of letters. What a find! she thought.

Feeling safer now than she had been for the past week, lodged in the tiniest of corners in the attic of this large manor alone, she opened the first letter. They were all musty-smelling and yellowed with age. She tried to peel the first one open carefully, but it was difficult.

After failing, she noticed it had a separate piece of paper inserted into a finely cut hole in the letter itself. She had read about this form of sealing letters before. It was a form of "locking" a letter from outside eyes. Had this letter never been sent or opened? Elizabeth almost wanted to set the letter down to maintain the integrity and honor of the sender. But based on the agedness of the letters, this person was most likely dead.

So, she carefully broke the extra bit of paper and slid out the tucked-over flap, eventually undoing the letter. The date on the inside was 1942. This was a letter from World War II and a woman who must have lived here during that period wrote it. She never sent this letter to her man, who must have been serving in the war. But her words were as warm and affectionate as ever.

Elizabeth read one and then another and then another until she heard the door below slam shut and Conrad was shouting her name. It was an abrupt yank out of the fairytale she was indulging in for the past hour or so.

Scurrying back down the stairs to the kitchen, she found that he did not look pleased. "What's wrong?" she asked, deciding to tell him about her discovery later.

"This job was hard to get. It took a lot of muscle to get him down, and he scratched me pretty badly." Conrad stuck out his strangling arm, which was covered in deep scratches.

"Oh, dear! Let me go get the hydrogen peroxide."

"Please, just help me with him first, and then you can tend to my unfortunate wounds."

Elizabeth grabbed the man's ankles.

This man was much thinner than the previous jobs. One could almost call him anorexic in the way his ankles felt in her hands. She could nearly touch her fingertips all the way around them.

"He's pretty light this time around," said Elizabeth.

"Yes, actually, he is. But I wanted your help all the same. You need to get used to touching the jobs," said Conrad, placing the man's body in the chair the way you would a scarecrow. He kept sliding down, so Elizabeth held him upright in the chair while Conrad bound his arms.

He bound them extra tightly this time, so much so that Elizabeth noticed: "Are you sure it needs to be that tight?"

"Do you know what this man has done?"

Elizabeth shook her head from left to right.

"He is a pedophile who used his relationship with his girlfriend to get to her daughter for the past three months that they have been dating. She only found out yesterday after catching him inappropriately touching her daughter on the couch while she was trying to watch the television. The mother walked in from the kitchen so quietly that he did not notice her entrance at all. Can you believe the *audacity* this creature has?" Conrad gave him a good slap across the face to see if he was awake yet. He did not react.

In hearing all of this, Elizabeth grew disgusted by the skinny man that she had just touched. "Men like that should be put in an asylum for the rest of their lives after actually offending against an innocent child." She spat for the first time on another human being.

"Good. I'm glad you are starting to understand what these animals deserve," said Conrad, pleased with his wife's apparent coming around.

"I feel like I need to scrub my hands raw now."

"Oh, you can, but I would hold off if I were you until we are finished here. You are bound to get messy again before too long," said Conrad, preparing to throw a cold bowl of water on the dazed man.

The water finally produced some signs of life from the pedophile, who, startled, tried to inch his way back into himself like a pill bug. Though he soon realized that he was strapped to a very strong wooden chair behind a locked door in an unknown place while surrounded by two masked strangers. He gulped and tried to plead even through the duct tape over his mouth.

To silence his attempts to explain away his crimes, Conrad only hit him harder with a closed fist against the left cheek and then the right and then the left and then the right again. His face distorted dramatically, and the broken blood vessels caused his cheeks to go from bright red to black and blue. He looked frightening so quickly.

Elizabeth shied away from staring at the job's wounds, though Conrad barked at her to look. Blood poured from his nose and down onto his shirt.

"Look at this sicko! Look at what he has done to his girlfriend's baby! How dare you touch any child who does not even know what sex is or what it entails. A little, innocent girl who cannot give her consent to your *sick* little fantasies. And people like you who *act* on their fantasies regardless of who else they hurt will *not* stop. It would have been sexual if I was not called in to stop you. You type of sickos never get better from rehab and 'talking about your messed up fantasies,' *no*! You need someone to *force* you to stop since you only respond to coercion. You are lucky that you were not caught by another criminal—you are in the hands of the good, just law—only in this court we use our fists, you bastard." Conrad swung with the full weight of his body right into the man's nose, an audible cracking sound was heard and Elizabeth covered her ears in shock.

Sinking down to the floor, she began to panic. It was too much violence for her. The emotions she felt were too new and overwhelming to understand. It forced her to place her head between her knees in fear.

Conrad noticed his wife, but he needed to dole out the most just punishment he could on this man. Her feelings could not dampen the pure rage stored up in his soul against this criminal.

Again, violent images flew through his head of what he could do to this man. He imagined him hanging up by his throat to the ceiling, but it was not enough pressure to kill him. He imagined flaying him alive or tarring and feathering him like in the old days. Conrad could envision placing a gun right in his disgusting mouth and blowing him away, but that idea seemed too easy for such a creature. Death was too good for a pedophile. No, Conrad wanted to destroy this man to the core.

The only way to destroy a man living in his fantasies was to hurt him where he focused the most—his own member. Conrad said, "Grab me my scalpel. The largest one."

The skeletal man began screaming like a banshee as he watched the second masked stranger grab the scalpel off the plastic table in the larger front room and hand it off to the stranger inflicting all the pain. The blade glinted and looked mighty sharp even under the dim ceiling light bulb. It was extremely long and cold in its silver sheen.

The bruised man lost consciousness, which meant that his blood flow to the brain had abruptly dropped, and as before, Conrad waited for him to wake up and take his punishment like a man. Elizabeth soon learned that once a job was taken under Conrad's purview, he did not let them go again until the fullest amount of justice was meted out.

Grabbing his ankles this time himself, Conrad's fingers actually did grip all the way around. He bent the heavy chair backward with the body in it to force the blood back up into his undeserving head. Then, Conrad threw ice-cold water over his face and that woke him up immediately.

Realizing that this was not a dream and that his face ached

immensely, the man tried to fall back asleep as if playing dead. Conrad scrunched up his face in disgust as he watched this cockroach try to trick his way out of being in trouble. He was probably a master of deception in front of the little girl and her mother too. Conrad spat on him and grabbed his ankles to lift his little frame back upright for more torture.

"A man like this who is a serious danger to society requires a much more severe form of punishment. Am I right?" Conrad said, standing before the pedophile and looking directly at Elizabeth.

"Of course. That only makes sense," she whispered, still sitting like a chicken on the floor. Eventually, she righted herself and stood at attention, though the next several minutes were the most scarring moments of her life to date.

Picking up the scalpel again, Conrad cut a line straight down the front of the job's pants. In a useless effort to protect himself, the skinny man tried to twist his body to the side. But his legs were tied to those of the chair and he could not turn much at all. In an instant, Conrad had pulled out his most prized possession and sliced right through it with his sharp blade. He went a step further to make sure that no other creatures could launch from his loins by dismembering his family jewels as well.

The man passed out within the same breath as the scalpel cut through everything he held in high esteem. Before this moment, all he cared about was down there—now, nothing. There was nothing left worth living for at this point. For he had built up his entire image, his entire *life,* on his masculine appendage.

Elizabeth could tell that the man just wanted to die when he came to again. He no longer wanted to live. She began to weep. Perhaps this punishment went too far. Conrad looked over at her toward the sound of her crying and looked back at his job.

"This man does not deserve your tears!" Conrad yelled, yanking a fistful of his hair back. "He only deserves your scorn! No matter what mental illness he has, no matter what sick fantasies he imagines about children, he *intentionally* acted on them. Those who act on what they know is wrong are liable and are evil. He is *evil.* There were so many ways that he could have gotten help. He could have gone to therapy. He could have gotten on medication. He could have picked up religion for all I care! Anything would have made him a good man. But, instead, he made a definitive choice to go after an innocent child to fulfill his hedonistic desires at the expense of her future happiness and his. Because now he will *never* be happy again—not without what made him a man.

"See, this man did not have a distorted perception of reality, like maybe a schizophrenic person may experience. No, he *chose* to tread down the path of evil. And we don't believe in leaving justice to a potential afterlife, do we?"

Elizabeth shook her head, "No."

"No, we don't. His punishment must be in the here and now. It must be served as quickly as possible for the wrongdoing, and it must be meted out with the same lack of empathy that he showed toward his victim." Conrad added an extra punch in the mouth for good measure. "This man is lucky to be alive. He needs to understand that this little girl who has just started on her journey through life will have trauma and years of therapy and nightmares due to this man's behavior. The least he can do is suffer physically for years from being maimed by the laws of justice," Conrad snarled.

The skinny man was bleeding profusely, so Conrad pressed a towel up against his wounds and motioned for Elizabeth to hold it there while he left to get something. He took his time unlocking the door and walking up the steps to the kitchen. There was an old poker next to the fireplace, which he stuck into the gas stove flame. It grew bright red after a while and he carried this hot poker back down to the basement.

The fireplace in the Queen Anne house, although replaced by furnaces, and then central heating, was still an important centerpiece of the home. There was beautiful tile on the floor around it and the woodwork of strong columns surrounded the pit with a full mantelpiece on top. Although they seldom used the fireplace, it still gave off a warm feeling with its presence. It was home. The furnaces were either hidden in built-in window seats or painted a gold color and detailed with scrolls and shells to make them more attractive. These heavy hunks of metal, also rendered useless over time, were still there to represent historical inventions of the period. The old phone system was there too. Conrad knew that some of the historic and heavier features of the house would someday become handy.

He took the poker downstairs and cauterized the pedophile's gaping wound. He screamed and the sizzling sound released fumes that flooded the basement with a wretched smell of burned hair and flesh. The work was done as the blood was staunched and the man would most likely survive this torture.

Conrad bent down close to his job's ear and said: "I hope you learned your lesson today, boy. If not, we will meet again." The typical procedure Elizabeth became accustomed to began with the chloroform and choke hold, followed by the hoisting and dollying-up of the job, and finally wheeling them to their residence. However, in this case, he had to be driven back to his home.

***

Neither Elizabeth nor Conrad spoke on their drive home. They had nothing to say to one another. They had said everything there was to say in the basement, though Elizabeth's face was still white. Nothing had sunk in yet for her as all the images of the day's job floated on the surface of her thoughts, submerging briefly and then reemerging only moments later in her mind. She felt ill.

Conrad was red with rage. He was upset from having to deal with such slime, but he was *more* upset that Elizabeth still was not completely on board with his career choice. How long did it take a woman to come around? he wondered, chewing on the inside of his cheek. She must know by now the routine and that what I am doing is just. I am *not* a criminal and no woman is going to tell me otherwise! he fumed internally.

He sharply turned the wheel, and they veered off into an empty field, barren of its crops that were freshly harvested. An icy wind and the smell of corn stalks squeezed in through the crevices of the car.

"What are you doing?" Elizabeth looked at him, concealing the first fleeting thought in her mind that he could kill her. It seemed that her already white face could grow still whiter yet as she leaned back, away from Conrad.

Meanwhile, Conrad grew closer. He knew that this area was open and next to the street. Someone was bound to come up asking questions soon. All that he wanted was a single moment alone with his wife—a single moment. An image flashed in his mind of strangling her right there in the passenger seat. He felt sick. His own two hands could destroy the highest value in his life, and, ultimately, end his own. Revolted by his imagination, he backed off, returning to the seated position as the driver of the vehicle, in control…always.

"You are scaring me, dear. What's going through your head?" asked Elizabeth, growing teary-eyed with each passing moment.

Conrad huffed. In reality, he was having trouble opening his mouth, afraid that his thoughts might come out like prophecies and things grew out of control from there. He was not a religious man, but at times he could fall prey to superstition. Instead, he turned the car back on and drove the rest of the way home.

Elizabeth looked behind her in the rearview mirror to behold a set of tire tracks in the mud they had created. The mud tracked them as they made it out of the field and onto the main roadway. The lines followed them for a mile or two before completely disappearing, and Elizabeth did not take her eyes off them until they had gone. She held her breath, believing that some policeman would follow them to their home and find out what they had done. Her gut still told her the court of law would prosecute them for their behavior.

"Turn around. *Now*!" said Conrad.

She obeyed immediately, frightened by his abrupt tone. He had never truly yelled at her before. There was something dark on his mind that she just could not understand. She sat there, twiddling her thumbs, trying to figure out what he was feeling all the way back home.

Before exiting the vehicle, Conrad turned once more to Elizabeth, gripping her arm. "On the next job, I expect you to participate."

"But I already do!" she stuttered, trying to pull her arm out from his grasp, but he clung tighter like a bird's talons piercing its prey. He squeezed and her flesh formed mounds in between his fingers. "I carried the job today to the basement with you, and I handed you the scalpel!"

"That's not what I meant. I want you to tell the job why they are criminals, and I want you to inflict the pain yourself," said Conrad.

"But this is not my job! I did not choose this line of work. I'm...I'm a woman! I'm more sensitive than you to violence. I can't. I *won't*!" she cried.

Conrad threw her arm aside, though he kissed it a moment later to express his apologies for being cruel to her. Still, a few kisses would not ease the tension filling up the car and then the garage and then the entire manor.

Getting inside, Conrad helped Elizabeth take off her peacoat, and he even hung it up for her. But he kept his eyes locked on her every move, watching for some kind of sign that she was going to do as he asked, but nothing came.

Nothing came from her until dinner that evening. The Fleischers sat there across from each other—each at the end of the table, where normally Elizabeth sat cozied up beside him when she could. Clearly, she was still upset. But after a sip of wine, she said: "I will do it. Just please be nice to me. I can't stand it when you are mean to me. Nothing scares me more than the idea of losing you forever."

Conrad stood up and came over to her side as soon as she had agreed. He held his love in his arms, gently patting her on the head. Finally, she felt his old warmth return. They both relaxed in each other's arms and all was right in the world once more.

"Promise me we'll go slow? Maybe not such a dramatic case

as today's?" she pleaded.

"Of course, of course. I will give you the most gentle of cases and we can plan it all out beforehand if you'd like!" Conrad was jolly. He practically glowed when things were finally going his way.

"Yes, planning everything out would help me avoid any surprises. You know I am not very good at handling those." She could not even utter the word "surprises" again because it increased her anxiety so drastically.

Husband and wife spent the rest of the evening laying in each other's arms, not thinking about much of anything serious at all. Elizabeth focused on the warmth and soft skin of her husband's chest against her face, while Conrad felt how small her frame was in his arms—she was safe there...always.

II

PART TWO

CHAPTER I

The Fleischers spent the entire weekend alone in their Queen Anne-styled manor—their garden of Eden, their paradise. They saw no reason to leave it, ever. Their home of comforts included indoor plumbing, central heating, hot and cold running water, their fridge was filled with food, as was the pantry, and every decanter filled with drink; they had everything needed to live in luxury.

Books covered several of the walls as if their house was more of a massive library than a living space. They had books covering every subject and ordered accordingly. Conrad and Elizabeth read page after page when the weather was warm enough out on the porch, or in colder weather, they read in the heart of the living room. But every season, there was at least one book in their hands at any given moment.

And when the books were set down, they occasionally opened their home to guests, though every time that happened Elizabeth made sure that the communal spaces were wiped clean of all evidence. Conrad told people he worked in some back room of a law office in town as something of a paralegal who had to be a man wearing many hats to keep the firm running. No one questioned it.

As for Elizabeth and making the unusual choice for the

modern-day woman to stay home as merely a wife, guests expected the children to come along shortly. For staying at home as a wife, to others, seemed rather lazy of her since she left the library.

"Yes, children are on our minds. Just not quite yet, we are saving up for them," Elizabeth always said. And they were, she thought. It was not a lie. But she did not know when that day may come and if he was still expecting her to live this double life forever.

It was easier for both of them to *not* have people over due to the very fact that only *they* knew the whole truth and could live their lives out peacefully in front of the other. There were no lingering questions or concerns to answer to. It was just the two of them, holding onto one another for a sense of security. In a wave of relief, Elizabeth often clung to Conrad as he grew to be her only light.

***

The day came when the next job was called in by a man who had caught his wife cheating on him. He wanted to see her suffer by watching her lover be tortured. On the phone, he called it his "marriage counseling" session, which would be conducted by Conrad.

Conrad agreed to take in two people to the basement, though Elizabeth had her doubts. How could they keep *two* people captive?

"This is the perfect assignment for you. You can take the lighter task of punishing the wife while I deal with the lover," said Conrad, his eyes lit up at such an idea.

Elizabeth could only frown and shake her head in disapproval, but she did not wish to lose her husband. She prepared herself that morning to go into the car and come back with two jobs.

They drove quite a while away, nearly thirty minutes. Elizabeth was told to get out of the car and ask to borrow the perpetrator's cell phone as hers had died. The plan worked as Elizabeth led the woman closer to the car. Quick as lightning, Conrad exited the vehicle and pushed the woman in and thrust the rag over her mouth and nose. Meanwhile, she had unlocked her phone and Elizabeth used it to message her lover for help.

It only took a few seconds as the woman's lover emerged from her *own* house, stumbling out, looking for her. He approached the Fleischers' car. Initially, he walked closer to ask if they had seen his "girlfriend," until he spied her in the vehicle knocked out, legs and arms akimbo.

"Hey! What do you think you're doing?!" he shouted. But the shouting soon was silenced with a knife in the lover's face held by Elizabeth while Conrad got around behind him and choked him out.

Both jobs were finally in the car. "Go apply the chloroform to the guy's face," Conrad ordered as he got back in the driver's seat and rode off to their home. She kept applying it every ten minutes to both of them, keeping her head far away from the fumes.

Thirty minutes with two people unconscious in the back of the car seemed ridiculous, an utter overstep in the bounds of the law. But Conrad insisted that this would be done jointly. It would be the job that brought them even closer together. Elizabeth wondered if he intentionally left off the end of the sentence, instead of saying, "...closer together in their crimes"? The closer they got in proximity to their basement, the more she was feeling hesitant.

"Conrad, I'm nervous," said Elizabeth.

"Don't worry, dear. Just do what I say and everything will work out fine," said Conrad, who had opened the doorway from the garage and was entering the mudroom with the male body. "Are you able to drag the woman by yourself?" Conrad called out over his shoulder.

Elizabeth tried to drag her under her armpits, but even this petite woman was heavy for her. She did not want to go by the ankles because then she would bang her head on the cement. So, she waited there, already feeling defeated, until Conrad came back for her.

He chuckled. "Perhaps you are not cut out for this line of work after all." Conrad hoisted the woman up and over his shoulder like he did Elizabeth on the way to their bedroom. A jolt of painful jealousy slashed at her throat. Elizabeth wanted him to drop her immediately, forget about her head. She wanted the pretty blonde whore to pay.

"Conrad…," said Elizabeth.

"Yes, dear?"

"Let me hold her ankles as we take her downstairs."

Conrad smiled.

The two of them carried her down and Elizabeth dug her nails into this woman's flesh hard enough to leave deep marks when she put her down.

"Now, our current problem is that we only have one wooden chair down here," said Conrad. "Will you go upstairs and get the sturdiest one you can find for the lady?"

"Why does she get to sit in one of our nice chairs? What if she gets her blood on it?" said Elizabeth.

"We aren't poor. We can always get another one."

"Not of these! They're antiques. We live in a historical

manor. Hello?" Elizabeth was feeling more hostile by the minute. How dare that "lady" even feel her husband's shoulders or his chest or his breath on her skin, thought Elizabeth. She deserved death. In her boiling rage, Elizabeth smacked the other woman so hard on the face that the entire basement rang with the force.

Conrad looked over, surprised. But he was not a daft man. He started to make sense of her sudden shift in behavior. He only smiled at his lovely, jealous little wife.

"Let's get this going already!" said Elizabeth, fuming.

The two of them split up some of the rope and began tying up their jobs. Conrad showed Elizabeth in a romantic gesture how exactly to tie the knot on her job's body. The arms and legs were tightly bound to the chair that was eventually provided to her. Elizabeth had chosen a less sturdy chair, but it was one that she had always found uncomfortable to sit in and could be replaced if needed.

The female began moving of her own accord. At first, it alarmed Elizabeth, who sucked in a heap of air before frantically looking around for her mask with which to disguise herself. About a minute later, the man also came to. Now, the process of justice was about to commence.

Both jobs had their mouths duct-taped before they could utilize them and the Fleischers sat on the ground apart, watching each of their jobs. They wanted to watch the horror on their faces as they discovered they were trapped in some dark hole, tied up, and next to one another's sinful and guilty pleasure. For the first time, Elizabeth could not look away, sitting on the cold, hard limestone floor, captivated by the facial expressions that her "lady" was making.

The woman at first kept blinking as if trying to remove

the cloud obscuring her sight, but then she visibly froze, as if doing so would make her invisible to her captors. She froze, while the wheels in her mind spun, trying to make sense of the situation she found herself stuck in. Then there was the attempt to move her right arm and then her left and her legs without success. The tape over her mouth was ripping at her peach fuzz and it hurt to yell out. Still reacting like a shocked animal, she managed to pry her eyes to the side enough to glimpse her lover, just realizing his situation as well. Then the flood of tears came.

"Stop crying!" shouted Elizabeth. "Otherwise, your tape might lose its stickiness!"

Conrad laughed. "I never considered that before." He was beaming. "We should begin, then, if time is of the essence. Give her a good slap. Maybe that will stop her tears."

Elizabeth slapped her across the other cheek this time. The woman became more hysterical, not less, to Elizabeth's chagrin. "Stop it, whore!" Elizabeth looked to Conrad for instruction as to what to do next, but he fully backed up and said, "Tell them what they are accused of."

"You are adulterers. You, madam, have cuckolded your husband to lie with this man over here!" Elizabeth pointed as obscenely as she was able with her pointer finger at the tied-up man. "You have committed the ultimate moral crime for a woman—that of betraying your husband and throwing her soul from that of an angel to a *whore* in an instant! And your lover is to blame too for allowing such a travesty to occur. His heart is black for taking what was not his and without coming man-to-man to talk about this to your husband. If you no longer wished to be with him, then you should have discussed it with him! But no, instead you sneak around, sometimes, like today, under your husband's own roof, you disgusting urchin! No mortal soul should even trust you again. You have murdered another man's integrity to satisfy your own base and bestial lusts. You deserve to die like the whore you are." Conrad clapped behind Elizabeth. She took the praise of her husband and waited for what seemed like several minutes before continuing: "But since you are in the hands of souls that are finer than yours, we will see a kind of justice that is measured and meted out only to the extent that your crimes deserve. You will not die today, but you both will feel the pain you have caused another man."

Elizabeth turned and walked over to the now infamous plastic desk with the surgical tools. This was her moment to determine what amount of pain each job deserved. She took a moment, facing away from them, both of whom were crying now, and imagined being the husband—walking in on them having sex. She imagined seeing Conrad there, sweating, breathing heavily, and moaning with the sound of his sticky skin slapping against her thighs. Elizabeth's mind only rang with *death*! *death*! *death*! but she knew such thoughts were barbaric. She stood there paralyzed because clips like from a film fluttered across her mind: cutting off her breasts, cutting off his member, stabbing one and then the other to death, forcing one to watch as the other died in a pool of their own blood, images over and over of nothing but red everywhere. Her emotions were on *fire*.

Conrad came over and watched her burn. He knew the kinds of images running through her head because he had had them since childhood. He gripped his wife by the shoulder and said: "You're afraid of yourself, aren't you?"

"Yes."

Elizabeth was afraid of seeing for the first time what she was actually capable of. She *could* kill. She could perhaps even tolerate such an atrocity—what a horrible recognition in a person. She was just as capable as a man of feeling such strong, murderous rage, only it may be fueled by different reasons. It was the jealousy over her own husband's fidelity that could finally cause her to desire to kill.

Taking in the whirl of emotion, how in the world was she ever supposed to mete out justice when she felt this on fire? She wanted to avenge *herself* now and not just for this paying client. It was dangerous, very dangerous ground that she was on. Elizabeth still felt too paralyzed by hatred to make a move and the time was ticking away. She needed help.

Elizabeth turned around to lock eyes with Conrad. He bent forward, getting the hint. "I need help," she said. "I tried to feel the pain her husband felt and now I'm murderous. I can't act rationally. Help me!"

Conrad wanted her to fight through the emotions. "Look, just take another minute to calm down. Would you like me to toss you some ideas since I've dealt with adulterers before?"

"Yes, please," she hissed, taking her anger out on Conrad.

"Okay, well, today under the law, only certain states make adultery illegal, and then they have varying fines and/or prison time. Now, historically, as in the 1600s, people were made to wear the letter *A* on their clothing and could be publicly whipped for such a crime on top of a fine. So, the physical equivalent then would be at the very least whipping. Allow me to go get my whip," said Conrad, "though we are not doing any of this publicly, still the two perpetrators must watch the other take their punishment."

After searching a while upstairs, Conrad came down with a

more modern whip that he most certainly found at a pleasure shop. Elizabeth wondered when exactly he had acquired the black leathery whip.

"Here," said Conrad, "do your bidding."

Elizabeth finally turned back toward her job, who had begun to calm down from the rather long wait. But she froze right back up when she saw what was in Elizabeth's right hand. To which Elizabeth replied, "I can see it in your eyes that you already know what this is. Perhaps you've already used such things on your man since your perversions probably know no bounds. Only this time, it won't be a painful pleasure to your body, I'll be sure to make certain that it draws blood and *only* pain." Elizabeth was breathing heavily over this woman's body, nearly salivating like a rabid dog over her, itching to launch at her with the first bite.

Elizabeth wanted to start low before she went higher, so she tore this job's dress up to her thigh, incensing her further because it gave her a more sexually suggestive look. Lashing at her thigh, right where it stung the most, the meatiest part of her leg was slashed by the whip, which made a buzz in the air and left an echo of the impact ringing around the basement.

The woman writhed in her chair, and the blood quickly exploded through the thick flesh. The whip had cut deep already, but Elizabeth was just beginning, though she felt a bit sick at the sight of her blood. However, that nausea was quickly overpowered by hatred when she saw a bit of her underwear from underneath her dress poke out.

Whack! Down came the whip, right on her most delicate flower petals, and she shrieked in agony. *Whack! Whack! Whack!* Thunderous beatings rained down on the woman's body, now leading up closer and closer to her pretty face.

Elizabeth made sure to draw blood from her hips and her stomach and each breast and finally, yes, even her face. Her body was covered in bruises and welts and blood oozing from all over the front of her body.

"You're lucky you're tied to a chair and I can't do the same to your back," said Elizabeth to her job.

She then turned her attention to the lover, who watched the entire fiasco from his seat. He flinched when Elizabeth turned to face him so suddenly, like the tips of a whip. She gave him one good smack with the whip and then offered it up to Conrad. Elizabeth's hatred had quickly piddled away in the face of the man. She only had one vendetta at the moment, and that had already been dealt with swiftly and mercilessly.

Conrad was indeed impressed. He knew he had married his equivalent when he met her. She had a darkness to her he could *smell*. It was just a matter of inflaming the right triggers to make her entirely his. After all, she was made from his rib and the Fleischers were meant to last forever.

He took the whip from her with a very chivalric nod of the head and turned his attention to his job. "Well, you saw what the lady got and deserved and now it only seems fair to give you the same."

The whip came down with explosive power. Conrad was much stronger than Elizabeth, but in order to make the same deep cuts through this man's thick muscles, he had to strike harder. Blow after blow, Conrad covered his job's body in the same decorative coloring as his lover. Though he had to pause after the man passed out from being hit so hard in his beloved jewels, Conrad had to check his pulse. He was still alive. It only took a moment and the cold water Elizabeth handed Conrad helped in his awakening.

Between the two jobs, the Fleischers began to grow tired and weak. It had been over an hour and their feelings had grown numb. In fact, Elizabeth had calmed down enough to become aroused by Conrad's strength. She watched him beat his job with vigor as beads of sweat ran down his face, like when he made love.

Elizabeth squeezed her legs together, trying to make sense of her feelings at this point. They had been so erratic throughout this experience of being an actual participant in the torture. In a ball of confusion, she only added to it by falling on her knees and kissing Conrad's feet. His fantasies had at that moment fully expressed themselves in her act of voluntary submission that he stopped his beatings to pat gently her head. The urge to have her right there had never been so strong.

Within two seconds of having the thought, Conrad stripped off his clothes and approached the love of his life. She responded equally in her strong desire for him. It shocked her to not even care that two other bleeding people were sitting there watching. In fact, the goosebumps forming up her neck told her that this would make it all the better since that whore could have stolen him away. She deserved to see that Elizabeth was Conrad's and no one else's.

A fury rose again in her breast and she pulled Conrad's head toward her nipples. Without needing any further guidance, he grabbed her slender wrists and pinned them back behind her as he shoved his face into her chest. A high took over all control as he breathed in her smell. Her skin was sweet and soft—the way a woman should always be, he thought.

Conrad climbed on top of her and inserted himself deep inside like he had a natural right to exist there. Her body was a temple and only he was allowed to light up all the candles inside of her soul. He used her just as much as she used him.

He squeezed her throat shut as she clawed away at his back. Both of them gasping for air. They were like two animals having a brawl with the way they bit and scratched. There was none of the mushy, romantic lovemaking. Both of them deemed that kind of love for the soft and weak and not for the lively and supple couple. They were, after all, the Fleischers, known to enjoy the flesh.

It seemed like an eternity had passed before the ball of sweat and moans fell apart to catch their breaths. Unbeknownst to the couple, they had rolled into the pools of blood that were starting to merge all over the basement floor. Conrad noticed the red splotches of it covering Elizabeth's pale body. He dipped his finger in the male job's blood and drew a more deliberate line around her left breast and then her right. Feeling compelled to baptize him in much the same way, Elizabeth dipped her finger into the paint and drew lines on his chest. They looked like claw marks from an animal.

He thrust hard against her as if she was a wall that must be knocked down. All the air in her lungs left faster than she had the chance to take in a fresh breath. Conrad was so brutal in his love, as if trying to tell her with his power how much he felt about her.

Knock after knock against her caused a soreness that she knew would form into a bruise later, but right now, she could hardly feel it with all the adrenaline racing around her body. In many ways, the two wished they could continue this moment in time without end, but he had gotten his fill and the dawn was fast approaching. They had to finish their work with the adulterers.

The Fleischers finally stood up, their hair in all sorts of wild, bird-like angles and the sweat and smell of sex filling the entire area, and tried to redress themselves. After they were done, they too looked like their jobs—all black and blue and covered in blood.

The tied-up pair knew they were going to be finally released and fresh tears formed. But the male got violent. He tried headbutting Conrad when he got close, and Conrad brought the force of his fist down on the side of his head.

"All right you two, you are going to be deposited back home together, back to the loyal husband that you both deceived. Just know that there are always eyes on the two of you and if you *ever* become lovers of the flesh again, you will end up right back here in hell on earth. And next time, you won't survive to see the finale," said Conrad, winking at Elizabeth, who simply blushed and looked down.

Conrad went, rather disorientated, to find the rag with chloroform and, with all the little strength he had left, knocked both of the jobs out one final time. The man fought with just his free head, trying to use it to knock Conrad out, but Conrad was able to take the pain on his arm. Elizabeth made a note to ice it later. She loved him so.

The couple swiftly unwrapped the bodies, carried them one at a time upstairs, and out into the car in the garage. Elizabeth, as on the way there, again, held a rag to their mouths a couple of times to keep them passed out before reaching the very house where they both came out. This time, the husband was peeking through the curtain upon their arrival. He must have been listening for a car to pull up since he got home from work.

Elizabeth stepped out of the car and the two covered their jobs just in case anyone was peering from inside their own houses. On the dolly, it just appeared like Conrad was delivering some oddly shaped bags full of stuff. To avoid further nosiness, the husband opened the door to the home and let Conrad dump them inside rather than outside on the porch.

The husband said nothing but looked pleased, so pleased, in fact, that he handed Conrad another hundred-dollar bill as a bonus. Their job was officially done for the day. Conrad entered the car, kissed Elizabeth on the passenger side very sweetly on the cheek, and the two headed home hand in hand.

CHAPTER II

It was another drive home in relative silence: Elizabeth was listening to the birds chirping, while Conrad was listening for the sounds of alarms. He was always on high alert when they were out in public. There were not many people in this world that could be trusted.

Once they reached home, Elizabeth covered her mouth to yawn and the two of them giggled like children about how they looked an absolute mess still.

"The blood will have to be cleaned up tomorrow, but for now, let's take a bath together; shall we?" Conrad said, offering his hand politely to Elizabeth, who took it with a coy smile.

They bathed together for the first time and watched the blood that was not theirs lift off their skin and swirl down into the drain. There was so much of it that Elizabeth was afraid they would stain the tub pink for a while, and it certainly looked that way.

But she was starting to accept their status as mister and missus, forevermore covered in the blood of others...

***

For having gone through such a violent array of emotions yesterday, Elizabeth slept through the night without a single nightmare. Although she often found that while she could slough off her emotions at the moment, they always came back around eventually, usually when her world became the quietest. For in that quietude, a chance for contemplation caused her to spiral into the ground. She may as well have buried herself alive and stayed in the ground until she could bear to open her eyes again to see the world with her still in it.

That sense of remorse came along a couple of days after their last job. Elizabeth felt a sense of shame when she even so much as looked down at her legs. Not too long ago, those legs were covered in another woman's blood and she did nothing of any substance than be the object of another man's jealousy.

Still, Elizabeth knew very well that at this point she could not tell Conrad. He seemed so happy since their last sexual union. And, as she proved to herself, she clearly could not bear to see him unhappy or dissatisfied with her behavior. So, she did what many wives have done throughout history—she repressed her feelings of remorse and moved on. Today was a different day from yesterday and, therefore, a new opportunity to act better.

At least, this is what Elizabeth told herself to help ignore what she had done and how she felt about it subsequently. Emotions were for weak women, she kept telling herself.

Meanwhile, Conrad felt so proud of his wife. She was truly becoming his soul mate. They were to remain together in health and sickness always. Though he told her repeatedly that the Fleischers do not get sick. She made note that sickness was also a sign of weakness and was not allowed. To maintain the appearance of her newly adopted surname, Elizabeth never complained about any aches or pains—she just dealt with them and Conrad did the same.

They were a couple that seemed to guests the perfect,

rational man and wife who could raise children into the world to become great. Their power emanated from their manor, and in how they each carried themselves.

This is what Conrad sought all along. He wanted to rule over his domain, his family, as the head of the household. He would raise strong, brilliant children with a wife who was his equal in mind and spirit. Of course, her body, he knew, was of the weaker sort, though she was strong and healthy for her kind. He loved the things that made her different, like her long hair and her soft, sweet-smelling skin. He would not change anything about her, especially now that she had come around to appreciating his job.

For Conrad, he knew, was a good, just man and one who kept society civil. He meted out justice in his neighborhood to maintain peace and a proper place for his future children to live in. This, he believed, was a man's job naturally: Men protect, while women defend. The men go out and prevent coercion of their loved ones, protecting them from any harm. The women defended their way of life and the morals that they teach from generation to generation of children. In this way, a household thrives and maintains itself over generations.

A family must have their affairs all in order to continue to succeed. Conrad had heard his grandfather repeatedly tell him the old proverb "from rags to riches and back again in three generations." His father had established himself here in America and his father before him for hundreds of years now. It fell on Conrad's shoulders to maintain their lifestyle for himself and his children without falling prey to the proverb. He was determined not to let any of his money go. No one would sully the Fleischer name.

Conrad wanted his wife to understand the pride he felt

about his family name, and he did. He bought this manor and showed her all of its intricate details. He made sure to keep and restore any historical relics given to him by his family members. They occupied every space in the house. And he modeled the behavior he expected to see from anyone who bore his surname, such as not complaining about the body and never showing emotion. A Fleischer was always rational and of a cool, somber mind.

He knew, especially with her nature of being a woman, that her emotions were going to be the most difficult aspect to train and overcome. But to rear children properly, he thought she must keep her head level and not blubber with emotion at everything she saw or touched. Elizabeth would have to learn that a weak person cannot maintain riches, and they will return to rags if they lose sight of it.

Conrad understood everyone out there in the world was looking for easy, fast money. He knew that if a man could hoodwink another out of his money, he would do so. And so, ever on the lookout, Conrad made sure that he hid his money well and never gave a penny more than he had to—the rest was saved.

He saved the majority in the bank there in town, but some of the money was kept in the gun safe, other amounts inside secret jacket pockets of his, and still other amounts in the little cracks and crevices throughout the home. There was money in all kinds of forms too, whether it came in gold coins or bars or paper or other precious metals or stones or even foreign currency.

In fact, many things were scattered throughout their home. Conrad always kept his guns in strategic places around the house, upstairs and downstairs. There were switchblades and knives atop mantles and door trimmings. Bits and pieces of the attic came off in chunks where he could hide things from the ceiling to the floor. Essentially, no place was off-limits for Conrad to feel more secure about preserving his money and his security. He lived like there was always a predator watching him.

His behavior made Elizabeth wonder if he really knew deep down that what he was doing was illegal. The "career" path he chose was one that subverted the law and brought emotional pain to those who may have a background story that he never took the time to understand. But perhaps he was right in that a person could have a difficult upbringing and still not choose to harm another. Maybe they had no right to empathy once they committed harm against another person.

Elizabeth grappled in silence with these thoughts as she found herself going through the typical daily tasks: cooking, cleaning, lots of cleaning, and doing laundry. All these tasks needed to be done because Elizabeth had neglected them while assisting Conrad with his jobs. The house was a mess and started to smell rusty.

Everywhere, the metallic smell infiltrated the manor. The smell even wafted up to the attic, where it mixed with the dead, musty odor of age. No matter how many times Elizabeth sprayed or hosed down the basement floor of blood, the smell stayed. The fear built up inside of her that she would no longer be able to smell the telltale signs of blood anymore just from being around it for so long. One day, she imaged the police would walk in and be blinded by the vile smells emanating from the manor. Within a second, they would both be under arrest, with nothing for evidence but the smell.

Having such thoughts caused her to reach for bleach and

other powerful chemicals which were preferable to the smell of blood. Over the next few days, she frequently went out of the house and into the side yard just long enough to take in the fresh air, clear her nostrils, and then walk back in the house to test out if she could smell blood still. Every time there was an awful mixture of rust and bleach—an even more damning combination.

Elizabeth knew that before the first frost came, she needed to keep all the windows of the manor open, but Conrad was too paranoid to let that happen. He allowed some of the upper floor windows to be opened a smidge and, even then, only during the daytime and for a few hours at a time. Elizabeth then had to do a walk-through of the house, checking every corner for intruders. Life in the Fleischer household was becoming *exhausting*.

The couple took turns checking the house after the windows were all closed. The fresh air did help get most of the smell of violence out, but Elizabeth had no clue how they could keep up with Conrad's work in the middle of winter, which was fast approaching. Rather than contemplating such awful outcomes, she tired herself out with the checks.

Often if she made too much noise, Conrad would shush her to listen for a moment to his surroundings, worried that perhaps someone was watching from their side yard or else hiding in the bushes that surrounded their property. It was always something. He even listened out for any bats or rodents in the walls. Nothing escaped his notice if it entered his property.

The bugs that lived another day could only stay because Conrad allowed them to. It was just too much work to keep on top of all the quiet little spiders who made their homes in the Queen Anne manor. Besides, he thought that the more foreboding the home looked, then the less it would be messed with by outsiders.

So, the bugs were given a break, that is, until Elizabeth sucked them up with the vacuum cleaner once a month. But she surmised that a whole month for a bug living in peace must feel like a lifetime in a bug's life, so she made an effort not to empathize with her victims as she sucked them up into the tornado of dust inside of the vacuum cup.

She imagined the cobwebs that went with them wrapping around their owner just as they wrapped up their victims before dehydrating them of all their fluids. In a sick way, Elizabeth found her own sense of justice among the spiders. She taught them a lesson about their style of capturing and eating alive their prey. In a twisted circle of life story, the spider became its own captive within the vacuum, and Elizabeth was happy to play the judge.

After cleaning the home and airing it out over the next several days, Elizabeth felt a bit more in control of the situation. No one came looking for them after the latest pair and no one had called Conrad either—everything became peaceful once again as the next day lulled into the next.

Elizabeth even imagined that this is how life will be when they slowed down from old age. They only attended to the household chores and nothing else. There were no jobs to go to or children left to care for—just the couple back in their home and tending to its needs.

But her fantasies could not last for much longer. Their adult lives together were still *just* beginning, and heaps of work had yet to be done. The Fleischers were not free quiet yet.

The next client contacted Conrad, in Elizabeth's opinion,

too soon. On the phone, she could hear the caller sounding frantic—a woman, she thought. Her voice was becoming screechier even from where Elizabeth was standing and she smiled as Conrad had to lift his ear away from the phone.

"I understand. Yes, okay, I will collect the job soon at the location you gave me. I'm writing it down now, yes. Yes, I am familiar with the area. No reason to worry, I'm a professional. Okay, and the money is expected beforehand. All right, very good. See you soon. Bye," said Conrad, quickly hanging up and sucking in his breath before turning on his heel to see Elizabeth.

"A wife has just been beaten to a pulp by her husband after she confronted him about gambling away all of their savings. They were saving up to start a family together and, well, now it seems he's ruined her dreams with his addiction. She thinks that the only way to get him back is to scare him straight. She said she had tried to send him to rehab before for gambling, but all their talking and therapy did not seem to change him much." Conrad shrugged his shoulders. "Sometimes men just need to be physically handled. Anyway, are you ready to jump in the car to help me? He's another larger job." Conrad gave Elizabeth the saddest pair of eyes and she just nodded.

She hoped that this time would be simpler and cleaner than the previous jobs. How much could a person pay for a gambling addiction, anyway? Dare she ask, she wondered in the car, waiting for Conrad to start the engine.

"So...what is the punishment for gambling?" asked Elizabeth.

"And assault? Don't forget he beat his wife," said Conrad.

"Yes, gambling on top of assault, then."

"Well, the Puritans of Massachusetts banned gambling. If

you were caught doing such, it would be the public stocks for you where trash could be thrown at you by the public for an extended period, and I'm sure some whippings were thrown in there for good measure. Again, we can't show this man out to the public. They would probably call such an act 'barbaric' but what do they know? They should have all heard this poor woman who just wants to raise her own children in peace!" Conrad's knuckles grew white as he gripped the steering wheel tighter, thinking about what he would do to such a monster.

"And will you be in charge of the punishments, then?" asked Elizabeth, still hoping that her test to him had been accomplished with the last jobs.

He stayed silent for a moment too long. She could tell that he was considering splitting up the responsibilities before he said: "Here's what I'm thinking. We could still humiliate him in my office by stripping him naked and bending him over the chair, rather than tying him immediately to it. You could play 'the public' and shame him and throw stuff at him while I give him periodic whippings from behind. How does that sound, dear?"

"I suppose so…but do you think that will really stop him?"

Conrad looked over at her in the passenger seat. "You little sadist, are you asking to up his punishment?"

"No, no! I just don't know how humiliated I could make him feel. I feel like I'd embarrass myself more than anyone else. I mean, who boos another person alone?"

"I could chime in. That makes two of us. Unless you have a better idea, my little sadist."

Elizabeth shook her head. She had no knowledge of historical punishment aside from what she had seen in movies, and even then, she was skeptical about whether those methods were actually used.

They arrived at the front door of the little house not too far from their own manor. It was only one story and had plain, white shingles that were turning brown from the growing amount of dirt on them. The house looked rather pitiful and poor. In Elizabeth's eyes, it was not really a fit place to raise children in. But the couple approached the door anyway and Conrad knocked.

A man opened the door up a crack, asking, "You a cop? What do you want?"

"No," said Conrad, "I wanted to see your wife for a moment. She owes me some money for cleaning up leaves the other day."

The man yelled out behind him for his wife, who ran to the front door. She clearly had bruising up and down her frame.

"I'll take it from here, thank you," she said and her husband presumably went back down to sit on the couch. Elizabeth and Conrad could both hear the squeaking of the plastic wrapped over the couch as he sat down. Meanwhile, doing everything in her power to signal to them that that was their next job, she nodded for them to enter. She pushed an envelope of cash into Conrad's hands as he took out a white rag from his jacket pocket.

Conrad was as swift and graceful as a dancer as he came up behind this woman's husband and put him in a choke hold from behind the couch, using the back of it to lean against as he held him. The man was powerful, but Conrad had the advantage of surprise. He slapped the rag over the man's face and, without needing either of the women's help, the husband finally went limp on the couch. The plastic whined even louder as he slumped right down it and onto the floor.

Elizabeth brought the dolly and the sheet without prompting once she had seen that the husband was out. The two hoisted him on and wheeled him out, telling the wife that he would be sure to come back home a new man.

The woman had never looked happier as she waved, smiling at the two people that had just knocked her husband out and dragged him away. She was vile.

"You know the drill now," said Conrad, "apply the rag on his face every ten minutes and make sure he stays down."

Elizabeth simply nodded, and she sidled her way into the backseat with the rather ugly man's snout on her lap. She had to feel his head lolling around on her thighs as they drove home. She hoped that at least he would not drool or vomit on her before they got there. As long as he just kept sleeping, then she could maintain her composure. Though the shirt he had on made her sick. It was checkered in red and white. He looked like a picnic blanket, ridiculous. Her opinions about this man, from the way he answered the door to the way he yelled for his wife to now how hideous his shirt was, were all solidified by the time they got home. She *hated* him.

Hating the job made it much easier, Elizabeth found, to carry out the punishment. She began to feel that it was measured and had to be done—not just for their current crimes—but for their behavior leading up to it. This job was an abominable pain, and it was surprising that he even had a wife in the first place, which perhaps speaks poorly on the wife herself. But Conrad taught Elizabeth pretty quickly that you cannot start questioning the client. The client showed enough proof already and should not be thought of again until the job is delivered. He said it made the work easier in that way too.

So, the Fleischers did the same old thing of hauling the body down the basement stairs and into Conrad's office. Only this time, Conrad ordered Elizabeth to help him strip the man naked. Elizabeth *really* hated him now that she had to see him naked. He was hairy in all the *wrong* places: low on his ankles, on his big toes, between his eyebrows, and other unnamed crevices. She shook in horror to find hair growing in places she had never even thought possible. They were thick, curly black pieces that she hoped would not be left behind on their floor once they were finished. The thought of finding those hairs stuck to her clothing—or in her food—made her want to vomit.

After he was completely naked, too much time had passed between applications of the rag to his face and he came to. Elizabeth noticed it first: "Oh god! He's starting to move. Where's the rag?!"

But Conrad ignored her entirely.

"Hey! He's waking up, don't you see?" she yelled.

But Conrad continued to drape his job over the chair and tie him up a little too slowly.

"Conrad, seriously. What has gotten into you? This man could *hurt* you," Elizabeth pleaded.

Conrad's attention finally shifted to his wife. "I think we need a little entertainment today. A little bit of a challenge."

"Are you *insane*? We mete out justice. We don't play cat and mouse!" cried Elizabeth.

But her yelling only made Conrad visibly slow down in his efforts to restrain the man who by now was starting to blink and take in his situation. The two of them did not even have their masks on.

Before the job could look up, Elizabeth turned around and

ran to the plastic table where the masks should have been laying. To her horror, they were not there. "Conrad, where are the masks?!" Elizabeth did a poor job of covering her face with her hands as she scurried over to him.

"We won't be needing masks today," was all he said as he looked her straight in the eyes.

"But…but he'll see us. He'll tell the police…," said Elizabeth.

"Remember what I've told you a dozen times? The police won't intervene. They know who I am and what I do to criminals. They won't say anything. Besides," Conrad broke his eye contact for a moment, "I didn't tell you everything his wife said to me on the phone."

"What are you saying?" asked Elizabeth, though when she caught him breaking his gaze, her heart sunk into the bowels of her stomach. "Conrad, what else did he do?"

"He killed someone last night."

Elizabeth knew what that meant, "an eye for an eye."

"I knew you would not take part if I told you everything."

Elizabeth broke down, her shoulders shaking violently, when Conrad pushed her down to the floor.

The job had tried to swing the chair he was attached to right at Elizabeth's head in that instant. She crawled out of the way, screaming, into a dark corner of the basement.

The job was given a chance to fight against his inevitable death. How much did he hear of their conversation? Perhaps he knew Conrad knew he killed someone. Did Conrad know who? The man swung as if he certainly knew the depth of his crimes.

The chair flew and a terrible cracking sound occurred, snapping off two of the legs of the chair once it came back down onto the limestone floor. A chunk of the wood splintered away and flew awfully close to where Elizabeth was trying to hide. Her head was in between her knees as she tried to maintain consciousness. This was all going way too far now. She was unprepared for murder. How could Conrad do this to her?

The job managed to free his hand from the ropes left on the shattered chair—still jumping around naked and vulnerable to Conrad, who wanted to hunt down his prey before killing him. He must have done this before…killed someone.

CHAPTER III

Conrad swung right and left hooks at the large man. He was leaner and faster, which meant that though Conrad lacked the weight, he could injure quickly. He knew that the surgical tools were just over in the next section of the basement, but Elizabeth could tell that this was part of the torture and it was only beginning for this man. There was no way that Conrad was going to stab him and have him bleed out just five minutes into getting him down in his office.

She clutched her own throat, trying to keep herself from screaming anymore and getting her husband in trouble. Conrad was going to force her to choose between helping him subdue the job or abandoning him in a crisis. With a numbness in her body, Elizabeth tried to pull herself up, using the dusty stones on the wall to help. Her feet felt like odd blocks that she placed in front of the other, nearing the fighting men. But Conrad threw her such a look that she stayed there in fear.

Conrad launched himself at the job, who was still standing upright after all of those punches. His nose dripped with blood, but he was still very much conscious. Slamming his fist into Conrad's lungs, an audible crack could be heard and a loss of breath.

"Conrad!" Elizabeth screamed. Frantically glancing around, she found the bottle of chloroform on her left side and she ran for it. Conrad was crouched on the ground, breathing funny. The job ran toward the door, trying to unlock himself from whatever situation he was in, but Elizabeth broke the end of the bottle on the stone wall and stabbed him once in the back. The edges of the bottle stuck into his flesh. He finally screamed. The man frantically tried to reach for the bottle while fussing absentmindedly with the door handle.

It was just enough time for Conrad, clearly injured, to smack him over the head with a bat that was by the door. He fell down finally like an ugly ogre, the glass bottle riding the waves of his breathing. It was a good way of indicating that he was still alive.

The second chair used on the female job was still down there and Elizabeth fetched it. Then she helped Conrad drag the man to the back of it and tied his legs together and his arms to those of the chair.

"This is what we should have done in the first place!" screamed Elizabeth. "What is *wrong* with you?! Now you are injured. Is that what you planned? To get injured? How are you going to explain this to the doctors?"

"*Shut up*, woman!" he shouted in return. "My head already aches without your shrieks! I will just tell the doctor, if I even go, that I tripped down the basement stairs. No big deal. No one has a right anyway to know about our affairs. Now, help me make sure these are tight before he comes to again, the bastard." And Conrad gave him quite the kick in the side for his putting up such a fight. He had not expected him to be so resilient.

The man woke up soon after they had finished tightening

the ropes.

"I've seen both of your faces!" the husband raged. "I'll report both of you *sickos* to the police!" His face grew red like a cherry. "Unbind my hands and feet *now*!"

Conrad just looked at Elizabeth and said: "It appears that in our struggle we forgot the duct tape. And as for our masks, well, my wife knows that any knowledge you may have of us is utterly useless—not only are the police on *my* side but your own wife. She paid us to torture you..."

Elizabeth noticed his withholding of the most devastating bit of news as she handed Conrad the duct tape.

"Now it's my turn to talk. You have said quite enough," said Conrad. The sound of the tape being stripped off the roll echoed in the office quarters. He slapped a large piece over his job's mouth, thereby ending all refutations for his crimes. "You have been accused of not only beating up your wife but that you spent saved money all on gambling, among other such horrific crimes that we shall speak of later. I am here as an angel of retribution.

"Did you know that in Puritan Massachusetts, the punishments were often physical? For adulterers, it could be anything from whipping to execution. For gamblers, it could be the stocks or public whipping, or both. For smokers, fines were ruthlessly administered. Just about everything had a penalty attached to it, and there were the good men of the law who distributed the punishments. You are face-to-face with a modern-day example of such a man.

"First, we are to shame you publicly in your most vulnerable skin and throw things at you as they would have in the public stocks. Elizabeth! Proceed."

Elizabeth had gotten rotten food from the trash can right

before they picked the job up. She had rummaged around a short time before finding the bits and pieces she needed: brown banana skins, green bread, squishy peaches, and even the familiar rotten tomatoes.

She opened the putrid-smelling bag and stuck her hand in what could only be described as food that gave in to the touch. It was all just decaying mush and the feeling would remind her of events that occurred later too.

Pulling out a rotten tomato, she hurled it from a short distance right into the man's face. The vein in his forehead popped out now as he was probably trying to scream about how backward this all was.

"Now tell him how *ugly* he is!" shouted Conrad, evidently enjoying the show.

"You're ugly!" *Splat!* Another tomato landed on his face. The muck shut his eyes this time. She imagined how they burned with the impurities living on and within the tomato skins.

But she hardened her heart to the scene before her, reminding herself that this man was a callous killer. He murdered his own mother for gambling money after all. To kill the one who bore you in their womb for nine months and taught you everything they know for years—it was just awful. Elizabeth remained strong as she stuck her hand in the bag for another rotten item.

This time she grabbed the old peach, which hit his face and as the pulp fell right away, it was the hard pit in the center that gave him a nasty scratch. It bled and burned his flesh, probably filling with more bacteria as time wore on. But, Elizabeth told herself, he deserved every bit of what he was getting today, every bit.

The flesh of the fruit was still slipping off his face when

Conrad told her to throw another and call him names. She picked out the brown banana, tore off the bruised flesh, and whipped the pulpy mush into his face, while yelling, "You monster! Feel every ounce of shame and pain you have caused your wife!"

The duct tape was starting to unpeel from the job's mouth as he was attempting to talk back.

Finally, a green piece of bread was left in the bag, and throwing it would not do much to this man. Elizabeth walked straight up to him of her own volition, tore the tape completely off, and, watching out for her own fingers, shoved the green bread in his mouth just as he tried cursing at her.

"You witch! Get the hell away from me!" was all that he could say before he was spitting out the moldy bread onto the floor. Conrad, in his mild surprise, handed Elizabeth a fresh piece of tape to put over his mouth before he managed to spit the rest of the bread out. She forced his open jaw up with her knee as she sealed his mouth back—his face turning green from the taste of the bread, which had soaked up much of the rotten tomato juices still dripping down his face.

"There! How do you like that?" said Elizabeth. Once her part was done, she looked to Conrad to take over, but he stayed behind his job. Suddenly feeling dizzy, she hoped he did not have another part for her to play. But, after some rearranging of the body in relation to the chair, he proceeded to whip the man on the bare back instead. Lash after lash from his upper back all the way down to his calves, all whips landed with a purpose to be hard enough to draw blood.

Elizabeth's ears had grown used to the sound a person made when they screamed beneath a piece of duct tape. She was not as fazed by such a reaction anymore to the pain. It was okay as long as she was not the one feeling it. After all, she reminded herself, she had done nothing wrong. The bad guys are the ones who deserve this pain.

Still, her stomach knotted itself up as she watched the blood start to trickle like a tiny river down the chair legs and around the man's feet. He mashed his naked toes in his own warm blood, like a child playing in a rainstorm.

Conrad kept whipping him and then asking Elizabeth: "Is he still conscious?"

"Yes, still conscious." And then *whack!* went another hit, *smack!* It caused audible gashes in this man's hide, which Conrad seemed pleased that he put there. He had thoughts of men being whipped before. He had seen movies where they showed slaves arching over in pain and being unable to hide their scars. As a child, he had remembered with awe the power that the man with the whip in his hand must feel. For he wielded the instrument used to distort the flesh. Conrad saw himself as someone akin to the local butcher in that way. He was merely providing a service for the locals of the town—beating those who could not play nice in society.

It was his job to beat those who kill and maim and shame others. And he took full responsibility for righting those wrongs. Conrad felt like an artist with a paintbrush, cutting up his canvas and causing the colors to bleed down in fanciful rivers, intricately woven together and falling apart. He masterfully used his canvas—not a single piece would be left empty. It would all be touched by his instrument.

Raining down blows, Conrad soon grew tired, too tired to make art. He paused. This was still the first act, and he needed to rest up if he was going to conclude his time with this pile of rot successfully. Every workman deserved his lunch break, so

Conrad knocked out his job swiftly, dragging his body to sit properly in the chair, making sure to press his bloodied spine against the back of it to inflict as much pain as possible once he came to, and tied him to the chair—using the holes in the arms and the chair's legs for the job's own.

"Good, now you wait here, you slime, while we take a break for lunch. I don't get paid enough to skip my lunch," said Conrad to the unconscious man sitting before him.

Elizabeth found it hard to find an appetite, knowing that the job was alone in the basement while they prepared for lunch.

"Should I check on him?" she kept asking.

"No. Besides, he'll be knocked out for at least another five minutes. Just go make our sandwiches," he said, sitting in the kitchen table chair and resting his hands on the back of his head.

"But what if he jumps in the chair toward the surgical tools and cuts his way out?"

"I would hear him and his fat body jumping around down there."

"But what about him somehow untying himself with his own hands?"

"Unlikely. Now can we just eat?" said Conrad.

The two ate at the small kitchen table in cold silence.

***

The food was too dry to swallow for Elizabeth as she tried begging her salivary glands to do their job. She nearly choked the dry bread down, visualizing the moldy piece that undoubtedly left traces behind in the job's mouth. Trying not to dry heave, Elizabeth got up to get a glass of water. She chugged it all before even sitting back down at the table.

Conrad ate with ease. He ate almost with a hunger, like that of a wolf. It was as if he had stolen Elizabeth's saliva and added it to his own pools forming at the sides of his mouth. His teeth gnashed and the bread, which turned to nothing in a matter of milliseconds, was swallowed in wet clumps. Elizabeth could tell that he was still hungry, so she offered up the other half of her sandwich to him in the hopes of appeasing her god.

He snatched up the food with vigor, as if one more bite would finally satiate his enduring hunger. But her half of the sandwich did not cut it and with a fury in his eyes, Conrad rose from the table, burning. He wanted more blood. What was he thinking right now, wondered a fearful Elizabeth.

All he had done was refuel his energy and the abundance of hate that Conrad carried for this murderer. His heart still felt heavy for the loss of the job's mother, and staring at the back of this disgusting naked man's body for hours already just made him more inclined to kill him. "An eye for an eye" is what Conrad believed in—only the perpetrator, the coercer, should feel much more pain before their final release. And Conrad would make sure of it.

"Let's go. I kicked my fatigue back with those sandwiches and in sitting down for a bit. My anger toward this man is becoming unbearable," said Conrad to Elizabeth as she got up to clean the dishes. "Oh, just put them in the dishwasher already, that's why we have one!" yelled Conrad, unable to control his anger any longer. He flung the basement door open, shocking the hinges holding it to its frame. The screw heads keeping them together were probably buzzing from the impact even after Elizabeth had closed the door once more.

The chair was gone.

Elizabeth panicked. Conrad, who was ahead of her, had already been looking for his captive, scouring his office.

Elizabeth turned around to double-check that she had actually locked the door behind her. There could be *no* chance the job had left the basement. Her head spun around at the sound of flesh hitting flesh.

It appeared that the man in the chair had somehow shifted the entire chair with himself on it into a dark corner of the office. What he intended to do once there was unclear, but thankfully it was in the opposite direction of all the surgical tools.

Elizabeth walked up to where her husband was eyeing his job. Tugging on his shirt like a child, she said, "If we leave him alone again, we need to take our tools with us. See how easy it was for him to scoot around?"

Conrad only nodded. It was such a silly mistake to make that Elizabeth was worried about his mindset right then. He wanted to get his job back under the singular light to see his work better. So, he hauled the naked man on the chair back under the light in the back section of the basement office. Back where he originally was and was meant to be. The man struggled and howled, but Conrad only took note and would punish him for it tenfold.

Conrad would break this man of all spirit before exterminating him from this earth. He started by beating the criminal's face in all black and blue—nothing spared: cracked nose, cracked eye sockets, cracked jaw, cracked cheekbones, cracked forehead. Once his canvas was colored in, he called: "Scalpel!"

Elizabeth handed him the item, and he gripped her close to him, telling her to watch. She must watch and learn what evil must endure here on earth. In her horror, Conrad first went for the man's right ear. The scalpel was so sharp that it did not take much sawing to detach. Blood drained out of his head as he screamed beneath the tape and Elizabeth was forced to harden her heart to the entire scene. These were not, she told herself, screams of the innocent but the wicked. This man did not consider the life that he had taken for money. He snuffed out a life that still had things to do in this world for lousy gambling money. He deserved no sympathy. The criminal was a monster, not her own husband.

Conrad chucked the ear onto the floor, keeping in mind not to throw it out of the man's sight. He wanted his job to know that he was losing pieces of himself, one by one. Then, the left ear came off with ease—more blood, more screams, a deafening silence that came with his loss of consciousness.

"Go get the cold water," said Conrad, pressing a wet shirt to each side of the man's head. Again, he was not allowed to bleed out just yet. He had much more suffering to endure, according to Conrad.

Elizabeth splashed the cold water over his face and he reawoke and, as if in a nightmare, he tried to blink several times. This was something he could not wake up from. The end of his life was near. Did he know it? wondered Elizabeth. Can a man tell when he is near the end? He must.

The shirt quickly soaked with red. "Get me another shirt to wrap around this worthless scum's head," ordered Conrad. This was nothing compared to what he was imagining would be the finale of this job. He kept seeing, as was his "skill," various ways of killing this man, from shooting to hanging to drowning to burning to choking, all manners of death were on the table. It was his job to select the most appropriate one for the crime.

But which punishment, which one? Conrad thought. Killing one's mother was probably the most heinous thing a person could do. And this job was full of excuses and fighting to struggle to escape, as if he had no regrets. At least an honest man would give in to his punishment. He would not fight like this man was. It means that he has not learned and if he has not learned by now, then he never will, concluded Conrad. It was just for him to seek the most painful way to die.

But what was the most painful way to die? To stab a man would certainly hurt, but depending on where a person was punctured, it could cause death to arrive rather quickly. To drown, thought Conrad, would be uncomfortable since a person would languish, trying to breathe but ultimately suffocating until losing consciousness. But their bodies are still intact. To burn to death would feel tremendously painful if you had to feel your blood boil inside and your skin peel away from the bone. Yes, that could very well be the most excruciating and long-lasting among some of the most common options. The least painful, he thought, must be falling from a height because a person would probably lose consciousness before landing and being choked to death since they were still in one piece.

Conrad glanced over at the job, still sitting there and taking stock of his injuries and pain. The most awful thing for a man who had the audacity to kill his mother, beat his wife, and go off to gamble with their money must be to know that their own life is over—that it was all meaningless and mean and small. The perpetrator had to understand that he had fallen, like Satan, from heaven. He had to *know* that his narcissism brought him to his early death and that he *deserved* such treatment.

The last punishment from Conrad must give the criminal enough time to *see* himself dying. He must not be as preoccupied with surviving as he was during life. He must just be there, even if it is for seconds, to recognize that his life is already irretrievably over.

"Conrad!" Elizabeth screamed.

The job scooted in the wooden chair toward her. Astonished at his speed, Elizabeth had become frozen to her spot, though he was still tied up. He could, in theory, squish her up against a wall or headbutt her in the stomach or try to land a chair leg on her foot. Any number of things flashed in her mind as the criminal approached.

Conrad snapped out of his contemplations to save Elizabeth. He ran up toward the back of the chair and forcibly dragged it back to where it initially was.

By now, it was getting late and dinner needed to be cooked. Elizabeth was in charge of that domain, but without a clock in the office, she had no idea what time it was. Only her stomach growls gave her a hint that it must be later than usual.

After Conrad heard her stomach, he motioned with his head for her to go upstairs to start cooking.

"What?! I'm not leaving you down here by yourself," she said.

"So then we'll just starve tonight?" asked Conrad.

"No, but how can we eat anyway when such a creature is down here and still fighting us?"

"You know I've had this job since before you."

"There is no 'before me,'" she emphatically declared, pouting now.

"I think it's cute that you want to forget your past like that and have me forget mine. Fine, I'll play along." He patted her on the head like a little pet. "Go around the outside of the office and grab the hammer drill that's hanging on the wall.

Its body is dark blue."

Elizabeth did as she was told. Hoping that the drill she found was the right type of drill that he was requesting. "Here, now what are you going to do with it?" She was afraid to hear the answer.

"Well, if I put him back where he was originally supposed to be in the middle of the room here, then I can drill holes around the chair into the stone, tie more rope around the legs, and nail them down to the actual floor. That way he cannot move from his "assigned seat." He glanced over at the man who could still hear but barely at this point with the blood-soaked shirts around his wounded ears.

"Okay, but shouldn't we check on him to make sure he doesn't try to escape? And I told you that if we leave him again, we are taking the surgical tools off the table and hiding them somewhere safe."

Conrad simply rolled his eyes, acknowledging his wife's nagging by going over to the tools and handing them to her. "There you go. Now you can take them with you while I start drilling."

Shallowly exhaling with relief, Elizabeth took the tools and left without another word. She could see that Conrad was already irritated enough.

Walking up the steps and into the darkness of the evening, with those tools in her hand, felt surreal, as if this was a dream that was happening. She placed the cold tools on her skin and watched the hairs on her arm stand up at attention. She was, indeed, awake.

The instruments were extremely sharp and were contaminated with their job's blood all over them. They needed to go to a place that was safe from all prying eyes. She saw a cupboard way high up in the kitchen, which was never used. It hung up there near the ceiling, much too high to be practicable. Why it even existed was always a mystery to Elizabeth as she rolled the tools up in a paper towel, stuck them in a plastic baggie, and placed them inside that cupboard after climbing a step stool to reach in. Climbing down and washing her hands gave her the first moment of calm in what felt like days. The objects of torture were safely put away.

CHAPTER IV

Their dinner and subsequent ascent to the bedroom were all done in a sterile silence; it was downright eerie. Once in bed, the Fleischers lay next to the other as if already dead and gone, buried next to each other right there. The sheet held their corpses out of pity. They were only feeling warmth in their deceased minds; there was only cold darkness outside of them. But their bed consoled the two lost souls as they tried with all their might to drift off to a more peaceful place.

But Conrad was filled with rage, as he always was beforehand when he had jobs that lasted days before. He remained angry until the job was done. Now, he was even more full of rage because Elizabeth had to see the finale.

While Elizabeth lay there filled with fear and sorrow. In a rush of confusion, she tried to make sense of why they had to carry so much burden in their hearts when this man deserved no pity. He committed the most heinous crimes...and yet, she felt *guilty*. She no longer wanted to witness pain or see her husband so upset, either. It was especially nerve-wracking to fall asleep with a killer in their house.

Rationalizing the whole situation made the pain less severe eventually for a drifting Elizabeth. She thought, Well, maybe if

I could focus my mind on something else like Conrad did, then I could help him mete out justice and still emerge with a clear conscience. Her fatigue made her reasoning more sensible than it was and she finally forgot the world.

Meanwhile, Conrad eased his heated mind by imagining a scenario where Elizabeth made love to him again, like with the last job. Only this time she was having sex with him in front of this villain and she thought *nothing* of him. She carried no moral weight around her neck, waiting to drown in the sea with her ship of values. Instead, she glowed, recognizing that this man was only getting what he deserves and no more. He imagined her looking up to him as a strong, just husband—her one and only. He would never mislead or betray her, and that belief caused him to drift off as well.

They slept in their manor peacefully after the clocks all struck midnight. The job in the basement shuffled and shook. He heard the bells ring, assuming that his kidnappers must be asleep since it had been hours since they had come down.

In a panic, he had watched Conrad drill holes into the floor and physically tie the chair down. To his horror, the ties were strong and he could go nowhere. How could he ever escape? he wondered. What would they do to him? He was in survival mode. There was no time to sleep. No time to recover his wounds. He had to escape.

The first thing he thought to do was to make himself as small as possible. He exhaled all the air he could to try to wriggle the rope down his chest and onto the small part of his waist. But the rope only moved a tiny bit. He tried to make his hands into fists to shrink his wrists and wriggle out, but there was not enough room. His feet could not squeeze out of the ropes in any way.

Hours into the wriggling, the man looked down at his body to see it was beginning to bleed from being rubbed raw. Everything burned. But if he had not passed out yet, then he had to keep trying. The clocks ticked by the hours as he tried to fall over in the chair. He had to change any aspect of his position in order to try other tactics of escape.

Eventually, he yanked hard enough to loosen the two nails on his left side and he fell hard onto the right. His right arm fell asleep quickly as he tried wriggling his left side free. The nails and the tugging had loosened the ropes on his left leg, which allowed him to escape. But what could he do with one leg free?

Although the chair was made of heavy wood, he hoisted it up on his back by using the momentum of his neck to right himself from his right side onto his knees with the chair still attached to his right leg and the rest of his upper body. Painfully, he pushed multiple times up onto the tops of his toes to try to right himself again back in the chair. The tops of his feet grew bruised and his forehead laid for what felt like hours on the cold, hard stone, resting. With enough momentum, he rolled up over his toes, which cracked from the force as he finally got back upright.

His focus now was to tug at the right ropes and pull away from them just like on the left side. He fell over, using all of his weight to the left this time, and had to repeat the entire process to right himself again—only now he had gotten both legs free.

Both legs made getting up a bit easier, though his toes were swelling by now. But his chest and arms were still attached to the chair. Only now he heard creaking from upstairs. Renewed panic set in as he realized that there was no more time to wriggle out of the ropes. He had to use what he had freed overnight to make his escape…or at least to kill his captors.

He walked with a crooked back, the chair up in the air and balancing on top, to the locked door. Regardless of the noise he made, he sat back down right in front of it and kicked with all the power of his legs—once, twice, thrice.

Elizabeth heard the knocks first, sitting upright in bed, while Conrad was coming back from his trip to the bathroom. It was about six o'clock and they were both getting up. But after hearing the first knock, she met Conrad in the hallway on his way back, hiding herself in his chest. "He's trying to knock down the office door!" she screamed.

Conrad knew that having a hysterical wife by his side was only going to make matters more difficult. "Go back into the bedroom now, lock the door, and hold on to the gun on the nightstand. Don't open it until I come back."

Crying, Elizabeth nodded and ran back toward the bedroom. She did exactly as she was told without hesitation. He made her feel safe, even though none of this would be happening if it was not his job in the first place. The emotional flurry messed with her stomach, and she worried about how long this situation would take. Where could she use the bathroom trapped in the bedroom? she wondered. Her eyes wandered to the little trash can by the bed and that solved one of the many questions buzzing around in her mind.

Skipping steps on his way downstairs, Conrad was livid. He did not want anyone, let alone this scum, to ruin the door he had just put in for his office. He envisioned all the paint chipped off because of this creature's body clawing and kicking away at it.

"Hey!" Conrad shouted at the door. "Knock it off! I have a gun, and I will shoot you if you don't stop right now!" The kicking proceeded. He thought that with the whole ears-cut-off thing that perhaps he could not hear him, so he only screamed louder, keenly aware that the neighbors might hear something from outside of his basement office.

With the blood rising in his face like a thermometer stick, Conrad was losing his patience. He even gave his new door a kick from the outside. But the kicking from the inside continued. Conrad pounded with his fists on the outside of the door in response. The door was weakening with every kick. Conrad decided to open the door in whatever state of freedom this man was in. Perhaps the door would hit the man in the face and stun him for long enough to take control of the situation again.

A single breath in and open the door went, knocking the chair with its occupant backward. Letting out a primeval scream, it took several seconds for Conrad's eyes to adjust to the darkness of the basement office. He could see that his job's body was still somewhat attached to the chair, aside from his legs, which he must have freed during the middle of the night.

"You sly bastard!" he yelled. Running around the now-flailing legs and dragging the back of the chair with the job in it, Conrad hauled him back to the spot where he had initially nailed him down. Conrad began mumbling to himself: "We cannot have this. No, your punishment is set to continue for a couple more days. Today is merely act two of our torturous play. Yes, you cannot escape tonight. I won't allow it!" Trailing off, he pulled the string for the puny light to come on as he looked wildly around for new bits of rope. There would be more rope and zip ties and more nails and more bondage to avoid a repeat. "You frightened my wife!" screamed Conrad, punching the naked man in the flabby guts with all of his increased rage. He went from a scale of zero to ten instantly this morning.

In his mind, the images of potential deaths preoccupied him as he set to work, making sure his job would never leave the spot assigned to him again. The thoughts grew increasingly more specific as he went over them again and again and again: from the way he would turn blue from drowning to death to the way his eyeballs would melt as he burned alive to the way his muscles would convulse if he was electrocuted to a crisp. Many additional details greeted him this morning, and he looked straight into the fearful eyes of his job the entire time, smiling. Conrad never hid the fact that he enjoyed the rush of his job. The adrenaline and testosterone coursing through his veins gave birth to a creature of ultimate control. Just like when he was lifting weights in the gym, the hundred-pound dumbbells became proof that he was in control of his body and his mind. He could move the improbable and change the impossible. Life, the world, was at his mercy.

Upstairs, Elizabeth bit at her nails. The knocks had ceased, but she was too afraid to venture down to the basement yet to look at what the outcome of it all was. She assumed since no one had left the basement that the job had not escaped and was probably under the control again of Conrad. Either that, she worried, or they were both dead. With shaking breaths in and out, ignoring her husband's final order, she made her way down each wooden step, one at a time, pausing between each to listen for any change from below. But hell had not opened up and swallowed her—she remained on solid ground in her own home.

Making her way further down into the bowels of the basement, she found blood spots on the floor of the office and Conrad was busy with the rope. "Had he gotten free?" she asked.

"Yes. The bastard somehow freed his legs from the nailed-down ropes and was trying to kick the new door I put up back down. Those were the knocks you heard. So, to make sure that does not happen again tonight—"

"Tonight?! You mean he's staying for another one? I could barely sleep through *this* night!" Elizabeth blew up, feeling the weight of fatigue pushing her down into the limestone floor.

"That's just too bad. We must follow this job through to the end to uphold our side of the deal with the client. Today is our act two and tomorrow is the final act three. You can make it another night," said Conrad, pulling some of the rope taught and this time he poked the man in the ribs to make him deflate himself before finishing the tying. "There will be no making yourself big to make yourself small and wriggle free tonight! No way. I know your tricks, you scum!" Conrad pulled tighter.

"Conrad, he'll lose limbs like that! The rope is not meant to be a tourniquet," said Elizabeth, watching parts of the man's limbs go white.

"Who cares?" said Conrad.

Elizabeth walked away, disgusted by her husband's callousness. She understood he was going to die...but, for some reason, she kept forgetting...kept *caring* about silly things that a dead man will not need once he is gone. She supposed killing just came unnaturally to her, as if such an act made no sense. How could there not be anything after when there were so many things now? And she cared about them all. She cared about not getting blood on her clothes still; she cared about concealing her face; she cared about not irreversibly damaging the body parts of a man who had no future. Was this what people called a "motherly instinct"? she wondered. The fact that she could cringe at Conrad's lack of feeling meant that her soul still rebelled against all of this.

"We need to go out to the local hardware store and buy more rope, zip ties, and nails. I will need more to keep this fool to stay put since apparently he is still fighting for his life," said Conrad, smacking his captive upside the head. Elizabeth and Conrad went to the store after she offered to make them breakfast. Her stomach was like a timer that reminded them both of their own needs to survive.

Upon arriving home from the errands, one of the neighbors stopped them before they managed to get to their front door.

"Hey!" said the lumbering idiot, his fat hanging out below his shirt. "I heard some loud knocking about and yelling earlier this morning. Is everything all right over there?" Panic rendered Elizabeth too paralyzed to speak, and she tugged on Conrad's shirt like a child.

"Yes! Everything is fine. My wife and I had an argument over a family heirloom that I accidentally knocked over, and it shattered. My wife was not happy about it. But we went out to get some super glue, and I'm going to try my darnedest now to fix it!" shouted Conrad back to his neighbor, hoping that it was just loud enough for the other nosy neighbors to hear. There was nothing to worry about—just normal, spousal spats going on inside the private sphere.

"All right then. Good luck with fixing that heirloom! Hopefully, your wife approves of the job you do. I know how that goes when you can't fix the problem," laughed the rotund neighbor, his belly visibly jiggling with his laughter.

Conrad and the paralyzed Elizabeth both smiled and waved back to their neighbor, opened their front door, and shut it and all the rest of the world out. What happened inside of their own property was nobody else's business, anyway. The two rushed down to the basement to make sure that nothing else had gone awry between the time they stepped out and the time they stepped back in. Thankfully, after all of Conrad's tying, the body had not moved. He was still wriggling but to no effect.

"I'm still going to use up half this stuff before we go back to bed. I don't trust him," said Conrad. Elizabeth merely nodded her head. By day two, she was starting to feel numb to it all.

"Today, I would like to focus on keeping him alive but still inflicting enough pain to make him wish he were dead already. It is a delicate balance," said Conrad. He paced before the job for a few laps before he turned and walked toward the plastic table to observe all of his surgical tools, which he made Elizabeth retrieve from the upper cabinet. Conrad approved of the location but neither of them could reach it without the step stool and so Elizabeth was sent as the official fetcher of tools. Every night she would put them away and every morning bring them back to the basement. It was a habit she was willing to integrate into her life.

Conrad picked up the sharp pair of tweezers, which Elizabeth had seen him use before. She knew what they were good for—peeling off nails and toenails. And that is exactly what he did. Jamming the sharpest tine under the bed of his thumb first, he dragged and ripped apart the flesh from the nail before tearing off the entire thing and dropping it to the floor. The job wailed in agony…first for the thumb…and then for the index...the middle...the ring...and the pinky of his right hand, only to have the agony repeated on the left hand and then both feet. Conrad carried out this torture for hours.

"Get me that bottle of hydrogen peroxide from the bathroom, dear," said Conrad.

She did as she was told. Utterly numb now emotionally to the screams of the job, she watched without flinching Conrad pouring the peroxide all over this man's body, probably as a way to stave off infection and disease for at least another day. The solution turned an angry, bubbly white as it foamed all over his body—increasing the burning sting of pain he must have already been feeling.

"Today, we are focusing on the extremities, as you have already seen. The nails and toenails are all gone. And now we must crucify this man. We must make sure he stays in his chair tonight like he was *supposed* to the previous night. Right?" said Conrad, pointing his finger right in between the man's eyes. He could only wave his head back and forth in response.

Elizabeth thought that perhaps the peroxide was also used to dampen the smell of urine and fecal matter covering the chair at this point, but it just made the smell more noxious. She held her hands to her nose as she watched Conrad's next move.

"We are now about to get a bit more biblical, Elizabeth. I would like you to participate in our religious ritual here. Come," beckoned Conrad.

Elizabeth walked toward her god and gave him her hand without a second thought, numb to one and all now. She only wished desperately for those simpler days when she could lie there in his arms and nod off, feeling so utterly comforted and warm. Listening to the steady beating of his heart, riding the waves of his breathing chest, with nowhere else she would rather be.

The best times were in the middle of the day, preferably spring when hope was in the air and the leaves were budding anew, the sun shone through the lace curtains onto their intertwined bodies, which pretended at that moment to know nothing of work or effort. In their lazy way, they rode the softest movements of their bodies lying there in unison, melting into one whole without any reason to move forward when everything in the world was right there already. Those moments of stillness brought Elizabeth the closest she had ever been to happiness.

She no longer needed to chase at happiness's coattails in those moments. She was there. She had it. And in her newfound numbness, she tried to recall that state of stillness that differed from this moment. It was different in that this felt like an enforced kind of stillness, like she was still running but against a wall of molasses that gave in to her struggles at such a minuscule rate that the change went unnoticed. Time did stand still now, watching Conrad hold out his hand for hers, but she did not want to stay there. She would rather go back to the sun and the warmth given to her by the closeness of their bodies and not in the darkness where they were divided by a bloodied and battered body.

That was her real problem—that body. That man who came in between them and their love, she thought. It was *his* fault. His fault for causing an uncomfortable rift between them, a rift so far apart that she could have hated Conrad and his hand she once admired. But if this *body* had not caused such a gap of feeling, then she would have never known what it felt like to be separated from Conrad. But now, *now*, with his hand sticking out for her, she felt consumed with hatred—hatred for feeling this way and hatred toward the thing that caused it.

Elizabeth thrust her hand into his like it was a life preserver bobbing around on a stormy sea. Her fingernails pierced his skin as he tried to escape quickly her grip.

"Nicely! You fiend," said Conrad, holding his hand and lapping up the blood dripping from his opened flesh.

Recognizing what she had done, her tongue curled. She wanted to choke herself with it. Believing that the next best thing was to fall to her knees and kiss him right where he bled. Painting her lips with the gruesome lipstick, she looked very beautiful there in her submission. Conrad's heart softened, and he lifted her up from the cold ground.

Kissing her on her red lips, his nostrils flared upon inhaling his own metallic fragrance. He knew it well. Burning brighter, his eyes looked hungry. And in her fit of jealous rage, she begged with a soft moan for him to take her.

Yet, again, Elizabeth found herself riding the high of a drug she could never escape—her husband, Mister Fleischer, a man of the flesh. And whenever a tear was felt down the middle of their shared soul, the only way to fix it quickly was to sew themselves back up with their thrusting bodies, working together to bind what was broken.

The job, the body, the *thing*, Elizabeth thought, was all tied up and forced to watch. He had to experience their love and remember what he *lacked* between himself and his assaulted wife. Their relationship was *nothing* like what she had with Conrad. For he always seemed to sense when their souls were torn apart as much as Elizabeth did. They did not need to speak to understand what they both felt.

A violent, animalistic attack of the spirit was the only way to put back together the eroded pieces. Their natural lubricants stuck them back together like glue. Elizabeth fit so well in between everything that was Conrad. Like a dance between serpents, they could easily intertwine and disentangle at will. They moved rhythmically, even if punctuated by bites from their fangs. Each Fleischer moved their long tongue around to better sense the other's current state, while their skins shed from all the vigorous rubbing.

The screams and howls of this morning had transformed their tune by the evening. Pleasure accented each rise and fall of their sexual song. The mixed scent of metal and sweat dragged the act out for longer because they each took a secret joy out of understanding what they had done. They were the predator and not the prey. They were the winners and not the losers. They were the good and *not* the bad.

Panting, sweating, breathing in the poison that bodies create, the Fleischers laid their heaving backs on the limestone. Having both satisfied themselves, they began to come down from their obsessive high. The fangs withdrew and their minds cleared, awakening to the fact that another body was in the room.

The man had watched the entire thing, and he even shared in their excitement, as both of them soon noticed. A hot wave of jealousy escaped from Elizabeth's hands as she swiped at the man's legs from the floor, hoping to sour his excitement. He was not allowed to gaze upon her husband's chiseled figure. He was not allowed to enjoy her breasts. He was the one who caused her such pain before the couple began sewing themselves back together.

"You. I *hate* you!" Elizabeth lashed out. She turned to lie on her side, looking at Conrad, who was still on his back. "What are we going to do to him now?" Surviving her little death had placed her in a space of delicious warmth mixed with cold numbness—a deadly mixture.

CHAPTER V

Conrad grinned like a teenage boy, youthful and careless and devilish all at once. "I believe that tonight's pain should ease your jealousy, my dear. As I was saying before, we are going to get biblical now with a little crucifixion of our own."

"Absolutely brilliant!" gushed out of Elizabeth's mouth before she could reconsider. "You are so creative, love." She was stroking his chest as he lay there on the cold floor, all while the man stared in worry. Did he hear his next punishment? wondered Elizabeth. It seemed not since his dopey face looked confused still and only streaked with anxiety.

The two helped each other up and got dressed. It was shocking to observe two healthy, attractive people in control of a situation that was so medieval and sick in its nature. They stood there, not decrepit like old hags with warts on their noses and ugly forms, but like Adam and Eve innocently playing in the garden. They exuded such innocence and youth. But inside they were growing rotten.

The idea that two attractive people could stand there and watch another ooze and leak without becoming sick to their stomachs would be astonishing to any onlooker. They stood there in front of the job, investigating his body as if they were not constructed of the same material. The Fleischers viewed this man as something *other* than a man. His flesh was not their flesh; his blood was not their blood; his organs were not their organs.

Conrad poked and prodded, quieting the curious voice in his head that wanted to know what this and that part did. He wanted to know how fast things grew just as much as how quickly they could die. He enjoyed his job of justice and controlling such situations.

Elizabeth, on the other hand, enjoyed having all of Conrad and his attention, and anything that got in the way would soon meet an untimely end. Once she found a job taking away Conrad's attention from her, they became the enemy. Men or women, it did not matter which caused their relational pain. Therefore, both were motivated to harm others for differing reasons.

"Get me the hammer and nails—four of them, please," said Conrad.

Elizabeth ran over to the plastic table, still riding on her high of numb ecstasy.

"Thank you. Right, so I will do one palm to show you and then you will do the other. The same will happen with the feet. There is no reason to do this quickly and there really is no 'right way' to do it," said Conrad, clinking the nails together in his hand. An extra sense of pleasure came from watching the man's nervous face, eyeing the rolling set of nails.

"Here we go," he said. He took one nail in between his thumb and index finger and placed the tip right over the man's right hand. It lay, tied by the ropes, on the arm of the wooden chair. Conrad picked up the hammer he had laid on the floor and raised it high. The intact palm that had remained whole for this man's forty-some-odd years of life, with its constant presence of new and dying cells, was to be destroyed in less than a second.

Down came the hammer and Elizabeth watched carefully, like a good student. She forced her eyes to stay on the destruction occurring in real time. The palm had seventeen muscles surrounding the bones to help articulate the fingers and thumb. But now a nail ripped through those muscles. It also divided the many tendons and connective fibrous tissue that attached the skin to the bones. Elizabeth could hear many explosive snaps inside the job's hand as all the intricate hardware was damaged by a crude nail. The force behind the hammer coming down and shattering a man's most helpful tool—his hands—forced a scream that was unheard of in Elizabeth's young years. It was a scream of pain mixed with sorrow.

Man's hands allowed the mind to carry on in the world of action. His hands were vital to creating and building things used for his very survival. Now all of that is ruined with the swing of a hammer. Conrad knew the devastation he was causing and so did Elizabeth, who followed suit.

Once the torture started again, neither Fleischer wanted to speak, as if it would ruin the moment. In an almost holy way, Elizabeth took the nail in her own functioning fingers and placed the nail on top of the man's left hand. Tears soaked his naked chest as blood gushed out of his right hand. But she continued on her journey to render him no longer human. Neither of the Fleischers regarded him as human anyway, at least Conrad had not since the day they picked him up from his house.

She lifted the hammer up as high as her husband, right above her own head, and swung it down with what had looked like the same amount of force used. The man's head swung back in agony as he felt the impact. But the nail had not gone completely through. The nail was stuck in the hand, but Elizabeth watched as his hand quaked. Her eyes grew large, and she looked at Conrad.

He nodded with the clear expectation that she would swing again and force the nail to go all the way through this time. She gulped. Choosing to swing much harder than she had before, she picked up the hammer and made sure the wounded hand was in its proper place.

One more time she swung and one more time his head flew back into the chair as if his life was being sucked out of him through the hands. This time, the hand was stuck to the chair. Conrad offered to wiggle it around a bit to test if the nail had indeed penetrated through the other side.

By now, Elizabeth's numb ecstasy was rapidly fading, replaced by a wave of nausea, which she fought back by breaking the silence. She needed to talk to another human being.

"Did I do it?" she asked.

"Sure did. He's stuck through like a pig," said Conrad.

The body writhed in its chair, droplets of red hitting the stone floor.

Elizabeth's hand trembled as she handed the hammer back to Conrad. He bent down to kiss her on the forehead in a moment of weakness, desiring to see his wife enjoy the process more than fear it.

"All right, ready for the feet?" asked Conrad. He squatted down over the job's bare feet. Taking hold of the right foot, he nearly gagged at his own work. The toenail beds were all red and swollen, and his feet were calloused and rough. With the size he was, he could probably not even reach his feet and so they went uncared for. This man deserved to die anyway, Conrad thought. Not caring for himself is revealing of how little he even desires to live.

Picking up the third to last nail, he placed its sharp head right up against the metatarsals running along the middle top portion of the foot. Conrad knew that the human foot contained many little bones and joints and over a hundred muscles and tendons and other sinewy ligaments, holding it all together, allowing a person to balance and walk and support their own weight.

This man's feet must be so overworked and uncared for, thought Conrad. His distaste for this job grew deeper the longer he stared down at the part of his body which was the most neglected. The foot would be the first part to touch hell if such a thing existed.

Taking up the hammer, the chosen instrument of torture for today, Conrad hoisted up the tool and landed the blow straight down on the nail's head. In his mind, Conrad imagined the nail puncturing the tough plantar fascia, utterly ruining his stability and arch. It would render any more kicking of his new door to be unbearably painful and walking nearly impossible. The ability to escape now was destroyed. The job's body in seconds was damaged and recovery was a slow process of several weeks. He would not be alive long enough to recover.

Everyone in the room knew that by now. This man would not live long enough to heal from his wounds. He sat there in the chair crying, probably begging behind the duct tape, but the words became trapped like flies to a web and neither predator heard them. Elizabeth was thankful for the duct tape. That way, she could not further rationalize his side of the story.

All she had to do was look at him and feel revolted, especially now when he was all discolored in hue.

"Well, this side is done. I would say it takes even more force to get that nail through that thick band of tissue at the end. Good luck," said Conrad, handing Elizabeth the final nail and the hammer as well.

"Thanks," she said, without another word. Her heart pulsed loudly in her ears as she placed the nail in a similar spot to Conrad's on the left foot. Then, lifting the hammer up high and bringing it down with all of her weight, the hammer wiggled a bit and fell off before it completely went through. Again, she had caused this man extra pain. In some ways, this made her feel like an expert at torture, but her stomach could only be controlled to a certain extent, and feeling the nail attempt to go through the bone she accidentally hit made her vomit.

She kept dry heaving even after solids from earlier had stopped coming up. Conrad simply sat there waiting. There was no need to rush on this job. He threw her a rag to wipe her face off with.

Conrad gave her the go-ahead nod as she prepared herself to hit again. Down came the hammer with the nail, moved in between the bones this time. The nail gave a bit against the main tissue like a trampoline and she had to beat down the nail once more in order to rip through to the other side and into the floor. Conrad had made two holes close to the other ones for the rope before. The nail somewhat stayed put in the floor where she hit it down for the last time.

Her stomach turned again, and she threw up harder, even with nothing but her own saliva as evidence. Elizabeth could not help but become acutely aware of her *own* feet and what they were made of, like she had peeled herself open for the first time and saw what was inside. The fact that she had insides at all was shocking. Skin was the only organ that registered in her mind when she thought about her body. Her outsides were beautiful and there was no need for a dark inside that squelched and squirmed and contracted.

At least she believed that all things inside should remain inside and hidden away—a band of tissue should never see the sun or a bone stick out of the flesh to greet the world. Those things did not exist for Elizabeth before this moment.

Now, the world was a terror. A terror with skeletons in it that were masquerading around, draped in tissue and blood. Living creatures latched onto the frame and animated by who knows what? In a flash, Conrad and all of his purpose looked so foolish, so silly…so pointless. She giggled amidst her own vomit, the spit strings still separating from her mouth on their descent to the cold ground, like a lunatic.

And yet, how could a person be a lunatic when they were joined in their laughter by another? For Conrad began to laugh too. They laughed together at the whole situation and at the body that was tied up and currently unconscious. They laughed at the whole charade as if it was the most hilarious joke they had heard in a long time.

The Fleischers supported each other in the echoes of their laughter. Nothing could be frightening when they were both laughing. Nor could anything be taken seriously if they were both laughing. A little comic relief never hurt anyone, they reasoned.

This was all *too* awful to be real—that their free will had failed them like this—to commit such crimes against the human body. They must not be in control. Lucifer poured poison in their ears as Claudius did to King Hamlet. They must have eaten the apple from the tree of knowledge against God's will. All those who judge must blame the snake and not the Fleischers.

Their laughter died out like a slow-dying flame—the rest of the wax beading off and laying to cool in the bottom of the candle holder. They were no longer able to continue. Their job tonight was done.

Conrad did not even care to throw cold water over the job's head or to check if he was even breathing. The bed called to them both. They had no appetite, only an acute hunger for sleep.

Staggering up each step like zombies, the two finally reached the bed, where they dragged themselves up on top of the sheets. They cared nothing for the blood transferring from their clothes to the bedsheets, nor for their shoes transferring hair and nails and blood and other damning evidence into their marriage bed. They lay there as if this was all a dream, like they would wake up in their sleepwear and be as clean as ever.

Nothing mattered to the sleeping couple, at least not for several hours, as they lay there unmoving and devoid of all dreams. That is, until Elizabeth shot up from sleep in a fit of terror. Her chest was soaked with sweat as she tried peeling away her dress from her moist skin. She looked over at Conrad, who was still fast asleep. Eventually, a cool chill overtook her body, and she shut her eyes once more, even needing to slide under the covers for warmth.

Her mind dropped her in what seemed like the middle of a dream as she watched her husband sobbing in front of her and pointing toward the door. She was being told to get out. But where was she to go? What was she to do? If Conrad pushed her out, then she would have nothing—no house, no car, no children, no status, no nothing. Even worse for her would be losing his warm touch and love.

Like the Ghost of Christmas Future leading her around her own dream, she watched as the seasons changed only once before Conrad was walking uphill with another woman. They even held hands at certain points and Elizabeth felt as if her heart was being squeezed in between their grasp.

Her fury made her sweat again in the bed as she watched this *other* woman move in and fill her closet and fill her bathroom and fill her place in the bed beside Conrad. She had blonde locks that cascaded across her back and blue eyes that reminded one of the sky.

Like a thunderbolt, Elizabeth took control of the dream, and quick insights into the gory mess left behind flashed in front of her. Elizabeth saw this blonde in the job's place. Her nails and toenails were torn off, her blonde hair ripped out of her head, and she was bound at the hands and feet.

The evening came along with a full moon and in her jealous rage, Elizabeth howled at it before driving the first nail in. There was no duct tape over the blonde's mouth, her thin torso doubling over from the pain. Elizabeth wanted to imbibe every scream of pain that escaped her lips.

Driving in the next nail, savoring the newest pangs of suffering, Elizabeth heard Conrad approach. She looked over in a fog to see that he was surprised, yet pleased. His pleasure slid from the back of his consciousness to the front as he smiled. Elizabeth felt ecstatic knowing that he still loved her. He had not abandoned her for another, less worthy woman. Conrad just needed proof of her undying love, that was all.

The final nails were all driven in by Elizabeth as Conrad

watched. The blonde, thin woman begged him to save her, but he stood there in silence. With a final rush of jealousy, Elizabeth chose to kill her enemy with fire. She wanted to inflict as much pain as she could before death.

The fire raged and her wailing screams increased the hotter it grew around her. Elizabeth soaked up the knowledge of watching her enemy's skin cook and peel away from the muscle, which once revealed was then new fuel for the flames that went to work on the muscles, and then the organs, and charred the very marrow in her bones. Her pretty blue eyes boiled and melted away before she finally passed out of existence.

Elizabeth never shut her eyes during this entire scene, and then she turned around to face Conrad. In her dreams, which she now controlled, Conrad grabbed her by the hair and pulled it back to kiss her lips with a passion that had been missing for *so* long. She vowed that if she had to murder brutally everyone on the planet that she would for another kiss like that one. Anything to satisfy her king, she would do.

A kind of peace came over Elizabeth's sleeping body, and she rolled over to get closer to Conrad. Her breath gently blew on his back as both of their chests rose and fell with ease.

Conrad, on the other hand, only got up once to relieve himself before getting back into bed. He had no sweats and no nightmares. In fact, his dreams began after he got back into bed in the middle of the night. But his dreams were of an entirely different sort.

***

Conrad also saw flashes of gore from the body of his latest job. At first, he saw himself as a teenager who would try to avoid the gory images by covering his ears like a child.

However, he learned rather speedily that the more he tried to avoid thinking about the gore, the more he thought about it. It was as if he focused too deeply on the images and his mind rang too loudly with the messages of fear and violence that they would somehow overpower his free will and force him to carry out such horrible crimes.

So he was stuck, akin to one of those Chinese finger traps. Eventually, he gave in to thinking about the blood and the bruising. And he learned as an adult that allowing himself to think about those violent thoughts made the mental images in his head softer, quieter. Of course, they were still on his mind constantly, but their power had seemed squelched, like he had squashed the thoughts under his boot.

The thoughts came through so softly that they no longer scared him like they did when he was younger. Now, the images fed him, even in his dreams. Laying there in bed, as at home as any other person, Conrad dreamed of the gore from the previous day.

He watched himself look at the nude job's body with disgust. His face contorted as he saw the rolls and his hunched-over back from years of sitting improperly. The man revealed was a slob. He beat up his wife and killed his mother all to play some silly children's games for even more money. But with those hopes dashed due to the facts of probability and the fact that the business needed to make money, all of that money was lost. So, on top of losing all his money, he also lost his mother and the respect and care of his wife on the same day.

The man downstairs deserved nothing. The *body* downstairs deserved nothing more than the loss of his own life since he lost the right to exist in society on that day of destruction.

In his dreams, Conrad watched himself lifting the hammer

high while holding the nail in place and then coming down hard. The job's hand in slow motion would have looked like a suffocating fish, flopping up and down on the chair arm as the nail drove through it. He was nothing more than fleshy skin, a sack of heavy potatoes, worth even less.

Conrad, through the fog of memory, could see this man's blood trickling down the arms of the chair to the floor. Conrad shuddered to think that he shared any aspect of himself with this scum. The ropes holding him down were dyed red, and as they dried, they turned a sickly brown color.

Even in his sleep, Conrad smiled, watching his beautiful wife take the hammer and nail from him. He wanted her right then and there because she stood in such stark contrast to the body next to her. She kept her dignity and treated her body well. This woman was always trying to live by a set of values, but they were not values that derived from some book listing them out or a deity telling her "thou shall not kill." Her values came from a rational place, a place where she used her experience and her mind to derive the most happiness.

Conrad felt guilty for damaging a value system that she thought by now was pretty much set, but her encounter with such a force as himself has kept her thinking. He could see it in her eyes as she watched him swing the hammer back down on the job's foot. Her pretty little brow was furrowed, and he wished she would stop that to avoid getting wrinkles. Women, he thought, should not have to trouble themselves with such serious thoughts. However, her undying curiosity and need to learn were values that drew him to her.

She worked in a library, after all, so it was no secret she surrounded herself with all the knowledge of the world she could at all times. Still, Conrad chose her to be his bride. She was a reflection of him and the more time passed, the more closely knit they would become.

He smiled, watching her hammer in the nail once, not being fully successful like a clumsy child, and then swinging again. Conrad enjoyed watching the worthless man, who could only correct himself with the most obvious method—pain. He had been too insensitive to notice all the warning signs he probably missed or, worse, ignored to attain his hedonistic pleasure. This was a dolt, a man without values, a man who did not care if he was alive or dead.

Conrad wondered if this man even regretted being killed by a stranger. Perhaps he believes he deserves it or he does not know why he found himself in this situation. The more of a dolt he is, the more likely the latter is true. Conrad hoped to find out this question before tomorrow night, when his world would end.

Dreaming about the different wails and screams of his victim, Conrad thought them all just. He could say to anyone on the street that he felt no sympathy for this man's final cries. A man can become no more than an animal without values.

A man with no values was simply a *worm*—they only responded to physical stimuli. They curl up when poked and are sensitive to temperature changes and light and moisture. They feel pain, but not in an emotional sense. When cut in half, a worm only moves according to its nervous system reacting. This man never gave a second thought to his crimes before committing them and now it seemed that only his body was reacting to the physical pain inflicted on him, but emotionally? He felt nothing, Conrad was sure of it.

Looking in that man's eyes for multiple hours a day over the course of two days, Conrad saw *nothing* there. He was a hollow person who had given up his values long ago. And giving up his values meant being "freed" to do whatever he wanted to get a second of pleasure in his life; otherwise, his life was meaningless to even himself. He became committed to his crimes until death's own stiff hand came out to stop him. Conrad felt obliged to take on such a role.

CHAPTER VI

"Well, today's the third act for this man," said Conrad to Elizabeth as they were eating breakfast at the kitchen table together. "Only his story does not end with 'he rose again.'" Conrad thought himself very clever and smiled at Elizabeth, scrambled eggs openly tossing around in his mouth.

Elizabeth shook her head, wearily mimicking back a smile. She was afraid of this day coming, but she also knew of the inevitable relief. After today, they could start over and forget what they had done. After this man's death, the Fleischers could rise again.

She stood up from the table to take their plates to the sink, determined to get this whole day over with. The sink filled with suds and each bubble that popped felt much more explosive than before because with each collapse came the end of an entity—the end of a world—and there were so many. *Pop, pop, pop!*

When Conrad rose from the table, Elizabeth listened for his steady descent down to the basement. This morning, he seemed even calmer than the past couple of days. Maybe he was sick and tired of this life too, she wondered. Perhaps Conrad would stop and they could turn their lives around before it was too late to fumble back.

"Hey! When you come down here, could you bring a bowl of cold water?!" he shouted. Conrad poked at the body, which seemed to have moved very little in the night. "I'm going to be so furious if you are already dead," he hissed at the job. Wriggling his fingers around the man's wrist, there was still a low murmur of a pulse left. "You just need a rude awakening, I think," said Conrad to his victim.

Holding the bowl of water, carefully tiptoeing down the steps, Elizabeth held the bowl out to Conrad.

"No, dear, you do it," he said. "You should know by now that whenever you can help, just jump right in and help!"

She cowered at his patronizing tone until she realized he wanted a partner, a *real* partner. Her flattered sensibilities helped in hoisting the bowl right into the job's face, to which he merely seemed to peek through his eyelids at us. The man was surely ready to die. He was going on three days now without water, aside from whatever he could lick up from his wet face, and no food. The job was feeling fatigued and probably in unimaginable pain, thought Elizabeth.

"Stop thinking and trying to sympathize with it," said Conrad, as if he could hear her own thoughts.

"I can think all I want!"

"Sure, but it's a waste on him. Look at him, remember what he did to his wife and his own mother! You need to look at the *whole* man—not the beaten one before you. Never forget that he is a murderer and is just getting what he brought onto himself," said Conrad.

"Right. I'll try to keep that in mind," said Elizabeth.

"Good. You will *have* to do it if you are to get through the rest of the day." Bending down to face the job, Conrad tugged his drooping eyelids up and then let them drop again. "There's some movement in there. He must recognize us still. I just think he's come to the realization that he is a dead man, which is good. That's what I wanted. Today, he should see the world for the last time through a dead man's eyes."

"So, what do we do now?" asked Elizabeth, trying to push this process along. For some strange reason, she felt like the victim walking the plank. By the end of the day, she may find herself unable to breathe.

"I think we spend the morning with our dead soul and give him some quality pain and suffering. Then, we take our usual lunch break. And afterward, we get down to the play's finale. Sound good to you?" asked Conrad, tightening up some of the ropes around the man's body. "Boy, he probably doesn't remember the last time he was this weight. A lot of people need the torture diet. They would be much healthier that way. I could be rich," Conrad laughed.

"It would most certainly have to be against their will, though; otherwise, no one would ever do it!" said Elizabeth.

The two laughed together in front of the condemned. If they laughed, then the world still spun. It gave both of them a sense of stability.

"Okay, now. Let's check on how his fingers and toes are doing. Grab me the sharp tweezers, please."

Elizabeth got the tweezers and Conrad poked and prodded at the black and blue, puffy nail and toenail beds. Once he poked deeply in the center of the exposed skin, the job finally made a sound. But this sound was more of a pathetic whimper. He had gone from such a burly, gruff man to this sniveling, whimpering child. Both of the Fleischers cringed.

"Don't let him deceive you. He's just trying this new tactic with us to see if we'll feel sorry for him and let him go," said Conrad. "Well, I don't believe him for one second." He spat at his face and stuck the pair of tweezers in harder until the body screamed and pulled deeper into itself. "Just like a worm," Conrad mumbled.

The pools of dried blood were released and poured afresh down the job's nails and toenails to the floor. The release of that blood may have even relieved the painful pressure he felt, and Conrad soon realized his mistake. The pain was only meant to increase, not the opposite. And so Conrad got up and stabbed the man in the stomach once, pushing his entire body against his prey's to the point where he could feel the man's heart beating against his chest.

Conrad pulled away just as quickly and released his grasp of the tweezers. They clanged onto the floor, drenched in blood. The job stared down at his blood once again featured outside of his body in front of him. It made him sick, and he vomited the little fluids left to his withered body.

***

The man began to look like a dried sponge. There were definite wrinkles in his skin now, and he looked ten years older. More thick gray hairs stuck out of his head, appearing to be dry and brittle enough to blow right off. Nothing was healthy about this man anymore. He had not seen daylight in three days.

The shirts wrapped around his head to stop his ears from bleeding were still there. Conrad pulled them off to take a look at his work, making Elizabeth nauseous. For the fabric stuck to his head and had to be pulled quite hard to come off and then the skin left around the holes in his head was all raggedy-looking and sore. He was probably still getting an infection, even after the hydrogen peroxide was poured over him.

There were bruises up and down his body from the rage-filled punches from Conrad and the face slaps from Elizabeth. And now his stomach was oozing blood from the latest stab wound to the gut. It looked like mincemeat, sitting there, half sliding down and no longer caring about much of anything.

And yet, after a few more minutes of poking and prodding it, like a child growing out of his favorite toy, Conrad grew bored. Both of them had always hated the term because there was always something to do in this life. But when tied to a job, one can inevitably get bored or tired of some aspect. Clearly, poking the dying was no longer exciting for him. There was no pleasure to squeeze out on a lower scale of pain from a man that was expiring.

"Do you want to go eat now?" asked Conrad.

"Yes, let's," said Elizabeth, who turned on her heels and walked back upstairs in an instant. She was ready to leave the sad man behind and brace herself for what was to come soon. They trudged up the stairs in silence.

They walked like funeral bearers, carrying the weight of the soon-to-be-dead man on their shoulders all the way to the kitchen. Without breaking the silence, Elizabeth assumed they would be eating the same for lunch: sandwiches made of cheap bread with a bit of ham and cheese in between. Really it was a child's meal, but who could eat anyway, Elizabeth thought, when death was upon the house? No one, even those excited by the prospect of death, could bear to choke down food. The private sphere of the Fleischers' manor today was a place for the skeletons to come out and play. There were no chubby demons with pitchforks out quite yet; they would inevitably appear later this evening once the mortal coil was sloughed off.

Conrad barely chewed his food. His hands shook with the jitters. Fueling himself and resting a bit had replaced his lethargic boredom with fiery excitement. He *wanted* to kill—he was ready for it. Having done this before, he knew what to expect. But poor Elizabeth's tremors came from pure fear of the unknown. What did a dying person look like before releasing their final breath? What did the process of death look like in a human body? How would their face contort when their muscles died? Did the maggots miraculously pop up from nowhere quickly to consume the flesh? What would they smell like after death? Her mind flooded with questions without answers; her heart was constricted by the lack of explanations. Dare she ask Conrad? Elizabeth debated in her own mind but came to no conclusion before Conrad shot up and left to go back downstairs to his office. She had never seen him more thrilled about work before. It haunted her.

After cleaning the dishes, she did a rather funny thing. Perhaps one would call it superstitious. Elizabeth bent her head and promised in a whisper out loud to help Conrad at all costs. After all, she reasoned, he was the only thing that made her life worth living. Being in his arms was where all her safety and warmth lie, and she would do anything—had done anything—for it. Her devotion to him would be tested here once more, and she was committed to following through. Before closing the door to the basement, she knocked on its wooden frame to seal her fate because once she came back out of that basement, she would be a changed woman.

"I'm here," said Elizabeth.

"Good. I'm thinking about exactly how I want to place him

for his final execution," said Conrad, tilting the heavy man in the chair forward and backward and sideways.

"Did you tell me what you planned to do?" she asked.

"I don't believe I have. Should we say it in front of him? If the old good-for-nothing can even hear us... I think we should. Give him some extra time to think about his impending, brutal death," Conrad smiled in the job's direction. The job was barely moving and did not seem to acknowledge the look at all.

"Okay, so..."

"I've been contemplating for a while the worst way for something like him to die. I believe that a man who could gamble, assault, and kill only cares for his hedonistic, momentary pleasure. So, I think it is only fair that he gets to *see* his death and have the ability to realize, even if for *one* second, that he is not omnipotent or special or desired by anyone any longer in this world."

Elizabeth wanted to cry. "That has got to be the most awful thing to feel, certainly. But how?"

"Well, again, going back to history, the Elizabethan era of England was from 1558 until 1603. Queen Elizabeth I used execution for criminals, though she was not nearly as loose with it as Mary Queen of Scots was. But beheading was one popular method. It is said that the tradition of holding up the head by the executioner was not really as proof to the crowd of the criminal's death but to show the *criminal* the crowd and his body lying there. Apparently, consciousness can remain in the severed head before they completely bleed out for up to *eight* seconds. Then, due to a lack of oxygen, the head becomes unconscious and then dies. But that criminal is punished even *after* their official death, and they knew that their head would probably end up on a stake for birds to relieve themselves on and people to ogle at and disgrace," said Conrad.

"Wow, that is certainly the most poetic form of justice I have heard of," said Elizabeth.

"Indeed. I think this man needs to feel genuine horror. He probably hasn't felt such a feeling in years. His heart's grown cold to emotions of any sort for him to be able to hurt the ones he loves so badly."

Nodding her head, Elizabeth felt better about helping Conrad bring a definitive end to this criminal's life. The job lay there in the chair without reacting much at all. Maybe, thought Elizabeth, he really had accepted his ultimate punishment…or else his mind was already elsewhere.

"All right, let's think about the tool we need to commit this with. In Elizabethan England, they used swords for the wealthy and axes for the poorer types and set their heads on a wooden block. The block had a crudely carved bowl shape to one side where the person's head would rest. The executioner, wearing a frightening black mask, tied their hands and feet together to avoid any of their extremities from getting in the way. I've also heard that it took several swings to sever completely the head from the body."

Elizabeth started to feel green; her emotions going numb again. "How many would you say, exactly?"

"Oh, I've read anywhere from one single blow up to a dozen. Of course, internal decapitation will most likely occur first before you get the entire neck severed. The earliest recorded execution in America was in Jamestown, Virginia, in 1608. Imagine what those public executions must have been like? How sharp were the axes that they may have used every day? I imagine not very sharp," said Conrad. He was looking around, trying to find something. "We have rope and an ax, but now we need to find something to serve as a block. Any ideas, dear?"

Turning to and fro, the little plastic table was too high, and it still had the duty of holding up the surgical tools. There was nothing block-like but the chair that was needed to hold the job in. "No, I can't think of using anything in here."

"Hmm, let's take a quick walk out to the side yard to look for a larger piece of wood. I could take the ax to it and cut out a little space for his head on one side. Come along, honey."

"Coming!" Before closing the door to the basement, she turned to look if the job made any further motions—he had not. It seemed that he was thinking of other places and other things now. Nothing would bother him much anymore, not even, it seemed, execution.

The Fleischers walked out of the basement, thankfully still the same people as they had been going down before, but Elizabeth knew they would not rise again once they had their block before this man's death. It was pure luck to be able to go up and get a breath of fresh air before descending once more.

Outside, the sun was shining and warming up the chill autumn air, which made the world feel a little less cold. Spindly sticks were mostly what was scattered over the yard. The nuts squirrels collected and the branches they broke caused the mayhem and bumpy walk through the grass for them both.

"What about this?" Elizabeth picked up a wedge of wood, but it was still small and low to the ground.

"No, that's too low. We need something more like a tree stump. Got it?" Conrad kneeled over by the hedge surrounding their yard to look for rotting wood or old trees. "This will just have to do," he said, dragging out from beneath the hedge a larger branch that had fallen with the last storm their neighborhood had. "Can you bring me the ax?"

Running back down to the basement, grabbing the ax, and hurrying back toward Conrad, Elizabeth was gulping for air as she watched him hack off the excess branches and shape the main branch into a square. Growing hot, he threw off his sweater and Elizabeth watched his arms shake with each strike and his muscles bulge with each movement. She could see the muscles flex just under the surface of his skin and she grew hungry and possessive of his body.

Elizabeth could not help but grow excited. To her shock, she was finding her own sense of giddiness among the madness. After about half an hour since getting outside, they had a wooden chopping block just like in the colonial days. It was a simple combination—the block and the ax—but a terrifying one all the same.

Conrad lifted the rather unwieldy block and Elizabeth opened each of the doors for him as a good wife should. He walked through and she carefully guided him down the dimly lit stairs, back down to the pits of hell.

The job was still lying there, unmoving. Dropping the block down with a clatter, the body jolted upright in its chair, as if out of reflex, and then sunk back down as before.

"All right. Time to bind him the proper way before making him lay his head on the block," said Conrad. He threw some of the already blood-soaked rope he had unwound from around the job's chest to Elizabeth, who caught it with arms way out in front of her.

She followed Conrad's *every* move when he was making the same knot around the man's ankles while she secured the wrists. They were raw and red from days of being bound down to the chair. It must have stung excruciatingly. But Elizabeth pulled her mind away from such morose thoughts and, instead, focused on Conrad's strong, calloused hands pulling the ropes taut. His fingers bled but for different reasons and she wished to lick at all of his wounds.

In her submissive state, she showed off her tying skills to Conrad, who nodded his approval. The Fleischers had properly secured their prey and now they would feed their captive to the devil himself.

"Are you ready, my love?" asked Conrad.

Elizabeth clung to his words "my love" with all of her willpower. She did not turn green this time. She turned off her ability to empathize with the already-dead-to-her man. This time, she would not allow herself to feel for anyone else but her soul mate. "I'm ready," was all she dared to say, as Elizabeth pushed the job's back out of the chair while Conrad took his feet and they brought him a little closer toward the front of the room with the chair in it. The light bulb hanging from the ceiling served as their only guide.

They both put him down without being gentle. Conrad made him get on his knees as Elizabeth pushed his back forward, with his head fitting perfectly in the curvature of the wooden block. The block was still a bit too low, and it wiggled around since it was skinner than the usual wooden block, but it served its purpose for today.

"Hand me the ax, love. You can observe the first blow, and then I'll let you take a swing. Okay?" said Conrad.

Elizabeth felt nothing, but she still held "my love" close, not taking her eyes off of Conrad. She simply nodded and handed him the ax. It seemed as if not a sound could be heard. But Elizabeth could hear the sound of blood circulating in her own ears and she wondered if Conrad heard the same. The creature lying there did not move a bit. He must not understand what was about to happen to him, thought Elizabeth; otherwise, who could just lie there limp and without any kind of fight? This man was no longer fighting for his life. And if they did not kill him tonight, then dehydration would.

Conrad checked the neck was nicely draped over the block and the head was laying in the guided curve of the wood. Then he raised the ax. It made a whoosh sound in the air before letting gravity take the force of the blade down onto the body's neck. The creature jerked around like a fish. It was terrible. Both Fleischers watched this man wriggle back and forth and it was impossible to tell whether it was all reflexive, like a worm, or conscious movement.

Clearly, the ax had bounced back off the fat and muscle encasing the bones, and more chopping was needed, as Conrad had predicted. The ax trembled dramatically in his hands as he shoved the handle into Elizabeth's. Nearly dropping it, she looked at her husband's face, which seemed transformed. He was not new to death, but he certainly was to beheading a man. His eyes were twitching with the stress of seeing someone so in pain and so near to death that the body became reactive. Conrad looked possessed, like he could not stop watching the train wreck he had created. Not for one second did he look at Elizabeth. No, he was in an interlocution with his soul.

Equally enthralled, Elizabeth kept her eyes on the writhing man while she clung to Conrad to serve as her strength. She touched his trembling hand before clutching both of her petite hands around the girthy handle and letting the ax fall for a second time. She tried not to make the wriggling man wait, though he was already dead to her.

Still, her weight added nothing to the next blow and the ax only made slight gains, cutting down through the gristle of the job's neck. The creature was moving less spastically now, though he was still very much alive.

Without a moment of pause, Elizabeth thrust the handle back into Conrad's manly hands. The ax handle fits so much better in his hands, she thought. He could wield it well, and all of his power was much more than hers. He should be the one to finish the job, she thought. She fell in love with those hands, she was married to them, and so she promised to still hold them dear to her heart, no matter what they did. She watched them closely now, with hyper-focus, noting that blood from the creature splattered all over them. Oh, how she loved Conrad so.

Hoisting the ax over his head once again, with the feel of this man's fat and muscle imprinted so recently in his memory, he knew how much pressure he would need to at least dig into the bones this time around. Using all of his power and with the help of gravity, he laid the ax head deep down into this job's neck. He had never known how far a human neck went, especially one of this size. It was as if the entire ax had disappeared. And with a little more pressing and sawing, the ax thumped onto the wooden block as the head descended to the floor.

Immediately bending down, Conrad picked up the head to show to the imaginary Elizabethan crowd, and his other half lying on the ground, as well as to Elizabeth who stood in horror at the number of bits dangling out of the neck of the human head. And the Fleischers watched together as those eight solemn seconds passed of the conscious head, finally trying to say something as its lips moved and eyelids fluttered, but nothing could be nor would be heard from that mouth again. The blood and oxygen left the face bereft of all consciousness and now the muscles relaxed, leaving the jaw slack and the eyes open, staring unknowingly into space.

The meaning of existence seemed truly bleak to the Fleischers. Elizabeth could not believe that she had the power to end another man's life. Conrad could not understand how he could be of the same material as such a weak form. Both watched as the body shut down in an orderly way, like a machine, since all men seemed to go in a similar fashion. Each replayed the decapitated head trying to speak over and over again, savoring the fact that perhaps there was a life after death that lasted even a short while.

III

PART THREE

CHAPTER I

Insensitively dropping the head on the floor, Conrad had to stomp his foot on the job's back to pull out the ax, which was lodged into the block. Once he freed the ax head, he wiped the blood and other grime off on his shirt, replacing the ax back up on the hanger where it resided before.

The two began cleaning up the stage, like at the end of a performance. Their principal actor, it seemed, had died and could be of no use anymore in the final cleanup. He could not be magically resurrected.

"I'm exhausted," said Conrad, soaking up the blood on his hands and knees. The rag he used was saturated with the red, metallic smell of blood.

"So am I," said Elizabeth, throwing items that could be used as evidence against them in a black trash bag.

"You know, we don't need to be cleaning up like it is a crime scene, Elizabeth."

"It is."

Conrad threw down his soaked rag, which made a sickening slap against the limestone. "How many times do I have to explain to you that the police know me and what I do? They look the other way. I am the good guy, remember?"

"But the law does not see it the same way. There can be no

room for revenge or retal—"

"Stop!" Conrad threw the smelly rag at Elizabeth, which struck her right in the middle of the face before peeling off much too slowly and leaving her seeing red.

"No, you stop! I'm tired of being shut down, especially when I'm so scared! I'm scared, Conrad! Don't you see what we've done? There is no coming back from this. I will never see you again! I love you!" Elizabeth wept. She wept violently, but not for the man lying there beside her. No, she wept for herself and the life she wanted to have with Conrad.

Conrad just shook his head, laughing under his breath. "You still haven't come around to viewing me as the good guy, have you? After all this time together, doing this job together, I thought you might understand."

"I do! I do. I don't care for this disgusting thing at all. In fact, I learned to hate him for you," she said, briskly wiping off her snotty nose and tear-stained cheeks. "I spent this entire day looking at you, loving you, doting on you. You are my true love, my *soul mate*. Don't you feel the same for me?" she asked, wringing her hands.

He looked down at her, even from his knees. For the first time, Elizabeth noticed a certain look in Conrad's eyes. It was a hidden, vacant sort of look. She spent the span of a few seconds in silence, staring back at him—not wanting to comprehend exactly what she was seeing. Her head leaned from one side of her shoulder to the other, puzzled. But, for the first time, he was letting her see all of himself.

To her horror, the eyes grew less and less warm and familiar. It was the most awful sight. He looked at her the way he had lifted the ax to come down on his job's head—coldly. Conrad did not love her. He *tolerated* her.

Now, an icy fear came down on her like a dark curtain. It seemed that their final act was not over yet. Elizabeth felt in fear for her own life. Her sense of self-preservation told her to keep her emotions hidden from him. She must keep herself in check. He must not know that she understands the shallowness of his love.

Instead, astonished by her quick thinking, her desire to live simply, she laughed. She laughed as if his lack of response was a joke, as if he had no option other than loving her, as if his love for her was unconditional. Elizabeth laughed at his silence, as if her soul had never died when she realized the truth. She laughed like the silly woman he thought she was, as if she could never possibly *dream* of him not feeling the same way as her.

After swallowing the rest of her laughter, she looked up to see Conrad's face warmer once again. He hid his momentary slip of apathy for her, as if the whole thing had never happened. They could both play pretend while the actual body that still lay there grew softer and colder.

"Well," said Elizabeth, using all of her willpower, "I want to clean up any evidence against us just in case. You know me, I want a clean house—a fresh start. Please? I'll clean everything up myself then if you don't care."

Conrad rolled his eyes and grunted, getting up off his sore knees. His pants were soaked with blood. "You can do all the nitpicky stuff if you must. But I will just be getting rid of the body and that's it. My job will be complete once it has disappeared."

"Deal," said Elizabeth, hiding her shaky hands behind her back.

The two of them got to work. The body, still being soft

and malleable, allowed Conrad to push it into three combined black trash bags. With one last look at the head, he threw the head in with the body. He was not trying to hide anything, so he skipped the idea of placing the head in a separate bag entirely. Each tie was tightly knotted in the hopes of keeping the air out and the smell in, at least until he found a spot to dig and bury the body.

Meanwhile, Elizabeth was finishing up with the blood-soaked stone of Conrad's office. She mopped and wiped and placed all the rags into a bucket, which she carried upstairs to sit next to the fireplace. Then she went back down to the basement, trying to focus on truly forgetting what she saw. Perhaps she had misjudged his look, she thought. Maybe they really could start all over again. Her steps downstairs felt lighter with each passing optimistic thought.

Entering the basement once more, Elizabeth carried with her some bleach and gloves. From all the movies she had seen, she knew there was unseen evidence everywhere—in the form of fingerprints and hairs and nails and other DNA—and all of it had to be scrubbed away.

Cleaning had always been therapeutic for Elizabeth, so she took to the obsessive scrubbing swiftly. She dumped out splashes of the bleach all over the stone, not caring to stain any of her cursed clothing. With every splash came the white spots appearing on her dress and all over her shoes. The bleach soon overpowered the metallic smell of the basement office.

"I'm going to get rid of the corpse now!" shouted Conrad a bit too loudly from the steps to the basement.

"Okay! I'll probably still be down here when you get back!" shouted back Elizabeth. He left her down there alone, now without even another body to keep her company. At times when she was sure she was alone like this, Elizabeth hummed to herself, and she did so now as a way of minimizing the horrors done moments before.

It felt like a century had passed and, yet, rationally, it could not have been more than an hour since it died. A nagging feeling of the need to check the time pushed her to pick up the last of the rags and ropes and other debris that could be burned and carry them with her upstairs. She passed the clock on the kitchen wall saying that it was nearly six o'clock that evening. It was already getting dark outside as winter was encroaching upon the land.

Although the need for a fireplace was no longer a necessity since the invention of furnaces and then central heating, the colder months brought the Fleischers back to the hearth. Occasionally, Elizabeth lit the fireplace back up after months of disuse.

Picking up the metal fireplace shovel, she cleaned out any old ashes from the firebox. There were logs ready to use beside the fireplace already, but first Elizabeth checked the damper to make sure it was working and held a lit piece of newspaper up to it. This was to make sure that the smoke would rise up the chimney and not into the house.

Then she balled up more pieces of newspaper and placed them under the grate, added some kindling, and lit the initial flame. But before it grew too much, she added her logs in a triangular fashion, just as in the old days. And although small fires kept the smoke at bay, Elizabeth needed a larger one to ensure that the damning evidence would be utterly destroyed.

The flames lapped up the newspapers and rose higher and higher. Elizabeth put the fireplace guard in front of it to prevent any hot embers from floating out and destroying their beloved home. The fire blazed up in the mirrors of her eyes as she watched it grow sufficiently. Once it was large enough, she started throwing the drier ropes in the flames, then smaller items, like the duct tape, which took much longer to catch fire. She left the rags in the bucket and set it by the fire in the hopes that much of the blood, or at least the watery bits, would evaporate.

Getting up off her knees, Elizabeth closed the sliding pocket doors of the Queen Anne to trap more heat in the room. But she could not wait there for much longer with the evidence-soaked rags beside her. It was as if she was holding her breath until all the evidence was gone. In her haste, she pulled up one piece of fabric and held it over the fire as close as she could without cooking her own fingers. Her flesh grew pink and warm. In her pain, she kept holding it until her fingers dropped the stained item into the flames.

An awful sizzling sound and smoke hissed as the rags caught fire. She hoped that the metallic smell cooking in the fireplace would not reach a nosy neighbor's nostrils. Elizabeth imagined that most people were eating dinner at six o'clock anyway. Their own noses were too filled with the steam rising off their plates to acknowledge anything that the Fleischers were cooking that evening. She even thought of what she would tell an inquiring neighbor.

"Oh, yes, we were just cooking a pheasant over the fire. We were interested in off-the-grid-style cooking and Conrad just went hunting for this wonderful, juicy piece of meat," she would say. It would be a satisfactory answer that simultaneously mocked the birdbrain standing right in front of her. Yes, that was her excuse. She would never let anyone come in between her and her soul mate...even if he felt differently.

Elizabeth concluded she had gone too far by now to leave him. He controlled life and death—both concerning others and herself.

Picking up another stained piece of fabric, Elizabeth went through the same attempt at drying without cooking herself and dropping it into the flame. There were plenty of extra pieces to go, but with each one disintegrating and flying away up the chimney, her breathing became a little easier.

By the time Conrad arrived back home, Elizabeth had finished burning all the most obvious items. She could even finish humming a whole tune now. Maybe by tomorrow, her demeanor would improve as well and things would feel like they did before she even met Conrad.

But her work was not done, and when the bucket was empty, she drowned it in bleach. The kitchen sink was full of the bucket and her scrub. Then, the now police-approved bucket was set back in its place in the garage with the other dirtier home items.

Walking back down the steps, she carried her scrubber brush to douse and clean the demonic chair off of every speck that body left on it. Conrad accompanied her just to observe her work before he sought out something to eat for dinner without her. For tonight, she would not stop cleaning until she felt confident enough to sleep once again.

Sleep, at this point, could only come to a conscience that was clean and Elizabeth's most certainly was not. Placing her hand over her mouth to stifle a yawn, guided only by the two singular lights attached to the ceiling of the office, Elizabeth kept wiping and re-wiping off every surface in her view.

She swung her arm around in circles, getting lost in the simple movement. Focusing on the rhythm of her body was much more productive at that moment than reliving that glare from Conrad—a man who was *supposed* to love her.

In her agony, she wept, scrubbing harder and harder against the stone surface. The scrubber wore through, bits and pieces of it laying all over the floor, though she kept rubbing until her fingers were being grated against the rough surface. Elizabeth only stopped scrubbing once she wiped over the area and red appeared again like magic.

Her fingers shook as she inspected them under the hanging lights—they were bleeding. The sting from the soap seemed not to reach her. Her mind kept her numb to the pain. Wrapping her hands up, she moved on to sweeping. Picking up a broom and dustpan, she moved air into it and flung whatever was supposed to be in it outside.

Sweat poured from her face as she ran up and down the steps, exorcising the basement of all the dirty evidence. Whatever went unseen, she made sure to eradicate. There was more bleach, a new scrubber, more rubbing down of the chair, the floor, the walls, each brick, even the light bulbs themselves. Nothing went untouched.

Conrad came downstairs once to check on Elizabeth.

"Are you coming to bed? You must be satisfied by now," said Conrad.

"No. It's not clean yet," said Elizabeth, soaking another brick with bleach. Both of their eyes watered from the fumes at this point. "But, dear, where did you leave his body?"

"Not too far from here, since we have nothing to hide. He's in the cemetery that is further up the hill from our house. I just dug him a shallow grave and threw his trash-bagged body in—threw some dirt back over him and called it a night."

"I see," was all Elizabeth said, "well, goodnight. I'll be up there soon, I hope."

Fed up, Conrad turned around, walked back up the steps, and closed the door with an excess amount of energy.

No longer distracted by Conrad, Elizabeth turned back to face the wet brick, applying her scrub brush to it. She repeated her movements, counting them as such: one, up, two, down, three, up, four, down, in her head. Like counting sheep to help with falling asleep, Elizabeth counted.

She was stuck counting until midnight. Her eyes kept trying to follow along a straight line made by the bricks, but the pattern kept becoming distorted by the differing amounts of the mortar used. She cursed Conrad under her breath. Just look at what a sloppy job he did, she thought. There is no *unit*y in this brick structure. It is a surprise that it could even hold anybody!

In her anger, her aching fingers gripped hard to her brush. She forced her hand back to the simplistic wall of brick, but her staring only grew worse. Looking at the lines in the wall repeatedly and the cracks that marred the bricks themselves caused her heart rate to accelerate dramatically.

Throwing her hand over her heart, Elizabeth dropped the scrubber but just kept staring. She felt like if she looked away for one moment, then life would stop. Paralyzed by fear, she stood in the same exact spot for what felt like days. When her heart finally calmed down, Elizabeth peeled her eyes away from the bricks and back out into the middle of the basement room.

There was a new level of darkness and silence that accompanied such a place in the middle of the night. It frightened Elizabeth. But she felt she had no right yet to cling to the one she loved and lie in the bed that sheltered her from harm while she slept.

Elizabeth had no right to peace ever again. At least that is what her soul kept shouting at her. But the basement was clean. Bleach fumes coated everything in its purity. It seemed to be the end for Elizabeth, and yet she still felt no peace.

Placing herself on the steps with the scrubber in her hand, she thought about what else needed cleaning. Perhaps I should clean the fireplace or maybe the entire house for good measure. Maybe I need to clean myself and bathe the sin off, she thought. Or I could go to pay my respects to that corpse in the cemetery. Yes, I am going to the cemetery.

Giving the scrubber a final good wash in the kitchen sink, she carried it with her as she quietly opened the side door of the house and walked out. Had anyone else been out at this time, they would have thought it quite strange to see a woman carrying a cleaning brush and nothing else up the hill. But it was past midnight and her only focus was on finding peace.

Instead of peace, her guts burned, and it was difficult to inhale. Perhaps getting away from the bleach would help, but clawing her way up the hill only seemed to make the symptoms worse. The hill felt so far and high up. Her legs shook with fatigue and she even sat down halfway just to regain some strength. Elizabeth covered another yawn while her soul remained wide awake.

The gates over the cemetery loomed just over the top of the hill. She could see the arch's curve growing larger with every step. The name of the cemetery was what the metal pieces twisted into and they glowed with the moon behind them. Elizabeth's wounded fingers reached out to touch the haunting words.

The climb was so high up Elizabeth leaned against one of

the stone pillars that stood tall by the gate to the cemetery. She laid her head back against the stone and watched the stars in the sky. For a minute, the stars glittered and eased her pain, but she was unable to forget completely her situation.

Getting up off the ground, she entered the cemetery by using what little strength she had to climb over the lowest part of the gate, abandoning her scrubber. It was not too difficult, though upon landing on the other side she scraped her knee—a small price to pay for her sense of inner peace to come back to her.

The graves poked out of the ground at varying angles, with the older ones following along the new hills and valleys formed over the years. Time made some of the tombstones ragged and covered with green moss. Elizabeth could barely make out names in the dark.

She tried reading the surnames, though she knew that the man she was looking for had no such stone above where he lay. Not too far into the cemetery, Elizabeth's foot went down a considerable amount into the dirt. It was freshly dug and not yet covered with grass or compacted by the feet of other living beings.

Her mind swam with images of blood and the corpse laying on the cold stones, unmoving. One does not realize how strange it is to see a body not even breathing. They become no more than a stuffed animal to the viewer. A sleeping person looks much different from a dead one, thought Elizabeth, who in her blinding fear began prying with her fingernails into the soft dirt.

Without hesitation, she felt this was the right thing to do. So, she kept digging and digging, getting herself dirty like a dog. Her knees grew wet and cold with the early morning dew. The ground smelled rich with minerals and her hand surprised the many worms under the soft ground.

She did not dig very deep, certainly not six feet under, before she heard the plastic trash bag crinkle and she hit something hard. By this hour, rigor mortis must have set in, for the body was as stiff as a board. Elizabeth grew frantic, not being able to decipher which part of the corpse's body she hit.

Regardless, she dug all over the spot, enough to reach in and tear open a hole in each layer of the bags. Nothing in her thoughts stopped her from her mission. She inhaled the scent of decay; she touched the stiff, cold muscles; she saw a body with sunken eyes, hinting at the skeletal frame underneath.

The body would eventually loosen once more and melt away back into the earth, but for now, it lay there as if still paralyzed by the fear of death—not wanting to relinquish the final bits of what made it human.

Elizabeth saw splotches of wetness cover the trash bag, and she looked up to see if it was starting to rain. There was no rain, only her tears coating the bag. She touched her cheek, unable to feel much of anything with her frigid, dirty fingers.

Eventually, the bags covered it no more, and the corpse lay there exposed to the night sky and morning dew. There were already maggots surrounding it on all sides, but Elizabeth hardly noticed. The voices sounding off in her head were currently much louder than the things she saw before her.

Trapped in her trance-like state, Elizabeth lurched forward and pushed herself up like a sprinter, jumping right over the corpse. She ran around, proving to herself that she was indeed still alive. During her run around and around the other graves, she found bunches of flowers for different bodies from families that were invisible and anonymous to Elizabeth.

She had always wanted a garden at the manor. Her heart

ached to envision picking a beautiful flower out for her child. She would teach her little one to tend to the garden and learn to love to take care of things. The soil would be as soft and tender as it was over the body's grave tonight and wonderful green stems would rise from its depths.

She found among the bouquets some flowers that allowed her to speak of her soul's regrets better than her lips could. There was a surprising find of asphodel, which normally did not bloom until springtime, and chrysanthemum, which bloomed in the fall as well as belladonna.

The asphodel was represented in Greek mythology as a symbol of peace and regret following a person to the afterlife. Its tiny white petals looked like stars guiding the way. Elizabeth felt a pain in her ribs, which she attributed to the feelings of regrets knocking around inside of her body, searching for an escape.

The chrysanthemum meant condolences and was a commonly used funeral flower, often placed on graves as a way to comfort the grieving who visited their loved ones. They were of the white variety and looked like white cushions for the ghosts to sit on. Elizabeth wanted to express her sorrow for all of this happening.

The belladonna symbolized silence, for it is part of the deadly nightshade family and could kill a man with just a handful of its black, poisonous berries. The flower itself was a beautiful purple that resembled a closed umbrella. Elizabeth felt that its long tunnel inside could hold the secrets she shared and keep them silent, laying atop the corpse.

Once she had bundled the flowers together herself, they formed a beautiful array of whites and purples. She wanted to share the terrible aching regret and sorrow while hiding it from the rest of the living world. Now, only the corpse would know that she felt miserable.

Laying the bouquet right over the corpse's own ribs, sticking out of its thin layer of decay, Elizabeth bowed her head for a moment in silence. Growing suddenly very tired, she kneeled down by the body and fell asleep next to it, with the maggots carrying on their busy pursuit of food. The whole world fell silent for the rest of that morning.

CHAPTER II

The sounds of birds chirping stirred Elizabeth out of her haze. She blinked several times and then shut her eyes tight. The smell next to her made her sick, and she vomited, making sure it was not over the body. Now, in the daylight, she could serve as a witness to her crimes, feeling even sorrier for herself. Conrad had never seen a body in decay, let alone one with a decapitated head. He never had to feel this depth of pain. Elizabeth's ribs soon ached with a groaning envy and anger. How could he let her feel all the grief? Was he soulless? Could he feel what she was? she wondered.

She whirled around, away from the exposed corpse, looking out over the rest of the cemetery. There were dozens of cypress trees surrounding the perimeter of the grounds where there were no gates to keep out the ill-intentioned. The trees stood at attention like soldiers protecting their borders. They were still lusciously green even with winter approaching. And their height appeared intimidating to Elizabeth as she tilted her head to look up at them standing there—thin, yet imposing.

Having read that cypress trees often represent death and mourning for those still living, Elizabeth felt the trees had a right to be there more than she did. She had spoken her regrets and sorrow in the language of flowers laying on the dead man's chest. There was nothing more to say to it, and now she was in the fight for her own life.

The sun was rising and the sound of an engine pulling up to the cemetery alerted Elizabeth just enough to cover the corpse back up with the black trash bags. Though she spent much of the time looking in the other direction, she used her dirty hands to throw small amounts of dirt back over it until the ground looked as it had before.

It appeared to be the groundskeeper who pulled up and was in the process of hauling all the tools needed from his vehicle for the morning's work. Perhaps he would find it strange that between yesterday morning and this morning a patch of dirt had shown up ruining his perfectly cut grass. Yes, thought Elizabeth, he would notice.

She was crouching down low to the ground. When he had his back to her, she stood up and ran to the nearest cypress tree. The trees would guard her against being seen by the only other living person there that morning—the only other human being who inhaled and exhaled.

Elizabeth figured that there was no way to cut through the cemetery at this point without getting caught, so she began walking around, being careful to hide behind each tree trunk as she went. But her sudden vocal inhalation foiled her plan when she accidentally stepped on the bones of a bird.

She had not noticed that the body of a bird lay stretched out over the roots of a tree there. Its feathers had fallen off and the tissue and muscle gone, revealing the long, bony spinal cord of the poor deceased bird. It astonished her that the spine was *so* small and yet it was not so very different from her own. The bird even had a small brain and lungs and a heart too, which became the food for a million tiny, unseen creatures.

Tears welled up in her eyes and the groundskeeper found her there with the bird by the cypress tree.

"Ma'am, are you all right? The cemetery is not supposed to be open to visitors until eight. How did you get in?" the groundskeeper asked. He was wearing a construction jacket and held his hat in his hands like a gentleman.

"I—I'm so sorry. I just came in behind the trees from my morning walk. And then I found this poor creature here and I—I stepped on him," she sobbed.

She had made the groundskeeper feel bad and rather uncomfortable on top of that. He had encountered grieving people before but never from a woman who cried as she did now over a bird. He watched as the snot dripped from her nose onto the ground.

"Look, I can dig a little grave for the poor fellow right here, but then you must go, okay?"

Elizabeth only nodded and watched as he dug a little hole for the bird and buried it in the ground. It only made her cry more as flashes of the decaying corpse only a few feet away came to the forefront of her mind. Yet, shutting her eyes to the world only seemed to make the images more powerful, so she peeled them open and barely blinked as she watched the tiny spine disappear beneath the ground.

"There. Now, go along. I've got lots of work to do this morning. I'm sorry that you had to see that poor bird on your walk, but that's life. We are born here and we die here. Circle of life, right?" said the groundskeeper.

"Yes, circle of life," whispered Elizabeth, turning around and walking outside the perimeter of cypress trees. There was a sidewalk nearby, and she walked down that and around the entire cemetery to get back onto her pathway home. She was exhausted. She wondered if that man noticed her dirty hands or her exhausted expression. He must have believed she was homeless, just trying to find a place to rest for a while. Well, let him think that, she thought. He just cannot know about the corpse.

The corpse that lay not even six feet under, who disturbed the grass with its presence, and who was wrapped in three black trash bags, and was now bearing a fresh bouquet on its chest. It would be a true testament to what Conrad told her if the police were called to the body and then did nothing once they spoke to his client. If the police were not at their house by this evening, then the weight currently crushing Elizabeth's chest might ease.

***

By the time Elizabeth got back home, Conrad was sitting at the kitchen table eating without her, as if he had forgotten she lived there too.

"You ate breakfast without me?" her voice trembled, as flashes of the decaying body and the bird's spine came to mind.

"Yes," said Conrad, spooning another bite of cereal into his mouth.

"Do you know where I've been?" Elizabeth said, not caring to leave her dirty hands out by her sides. She smelled heavily of the outdoors.

"You smell like a wet dog, so I imagine you were at the cemetery."

"I was. I couldn't sleep."

"Really? I slept just fine."

"Well, I couldn't...how could you?"

"How could I what? Fall asleep? The man deserved

everything that came to him," sneered Conrad.

"But we managed to destroy a body that took nine whole months in the womb to form. We made maggot food of something that had a brain—something that knew what was coming. We ripped and tore and tortured some mother's baby! We took away any small chance they had to change. And we stole—"

"Quiet!" yelled Conrad, slamming his fist on the table, the vein in his forehead pulsing like an angry snake. "If I had only known that you would react like such a woman to my job, then I would have never, *ever* brought you along. I thought you knew me. I thought you would understand me. But I guess I was wrong."

"I love you! I love you more than anything or anyone. I just can't understand how you could love me if you can turn around and then destroy another human being. Is it possible to kill and still love deeply?" Elizabeth paused, questioning if it was possible but emotionally doubting it.

Conrad stayed quiet too for an uncomfortable amount of time, playing with his spoon, before saying: "I love you, but perhaps it only goes so deep. When I kill a criminal who deserves it, I don't allow myself to think about how his mother would feel; I don't wallow over the fact that his body is out there right now deteriorating; I don't waste emotion on what is not worthy of my time.

"Do you think that soldiers who kill their enemies in war don't love their wives? How dare you tell them they cannot love another if they have to kill another? They go to war for exactly those reasons—because of love. They kill to defend their countries and their families. So, don't tell me I don't love you." His face looked pained for the first time.

Elizabeth shook her head. "But you looked at me yesterday without a soul, without any love at all…"

"I was tired. I *am* tired. So are you, I mean go look in the mirror. Your hair is scruffy-looking and your hands are filthy, your dress is dirty. You look like Ophelia just dragged herself through the brook to come back home."

She looked down at herself, humming with a new and curious buzz of fear and excitement. "I do look a mess. But there are men who kill and use love as an excuse, don't they?"

"Do you believe me to be so low? Those are the *real* criminals, dear. Not me. I've told you this ad nauseum. I think it is perfectly possible for a good man to kill and still love at the same time. It seems that *you* do not.:." Conrad looked seriously at Elizabeth, knowing that this uncertainty could break them apart forever.

"I—I don't know. *I don't know*!" she cried.

For a long while, her sobs were the only sound filling the rooms of the Queen Anne manor. It painted the walls and floors fittingly since the rooms were dark and had seen many lifetimes of sorrow. The house carried on standing tall while the people filling it wept a thousand tears.

Conrad eventually put his hand over hers. "I am not a de Sade figure, Elizabeth. I am stronger than that. I have a sense of self. I am in control of my own life and the choices that I make each and every day. I am highly aware of what actions I have taken."

"But killing is morally wrong! *It just is*!" cried Elizabeth. "I thought I could coax myself into it and commit the act without feeling any repercussions, but I simply can't. My conscience won't let me. Maybe I'm just a weak woman…"

"You talk as if 'thou shall not kill' from the Bible is the only way to look at morality. But you would be wrong. There is no god to save us. We must save ourselves, and that means killing those who have forgone all value and harming others. The good kill in self-defense."

"But what you are doing is not self-defense at all! You are taking money from paying clients, not giving the criminal a fair trial, and killing them without even allowing them to explain or defend themselves. What if that man really didn't assault his wife or kill his mother or gamble all their money away, Conrad?"

"I always sit down with a client and we go over thoroughly the criminal's history and then I make a judgment. Are you trying to suggest that more people voting or judging about a problem makes it a better conclusion?"

"Not necessarily…I guess, no. But who put you in charge?" asked Elizabeth, feeling relieved that she could finally express her true thoughts to Conrad.

"So then, a single individual can do a lot in this world. Why can't he be moral and weigh the crimes rationally and then execute the punishment himself?"

"There is already a system put in place for that. It's called the law! Why should you meddle or reinvent the wheel?"

"Because I can and I find I am good at it," said Conrad, offended that she did not trust his judgment.

"Then become a lawyer!"

"Why should I when the law never punishes the criminals with what they deserve, namely torture?" asked Conrad, still stirring his spoon around absentmindedly in his bowl of now mushy cereal. "Besides, the killer has the time to kill with intent, while the victim of the killing does not. So, if the victim pulls out a gun and shoots, then their killing does not even fit into the moral realm since morality is only available to a person who can make a *choice*. The killer is playing in the field of morality; the victim is not. So, the onus of proof is on the killer and not the victim. The act of self-defense cannot make a man good or evil—it just is the act necessary for survival, just as is putting your hands out reflexively to stop a more damaging fall. Do you see what I am saying here?"

"Yes, but this is *not* a case of self-defense, like I said before. You chose to murder this last job because he allegedly killed his mother, among other illegal things. Is there room for 'an eye for an eye' kind of retribution here? Does the criminal forgo the right to life once he has taken the life of another?" asked Elizabeth, furrowing her brows in considerable concentration.

"Yes. I believe that there is no moral grayness that people, especially artists, like to describe. There may be a series of gray actions that lead to an overall morally good or morally bad human being. And I think that this can change over time. Maybe this man that we killed yesterday started as morally good and perfect as a child, but then he chose to pick away at this goodness one poor action at a time. Now, he has worked up over the years to the point of killing his mother—killing being the ultimate crime. As soon as she stopped breathing, he lost his rights. Then, people like me come along and take them to serve justice."

"But the legal system is there to do that! Not everyone has a moral compass like you do, dear. That is why things can get out of hand quickly when all of society starts to 'take the law into their own hands.'"

"Don't you think I realize that, Elizabeth? That's why not everyone does what I do as a job."

"Then why not work with the police and the legal system?"

"Because they have gone soft on crime in this country."

"Well, then you want us to go back to our colonial days of hanging witches and heretics?"

"That's not what I said," growled Conrad.

"Then what you are doing still makes no sense to me," said Elizabeth.

The two were back at a standoff and neither looked like they were about to back down.

"I still love you, Conrad. But I don't know how to feel after this conversation. I don't believe in unconditional love—it has to be earned. I think love, in its pure and limitless response, can vary in intensity based on shared values. I love you for your values. I love that you care about being morally good. I love that you want to see justice served. I love that you are emotionally strong for me. But my love for you is not static. It changes every day, just as you and I change.

"As you said about morality—a person can start off being morally good and then turn bad later or vice versa. And my love for you reflects that. I loved you more before all of this started."

Elizabeth had to look down to avoid Conrad's teary eyes. He had never been so close to tears in all the time they had known one another.

Still, she persisted: "I felt more intensely about you before all of this torture and killing. Now, I feel as if I've been sucked away from you and forced to live inside of my own head, struggling with my conscience and paying attention to how my insides feel all day long. The torture you…we participated in is having its effects on me long after the physical bits cease. Conrad, I'm too shaken morally to love you as deeply as before, though I want to. But the law does not allow random civilians to take their revenge on others. We will get in trouble and what would I do then? You are choosing a series of morally bad acts, and I am afraid of losing you entirely to them." Elizabeth wiped the tears from her cheeks, but they kept coming, falling faster with each moment of icy silence that passed.

Conrad felt numb. He could not bear to feel what she was saying to him. He wanted to be the man she fawned over forever. To lose her love was devastating. To lose the love of her soul was worse than death.

Finally clearing his throat, he said, "Take a look out the window, dear."

"What, why?" Elizabeth was suspicious and another wave of distrust made her hesitate to turn her head around and away from him.

"Do you see the dogwood that is outside? It is all fiery red and if you inspected it up close, then you would see its crimson-colored berries?" he said.

"Yes. I am fond of that tree. I didn't know what it was called before."

"It is a dogwood tree, and in the Victorian era, couples exchanged the white flowers that bloomed in spring to show that love could endure any trial that came in their way. My point being, love, that this too is just a trial. We can learn to overcome it. Not all is yet lost." Conrad gently cupped his palm over her hand, encapsulating it entirely with their larger size. Elizabeth felt the warmth emanating from his skin and she felt the sweet tinge of home. She so *desperately* wanted to go home.

In her desperation, Elizabeth told herself that this was merely an obstacle over the next few days. All of this was just a learning experience for a couple of rational beings who had to learn what secular morality was all about.

Her rationalizations only went so far in helping her emotions. From one moment to the next, she could be feeling almost normal and then a captive of her own internal slideshow. Elizabeth felt cool to the touch, but then she would sweat profusely. In her mind, there was no more silence. Oh, how she *longed* for silence!

But peace did not come. Rather, cleaning the manor over and over again soothed her aches and pains to a degree. And Conrad watched her unraveling uncomfortably.

He tried to put his hand on her shoulder, but she pulled away. Then he would attempt to help cook their meals only to frustrate her and only manage to get in the way. Her unhappiness in the home tainted all thoughts for everyone. There was no more room for happiness.

"Elizabeth, *please*, how can I get out of this purgatory you've put me in? I haven't worked in days for you."

"Try quitting. Try proving to me that at any minute, the police won't be knocking on our door. Try giving me a new soul—one that is untainted by the sight of death." Elizabeth was putting the dry dishes away, and she made sure to place them back with as much force as was possible for a woman. The incessant banging set Conrad off.

"All right, *enough*." He grabbed Elizabeth's wrist and held her to his chest. Conrad did not let her go and kept her there. He knew that the way to soften her up was to hold her. She finally sobbed with fresh tears onto his chest.

"I'm so miserable and tired, Conrad. I don't know how long I can go on like this. Nothing in this house will ever be clean again…"

"I never wanted you to feel this way, dear. I'm so sorry. I—"

Both of their heads whipped around to the door. A stern knocking came from it and the Fleischers knew who it was.

"Open up! We have a search warrant for your address," shouted the male voice from outside of the door.

"I knew it. *I knew it*!" cried Elizabeth.

Conrad shook his head, the look of fear flashing across his face, but only for a second as he headed for the door. He passed from the dainty, feminine kitchen with its petite wooden chairs through the more masculine parlor with its strongly colored walls and up to the front door. His opulent wealth serving as the background, he hoped, would dissuade the police from messing around with anything.

"How can I help you, officers, today?" he asked, squeezing his fingers into a fist behind his back.

"May we come in?" Two male officers stood in front of the doorway, one with a foot already halfway in.

"Yes, just please make sure to remove your shoes. My wife just vacuumed the floors," said Conrad, watching the officers deliberately ignore him as they entered. His fist clenched even harder than before.

"There was a body found in the nearby cemetery this morning and the groundskeeper said he saw a young woman fitting your wife's description in the area before opening to the public. He said she claimed to be walking this morning and happened upon a dead bird in the cemetery, causing her much distress. We have taken the body out of the freshly dug up earth and sent it to a doctor for a proper autopsy. We need to know what you were doing between last night and this morning." The second officer withdrew a pen and pad to take notes. Elizabeth began sweating and Conrad squeezed his fingers so tightly into balls that they cracked.

"Well, last night we were at home, officers, eating dinner, watching something on the television, and then going to bed. My wife was out for a walk this morning because she was not there when I went downstairs to eat breakfast. But she came home without a word about seeing a dead bird on her walk," said Conrad. He was so calm compared to Elizabeth, who was now seeing stars and black patches obscured her vision of the men.

"Ma'am, do you usually walk in the morning?"

"I—" but she could get no more out as she fell unconscious to the floor. Conrad dove first to try to catch her and he managed to keep her head from hitting the floor. Propping her legs up with a pillow, he went to the sink and wet a towel to place on her head. The officers watched from a distance as Conrad took care of his wife. The second officer took a note down that must have been damning of her guilt.

"Please, you are distressing my wife. As soon as she comes to, can we have this discussion outside without her?" pleaded Conrad.

"We can start questioning you and then question her separately. I'm afraid she cannot be excluded entirely from our investigation," said the head officer.

After several seconds had passed, Elizabeth woke up on the floor, looking around in her dismay.

"Everything is okay, you just passed out," said Conrad to her. "Let's get you to the couch and I will go speak to the officers. Okay? You just rest."

She nodded weakly as he helped get her up and over to the safety of the couch. He covered her with a blanket and accompanied the two officers out of the house and onto the long wraparound porch.

"Please, take a seat, officers," said Conrad, maintaining his calm.

Then, the Miranda warning came: "You have the right to remain silent. Anything you say can and will be used against you in a court of law. You have the right to an attorney. If you cannot afford an attorney, one will be provided for you. Do you understand the rights I have just read to you?"

"Yes," said Conrad.

"With these rights in mind, do you wish to speak to me?"

CHAPTER III

Conrad paused for quite a while. He knew he was in the right. But he also knew that he should stay silent and ask for his attorney. Then an image came to him of one of the officers hanging in the formal parlor. The image grew in size and detail the longer he sat in silence. It was just awful. Conrad's mind was a frightening place, and yet, he used it for good. He was the equivalent of a cop himself. He should have nothing to fear, he thought. It was all a misunderstanding, and he had to prove that concept for his own sanity, so he said: "Yes."

"Did you kill this man yesterday and bury him in the cemetery?" asked the primary officer. He looked up at Conrad and his bald head formed wrinkles like those of a shar-pei. The other officer kept his head down, looking at his notes. He was much younger than the other cop, probably even in training, and he still had all of his hair.

It was time for Conrad to explain the misunderstanding. He cleared his throat and sat up straighter: "Gentleman, I am like you. A citizen of our community hired me to serve justice for those who have been wronged. I researched this man's background. He murdered his own mother and assaulted his wife in order to steal money from them to gamble. He was a criminal."

The officers remained quiet, plucking at the delicate nerves holding Conrad to his seat without trembling. Their silence was meant as a signal for him to carry on. It was neither an approval nor disapproval of his actions. They just wanted him to keep speaking. But he had to know from them he was good.

Conrad flexed his shoulders back, attempting to stretch while increasing the length of his spine. Even sitting, he wanted to appear powerful and sure of himself. He carried on, saying, "I realize that I have free will and I had the choice to make about whether or not to help out my community. Maybe I should speak to one of your higher-ups? I mean, this is not my first time dealing with the police. I have taken justice into my own hands before, and you guys never felt the need to come after me. Sometimes the law does not dish out punishments fairly. Am I right?"

He paused, observing the faces of the two officers, but neither moved much. They were trained not to show their cards.

"Look, I know what you guys are thinking, even if you cannot admit it here. The law needs men like us. We are the aggressive good guys, if that's how you want to see it. We make sure that the criminal knows what wrong they have done. We stick their faces in it, 'an eye for an eye' style. Right?"

Still, there was no answer.

"Yeah, well, those who are evil commit crimes intentionally. This man knew that killing his mother and assaulting his wife was *wrong*. He was not like a schizophrenic man who was having a psychotic break from reality. He made certain calculations and acted on them, presuming that he would get a simple slap on the wrist or, at worst, sit in jail and be fed three meals a day with an added recess. He committed a crime because he thought he could get away with it. Well, *I* made sure that he knew what he did was wrong. The law would not have given him the physical punishment he deserved."

"What about all the other prisoners?" finally added the secondary officer. "They often harm other inmates, especially when their crimes involve children. Of course, the guards are supposed to stop it, but sometimes those criminals get taught many physical lessons repeatedly in prison."

"Right, but I don't want to take that risk of them never finding out how wrong they were," said Conrad, encouraged that at least one of the officers responded to him. "The morally bad just stand by and follow along, while the truly evil people intentionally harm others. This man was *evil* and since he was deemed so, he gave up his right to life the day he murdered his mother."

"That's not for you to decide, sir," said the main officer, speaking up for the first time.

"What do you mean? An individual cannot decide, but an anonymous, nebulous body called 'the law' can? That's ridiculous!"

"The law does not permit any kind of retaliation or revenge from civilians. What you did is illegal. Do you understand that?" asked the primary officer.

"No. What about soldiers who individually kill enemies when at war? Are they not allowed to kill?"

"Soldiers are representatives of the government. They work for the legal body. You are a civilian who has no right to coerce or harm another human being. And even if you were in the army, let's say, you could not just kill anyone—you have to kill the enemy targets that the government tells you to. There is not meant to be any revenge, or even emotional killing, committed during times of war either. There are rules."

"I'm not the one with emotions while I kill. I am doing it for the victims. My methods are all measured out according to the crimes committed."

"Sorry, but it just does not work that way anymore. Things like honor killings in the Middle East and societal mob killings are atrocities committed by third-world countries whose laws are not just in the first place. You are opening the door to more people who believe that they can represent 'the law' alone."

"I have been an asset to the police force. Just hire me on the team then. I have proven myself to be useful and just. I am a *good* man," he said, running his fingers through his hair. "I'll become 'legitimate' in whatever way you guys want, but I am not a criminal. I am *not* the bad guy."

The officers glanced over briefly at one another before asking to speak with Elizabeth. It was her turn to speak up.

"Sure, let me see if she is well enough to get some fresh air out here with you two," said Conrad, wiping his sweaty palms on the front of his pants before grasping the ornate doorknob. "Elizabeth, honey, the officers would like to ask you about the man they found with you outside."

Elizabeth sat up on the couch. Her hair was matted and scruffy. She looked in no shape to be speaking eloquently for herself in front of the police.

"Maybe I should tell them to come back another day...," said Conrad, feeling her forehead. "Would you like me to try?"

"No," she said, "I'll just worry about them for longer if I don't say anything to them now." She pulled herself up off the couch and shuffled toward the door. The light poured into the dark manor and blinded her.

The officers glanced up at her as the front door creaked on its hinges. The heavy wooden door was carved with intricate floral patterns. There was the poisonous hemlock carved in its white clusters, which would make Socrates quake, for death was behind this door that kept all the living out. Along with the hemlock was honeysuckle, with its long insect-like flowers protruding in all directions. To the Victorians of the era, it was meant to represent devotion and affection. And the final floral was hyacinth, begging for forgiveness with its cheery-looking head of flowers. It looked like a cotton candy treat on the door. What was the woodworker trying to say? That something horrible was happening inside but out of love, which must be forgiven? Yes, Elizabeth had now understood that her fate was already written in the manor's facade.

She strained to walk forward, one foot in front of the other, paralyzed by her own body as if it knew that she was walking toward death. Life in prison, for instance, would certainly be akin to death, she thought. "Hello," she coughed, "may I sit here?" Elizabeth pointed to the swing, which she hoped would finally break from its rusty chains before the questions became too damning.

The main officer cleared his throat and read her her Miranda rights before asking: "Ma'am, we have reason to believe that you know about the murder of the man that we found buried in a shallow grave this afternoon. Is that true?"

For a brief second, Elizabeth looked up at Conrad.

"Eh, eh, eh. No looking to him for any guidance. We want *your* testimony. Sir, please step back inside the house," said the leading officer. The secondary officer guided him firmly back into the house, keeping an eye on him while the questioning continued outside.

"Okay, now, do you know about this murder?" asked the officer.

Elizabeth shifted uncomfortably around. She had a chance here to choose whether to save herself or Conrad. "Can he hear us?" she suddenly whispered.

"No, the door is closed. Tell me what's on your mind."

Elizabeth's voice seemed to shift up an octave and as she spoke more softly, in no more than a whisper, she sounded like the most innocent child. "I love him so much. I would *die* without him. But he made me help..." She would not continue unless the officer prompted her with a more direct question, proving that he knew more.

"Help...do what exactly?" He had his pen at the ready for any incriminating statement she was about to make.

"Kill him."

The officer wrote the statement down before asking: "How did Conrad kill him?"

"An ax."

"An ax to what part of his body?"

The officer observed Elizabeth's face turn green, and she hurled herself to the porch railing to vomit up everything inside of her stomach. The rocks below the front of the house were covered in her sickness, which the officer got a waft of when the wind blew.

In his disgust, he moved his chair back to save himself from the odor. He took notes about her behavior, and she noticed.

"Can I just say that I would *never* have helped if it wasn't for Conrad? I love him. I am his devoted wife. We made *vows*."

"Ma'am, you didn't answer my previous question: How did Conrad kill the man found today?"

"An ax."

"I got that. What body part?"

Elizabeth just shook her head.

"An ax to his legs?"

There was another shake of her head in disagreement.

"An ax to his torso?"

Then came another shake of the head.

"An ax to his head?"

Another shake came, though it was noticeably less forceful this time.

"An ax to his neck?"

Feeling nauseous once more, Elizabeth only nodded her head up and down. Verbalizing such a crime was too much for her, even if she was forced into it.

She stared at the wooden door and wished that she could consume hemlock right now to hurry on the paralysis she was already feeling and only death would loosen.

"All right, so Conrad killed the man by cutting off his head with an ax?"

The rocks were plastered with fresh sickness.

The officer waited, figuring that the more exhausted she became, the more she would reveal. "And what did you do exactly to help?"

"I mean, the only thing I did was help get the things needed to bind him..."

"He was bound to what? Where?"

"To a wooden chair downstairs in the basement. All I really remember was being upset that he would ruin one of our nice wooden chairs. Chairs can be expensive, you know?"

The officer nodded and smiled. He knew when a criminal was trying to change the subject. "Okay, I think we got a good start here. I am going to be taking you two down to the station for more questioning, while I get a team out here to inspect the basement further. Please turn around with your hands behind your back."

***

The handcuffs were cold and hard around Elizabeth's wrists. In shock, she followed the police officer like she was struck dumb. Conrad understood the gravity of the situation when he saw the cold steel behind his wife's back.

"No," he said, "take those off her right now. She hasn't done anything! This is about me and my job right now."

"Please turn around with your hands behind your back. I would like to remind you we are armed."

Conrad began shouting, "This is preposterous! I am on your side! What did you *think* I meant when I said that? I am not lying. I took care of a bad guy *for you*. Besides, this is *not* her fault. Elizabeth, what did you tell them?!"

His ire turned on her now as they were both taken to the police vehicle outside of their front door. The door that warned all the neighbors in its own quiet way about its inhabitants.

Some curious people watched as the two attractive individuals who were rarely seen outdoors were being escorted into the well-known vehicle with the red and blue lights. Within the hour, the entire block would know who was arrested.

Elizabeth sat next to Conrad, her hands uncomfortably still behind her back. She wished she could give Conrad a bouquet, something in it with hyssop and ivy. The tall purple flower would remind him that this was just a new beginning, perhaps a cleaner one, and the green, luscious ivy, her pure attachment to him, no matter what happened to them while waiting in jail. But there were no flowers in this confined space that smelled of vinyl and cigarettes.

All she could do was look at him, or at least try to, for he was keeping his eyes purposefully averted. He knew she had betrayed him. And his only form of revenge was to not say goodbye. Large tears rolled down her cheeks. The officers glanced in the rearview mirror, watching her silently weep. They both knew that she was racked with guilt. They were guilty.

It did not take long to arrive at the police station. This was it. The last time that Elizabeth may ever see her love, her soul mate.

"Conrad, please, look at me," she whispered, as one officer opened the car door for her. "Please!" she screamed in his face. Her spit touched his cheek, and he wiped it off without hesitating. It seemed he wanted nothing to do with her anymore. Did he no longer love her? Was it possible? She felt out of breath all of the sudden, a weight dropping on her chest, growing dizzy without oxygen. In a way, she was glad that the handcuffs were on her and the police were watching because she was afraid of imploding. Right there, she would have found the nearest ledge to jump off or the closest body of water to drown herself in. Or what if she could self-combust? Losing Conrad's love was worse than dying in prison. In her current state, she knew it must be true.

The assisting officer pulled Conrad from the other side of the car. He walked straight away from Elizabeth, his back turned to her.

She could not take this insult. She had killed for him. She had felt the flames of wild jealousy for him. For what? To die alone in prison? No, no, *no*. Elizabeth screamed, "I love you!" But he kept his back turned, and that was the last she saw of him.

***

The officers kept them separated, even during the intake process. Both of them had to repeat their information separately to the police, have the items on them sealed in a bag and taken, and their fingerprints and faces recorded into the system.

Each of them was led into different interrogation rooms. The white walls and plastic chairs and table, with the hideous fluorescent lighting, made them both feel sick and cold, an awful preview of how time stops in prison.

Both Fleischers waited in their rooms for hours, marinating in their own feelings. The police seemed to be waiting for the sense of shock to thaw, though they knew that the shock may very well never disappear for either.

Elizabeth sat in the corner of the room, making herself as small as she could, trying to render herself invisible, like an insect. The camera showed her trying to press her head down in between her knees, like in a sitting up fetal position. Perhaps sleeping would cause her raging headache to quiet and her intestines to unwind. She had already glanced around the room for anything sharp or useful to end her current misery, but there was nothing, nothing at all.

Meanwhile, Conrad sat upright in his plastic chair. It was hard and uncomfortable, which is exactly what he wanted. He pressed his thighs against the edge of the seat in the hopes of cutting off circulation, allowing him to take his mind off any pain he was experiencing. And at that moment, *everything* was in pain. His soul was on fire. But he sat upright like a tin soldier, waiting for his time to speak to someone in charge and prove to them he was not the bad guy. It was all a misunderstanding. It was a bunch of men just doing their jobs. They would agree with him once he proved that his work was sound, and the law was soft on crime.

The Fleischers remained lost inside their own minds, as if the strength of their thoughts could be shared across walls. As the time spent separated wore on, they both craved the other's touch. Elizabeth wanted *nothing* more than to be back in their home and laying in each other's arms. Conrad desired the same. Without the cloud of morally questionable actions hanging over their heads, they both still believed that they deserved love.

But love was no longer offered in the four walls that kept each of them separated from human touch. Human interaction was going to be heavily limited from now on, it seemed. The couple still felt connected by the bonds of marriage, but how long would it last when separated?

Hiding in between her knees, Elizabeth imagined the story of Lamia, a bride from ancient Greece who is about to marry a knight, but he discovers on their wedding night that she is, in fact, a half-serpent. After his shocking discovery, Lamia disappears, and the bridegroom dies from grief.

Elizabeth felt very much like a snake hiding in the lavender, betraying Conrad as she did to the officers today. His look of shock and anger burned into her memory. She was not a person to be trusted, and yet she did not realize that about herself until today. Women were just snakes in lavender fields.

She imagined making amends with him, though, by carrying in her serpent mouth a lilac as a symbol of reminiscence about their first love. What they shared, in the beginning, was perfect. *Life* was perfect then, before his job ruined everything. She sighed, reflecting on what they had.

In her mind, Conrad took the delicate flower and held it to his nose. Then he would kiss the very end of the bundle of petals and this would turn her back into a woman. The magic of his love could make her worthy again. She had to earn it back.

Between her knees, she promised herself that one day she would earn his love back. Elizabeth refused to consider another man—there would be no *other* man after what they had done together. For killing bound them together in sickness and in health. She only hoped that he felt the same.

At the same moment, from across several layers of wall, sat Conrad in his chair, losing the feeling in his legs. He concentrated on the numb feeling, imbibing it like Bacchus to wine. There was no room allowed in his mind for the flashes of the ax or the sounds it made cutting through flesh and gristle. Nothing inside his mind could bear more images of death. He was a man, and a man did not break down under pressure.

After all, he thought, this was all a mistake. Once he explained himself to a higher-up, he would be let go and so would Elizabeth. Elizabeth...her name should not be allowed in his mind either—no room. Conrad thought about her confession to the officers. Did she try to blame it all on him? Did she just break under pressure? What caused her to say anything to them? He wished that he could have told her before she went out there to just ask for an attorney and stay quiet. But he was wasting precious mental energy on what was hindsight.

Sitting there heavily leaning on the edge of his chair, he could not help but imagine the last job he tied up to a chair, forcing him to sit in the same spot for days on end. This brief glimmer of how much pain he must have felt just sitting in the same position gave Conrad a strange electricity of pleasure down his spine.

He recognized that even small things like sitting for too long can cause pain for a human being. And now, it seemed, that Conrad was experiencing the same feeling. He wished he could have Elizabeth here, stuck in the same position. He wanted her to feel pain at that moment.

She lost his respect the moment she opened her mouth. How could she betray him...them? he wondered. Perhaps women were just weak-willed. If he had only refused to go inside, then maybe she would have kept her mouth shut. Stewing in his own anger, Conrad shifted his weight just slightly onto his right leg, imaging the moments when he nailed down the man's hand and foot. The nail drove through the skin and sunk deep, deep down to Conrad's satisfaction.

Enjoying the sense of control, Conrad allowed himself to fantasize while sitting there. His left leg began to get pins and needles, adding to the intensity of his pain. He gave himself goosebumps.

Elizabeth should have adorned some nails in her for what she had done. Maybe the physical pain would have knocked some sense into her thick skull, he thought. Now, here we are, sitting in frigid rooms without a soul anywhere. He would not allow himself to believe that prison was to be their home for life or even something like an execution.

Death was not permissible for those who were in control. The phantom lost its kingly powers when a man proved himself fearless. Convinced of his worth, Conrad did not fear death.

In a way, his mind, the way it was wired to see images that frightened and boggled itself, must have come from the devil.

And the devil, as everyone knew, was the ruler of death. Either way, Conrad believed himself to be a good person and in control, and he would make a Faustian agreement if the offer was ever made.

He considered himself a survivor type above all, and he would make it through this hiccup too. With a rush of intense energy, the cameras showed Conrad standing up. The pins and needles made standing unbearable, but he committed to standing on his two feet until the sensations subsided.

Standing in that interrogation room, with his two feet firmly fixed to the solid ground, Conrad felt invincible. No one would tear him down. Nothing would make him bend. He would never, ever turn to a god figure to beg for forgiveness when he knew that what he did was right. The world around him was wrong, that is all. They were always slow to realize a man of genius.

Socrates was executed for "corrupting the youth" with his intellectual ideas. Writers of all ages died before ever being read by society. Artists and explorers and inventors of all stripes perished in obscurity and abject poverty. Conrad felt this to be no different. He had explained himself to the general populous who were too intellectually *lazy* to see that what he was doing was not opposed in any way to their beliefs—it was just different.

CHAPTER IV

Conrad was still standing up when the door opened and two officers appeared. They were the same ones from earlier.

"Hello, sir. We are here to ask you more questions about the body that was discovered today. We will read you your rights again first onto this recording device we have here." The officer read Conrad his rights for what seemed like an excessively large number of times already. "Let the record reflect that this is the time and place set for the interview of Conrad Fleischer. We are starting at twelve thirty in the afternoon in interrogation room 1A."

Conrad sat there, upset, folding and unfolding his hands in his lap. "Are you done? Look, I've already spoken to you two. You know I am on your side. Get one of your higher-ups to come in and talk with me."

"I'm sorry, but you're stuck with us for now."

"Then get me my attorney. I won't say any more." Conrad crossed his arms, closed off to anything more the officers had to say.

But the officers did not leave, rather they sat there for an uncomfortable amount of time, waiting for Conrad's fit to pass, and it did. He began unfolding his arms, slowly, ever so slowly, agonizingly hot in his body and mind. He uncoiled and asked: "So, what? I get nothing? No help? I asked for my attorney, you have to comply legally with that request. You said it yourselves multiple times now. I know the law."

The younger officer with the hair wrote something down and said before exiting, "You know the law says everything." Then, he went away, presumably to get an attorney for Conrad, while the older officer stayed in the room with him. He smiled at what his colleague said. "You know, he's right. You just admitted that you understand the law, which means you know that what you did was criminal. You killed another human being. You must face the consequences now for it."

Everything inside Conrad wanted to scream out and explain. He wanted to eradicate the festering going on inside his ribs. But he remained silent.

After what seemed like several more moments of awkward silence, the young officer came back with an attorney and some kind of detective. They all shook hands, exchanging pleasantries that nobody cared to hear. The men stood up like magnolias, each puffed up with the pride of dignity and goodness, as if no one in the room had perpetrated anything heinous.

"Let's try this again, now," said the detective. "We found the body in a state of decomposition that is commensurate with a body that has been dead for at least seventy-two hours, during which time the internal organs are all decomposing and bacteria are causing bloating of the body. Here are some photographs from the scene."

The detective knew that the shock value of Conrad seeing such images from the get-go might loosen his lips.

Conrad had never seen a body before after being dead for so

long. It made him sick and utterly disgusted with the thing that he regarded as disgusting enough in life. He looked for only a second and no more. Perhaps, if that is what Elizabeth had seen, she could not remain silent. She opened her mouth and only horror came out. Maybe she did not even say anything, but her behavior said it all. In those moments, lost in thought, the detectives watched his reaction closely. Conrad had never received so much attention in his life.

He sat back in his chair, attempting to maintain his calm. "Yes, that is him, and I imagine that is what he would look like after a day or so. I find it depressing we could even be made of such liquid stuff. But aren't you all forgetting what this man did?"

The detective spoke up again. It seemed he was going to be in charge of the rest of the interview: "The officers briefly told me about what your 'job' is. Have you done this before, sir?"

"What? Killing or torturing or what?" he asked.

"Anything of the sort," said the detective.

Conrad looked toward his lawyer, who just sat there like a blank slate, watching him, taking notes like they all were.

"Will you all stop taking notes?!" Conrad yelled. "You are recording this whole thing. Why do you need notes? I'm on your side. I only served criminals the justice that they deserved. I told you this time and time again."

"But you do realize that if everyone took the law into their own hands, then many more innocent lives would be taken than criminals? Is that what you want?"

"No, but I am not suggesting that all people do what I do," said Conrad.

"And who gave *you* the authority to take lives?" asked the detective.

"Who gave *you* the right? A body of people, I suppose? Some collective of morons who think they all have a larger brain together than separately?" Conrad replied.

"No, we follow the law that is written in books that many minds have updated throughout human history to help us make better-informed decisions with every case. The law is the most just way that we have to assure everyone is given justice. You have no such system."

Conrad shifted around, wiggling, in fact, in his seat. "I have read a lot about the law and it does not take a genius to know when someone has committed a serious crime."

"Do you realize that about yourself?" asked the detective, staring directly into Conrad's eyes.

"I am not mentally ill. I have a clear conscience, and I am sure that what I did was just, regardless of who here believes me. At the very least, I will not be sentenced for anything like that murdering, assaulting, gambler would have had he lived."

"Well, the legal system will decide what punishment you should get in due time."

Conrad dropped his head and visibly curled inward like a marigold. The men watched this man droop in the darkness of his own mind, unable to imagine the film playing inside of his head, while he grieved over his lost freedom. The law would deal with him unfairly. He was to become a martyr.

***

"Conrad, Conrad," said the detective, pushing his arm with a finger, "are you there?"

Conrad unfurled, tears rolling down his cheeks for the first time. "I realize now that the legal system will crush me regardless of whether or not I am right."

"No," said the detective, "it will give you the proper punishment for your particular crime—no more, no less. You could have made a citizen's arrest, acted as a servant of the law, and then given the offender over to the police. That would probably have been legal. But killing them without the right to a fair trial? What is to say that his wife wasn't lying to you? Do you know for sure he did all of those things? Can you sleep comfortably at night knowing that that is only one side of the story you heard?"

"Men like that are obvious. They do not need to be put through a trial that drags on for years and then the appeals process and, finally, an execution decades later."

The detective pursed his lips together before letting out a sigh. "Look, I can see your point. The legal process is always agonizingly slow, but it is the best method we have for making sure that everything is logically dealt with. Coming to conclusions based on little evidence is not enough to coerce another man, let alone *kill* another person."

"I wish I could have beat him with stinging nettles before I even killed him..." said Conrad. Then I would have sprinkled his body with mint to mask the smell of his decomposing corpse and stuck him somewhere less obvious. I didn't know until this morning that Elizabeth had been anywhere near the body. *Foolish* girl..."

"Okay, so clearly you are admitting to guilt. You killed this man with an ax to the neck in order to sever the head from the body. Did your wife do anything to assist?"

"No, let's leave her out of this... She doesn't deserve punishment. I dragged her into it."

"Which means...? She participated?" asked the detective.

"No. That's not what I'm saying. Please don't put words in my mouth. We are on the same team. I'm not lying to you.

She had nothing to do with my job."

"But she knows about the murder. She told the two officers here that it was with an ax that you brought down on his neck."

A sense of betrayal flowed underneath Conrad's skin. It washed up and down his body, causing him a series of uncomfortable goosebumps. "I mean, yeah, she knows about my job…but, well, have you talked to her yet?"

"She is next on our list here. Now, I have a few more direct questions here for you. Did you know this man who we are still in the process of identifying in the autopsy room? What was his name?"

"I never cared to ask. Makes my job easier, I guess."

"Okay, had you ever met him before?"

"No."

"So, how did his wife contact you? How did she find out about your 'services'?"

"Word of mouth, I suppose."

"And what exactly did she request you to do?"

"Punish him for his crimes. Serve justice."

"Did she specifically ask for you to murder him?"

Conrad looked up from the floor and stared at the detective: "Yes. As I said, I am a professional. I try to stay out of the whole thing emotionally, like any servant of the law."

"Well, just so we are clear, for the record, you are not actually a servant of the law, correct?"

"That is correct." Though Conrad glared at the detective for making him say it.

"Okay. I appreciate you sharing all of this with us without having to go around in circles, as many other people do in interviews."

"And what kind of people exactly are you referring to?

Criminals?"

"Well, the interview does not mean you have been charged with anything. We are just gathering information, so not everyone who gets questioned like this is a criminal, no," said the detective.

"Good, as long as we're clear on that. I am *not* a criminal, and that is why I am being open and honest about everything. Now, when you speak to Elizabeth, you need to be more careful. She is overwhelmed right now, probably in shock," said Conrad, feeling slightly better about belittling his betraying spouse. "She may say things that are just incorrect or inaccurate about me or about what I did. But I can assure you that I am calm and clearheaded about the jobs I have taken."

"I appreciate the warning. Is your wife always anxious or is this her state just due to the circumstances which are understandably very scary?"

"I would say she has always been anxious. She is a little woman out in a world with big men. That's part of what attracted me to her. She needs protecting." Conrad felt a pleasurable rise up his spine. He shifted his weight in the plastic seat.

"Right, so she may embellish the facts? Is that what you're saying?"

"I don't know, maybe. I mean, I've never seen her this anxious before, for obvious reasons. She's been ill more than I have ever seen her, just from her anxiety. The officers saw her faint." Conrad glanced over in the officers' direction, and they both gave a slight nod.

"All right, well, I'm sure that we will have more questions for you once we talk to Elizabeth. So, for now, the time is one o'clock and we will conclude this section of the interview. Off the record."

The detective took the recorder and pressed the off button. He stuck the entire device in a box and placed a sticker over the edge, sealing it closed. Then, everyone in the room signed and dated the sticker. The primary officer took the box back to the evidence room and everyone shuffled out after him. Not *one* person looked back at Conrad, and he was left alone once again. This time, though, he felt the fresh sting of loneliness.

***

The string of police officers, the lawyer, and the detective all went down the hall and entered Elizabeth's room. She was sitting in the corner, still with her head between her knees.

"Good afternoon, Ms. Fleischer," said the officer she had spoken to earlier. "This is our lead detective who is going to speak with you some more about the man we found today in the cemetery." He took out a similar-looking recorder to the one used with Conrad, laying it on the table. "Let the record reflect that this is the time and place set for the interview of Elizabeth Fleischer. We are starting at one fifteen in the afternoon in interrogation room 3B. Ma'am, can I ask that you please come take a seat up here?"

Elizabeth looked up at him from her lowly spot on the ground, like a child. She could no longer stand being an adult, especially not without Conrad around to support her. Her voice came out high-pitched and as fragile as birdsong. "Sure, just give me a moment." Crossing one leg awkwardly in front of the other, like a newborn doe, she staggered up and walked cautiously toward the chair.

Her eyes stayed secured to the floor as the detective tried to meet them with his own. Having given up his attempt at eye contact, the detective resumed: "Did you know the man before at all?"

"No."

"Did you know his name?"

"No, sir."

"Did you help your husband get this man to your house?"

Elizabeth pulled her head away slightly, before answering: "I watched."

"You watched? From where?"

"Inside their living room. He was watching the television."

"Who let you in?"

"His wife."

"Did she ask you to do this?"

"Not me, Conrad. Conrad did it. It was *Conrad*." This was not her speaking. Elizabeth had gone somewhere else since arriving in this white box. She felt like she was speaking to the wall, all alone. There was no way Elizabeth would be concerned over her own skin. She loved Conrad too much to blame him...right? In her confusion, her words fizzled out like a flat beverage and she remained quiet.

The detective wrote down some notes and decided to show her no mercy. He pulled out the pictures of the body right away and placed them in front of her. Perhaps this was a mistake, for Elizabeth's face went white.

"Did you kill this man, Elizabeth?"

No answer.

"Did you kill this man?" asked the detective, a bit firmer. "Do you know what you have done?"

"Me?" she asked. "It was Conrad. He did this..."

"Why?"

"Because it's his job."

"It's his job...okay. Do you think this kind of work is legal?"

asked the detective, carefully watching Elizabeth.

She squirmed about uncomfortably. "Not exactly…we argued about it."

"What exactly did you argue about?" Getting answers from Elizabeth was much harder than from Conrad, but the detective was patient enough to pull at one string at a time.

"…about the legality of it all."

"What is 'it all'?"

Elizabeth grew smaller and smaller in her seat. She needed an oak leaf for bravery, oleander for caution, some mistletoe for overcoming obstacles, myrtle for love, or even better, orange blossoms, like at a wedding for eternal love. Any of those plants would surely help to guide her now through the dark. Her throat closed, making it hard for her to say anything. Eventually, all that came out was a puny: "…his job."

"So, you thought his job was illegal, and he thought it wasn't. Is that what you are saying?" asked the detective, closing in on her minimal bursts of answering.

Elizabeth sat there blinking, frightened of what consequences lay ahead for her. She soon saw an image of nothing but a black square—a prison cell with no light or stimuli at all. She blacked out.

Waking up a few seconds later, the officers were fanning her with their notepads and just waiting around her. She had never lost consciousness so many times before. That also scared her.

Finally, a nod escaped and confirmed what the detective already knew. He decided to play nice now. "So, you are not in trouble. You did not take this upon yourself as being your 'job' and you only did as you were told by your husband, right?"

Her ears perked up upon hearing "not in trouble" and she

more quickly and easily responded in the affirmative.

"Did he physically hurt you in any way?"

"No."

"Did he emotionally hurt you in any way?"

This time she took longer to respond as images of his frustration and belittling talk rolled by like waves in her mind. Still, she said, "...no."

The detective noted something else down on his notepad. It was one of those black, waterproof pads that the officers always liked to use. She watched the notepad intensely, as if it was talking back.

"Okay, ma'am, now did you assist your husband? Tell me why you got in the car with him to watch in the living room and, apparently, witness other aspects of this crime occurring."

"I had to."

"Why?"

"Well, I *love* Conrad. I wanted to be a good wife and follow his orders. I'm also not the one who initiated any of this. *Conrad* did. I just wanted to be with him and, I guess, I was afraid of being abandoned. I *love* being his wife."

"You wanted to follow him off the proverbial bridge?"

"If he asked me to, *yes*. That's what love is to me. It is unconditional...I just wonder if he feels the same." Elizabeth closed up again, feeling wounded by her own half-truthful confession. She could only maintain her sanity through this trial if she believed that he still loved her. Otherwise, the end of her life felt too near. But could Conrad love her if he could also kill another human being? she wondered. Was deep love possible for a murderer? Could he feel both love and hatred at once?

***

She continued to sit in her plastic chair as if in a daze. There was no absolute proof for her to believe. Perhaps, like many soldiers coming home from war, they learned to live with the hatred for their enemies, all while still loving their wives and children.

Sitting on the edge of her seat, the rim cutting into her thighs, Elizabeth feared she may never get to ask him if he truly loved her as she loved him. Surrounded by four white walls for an eternity, left to contemplate his answer, would be the only activity allowed. Being left to think over and over again about her crimes. She became determined to not rot away in prison. Besides, she thought, none of this would have happened if Conrad had just quit this "career" of his and switched jobs. It was his fault.

Her facial expression darkened in front of the detective, who was concentrating on her every move. "So you would have done anything he asked of you?"

"Correct."

"Did you enjoy the process of his work at all?"

Elizabeth scrunched up her nose at the question before answering, "*No.* I got sick and felt awful many of those days. I *hated* it." But suddenly a whirl of images of her being thrust into on the basement floor, covered in that woman's blood played over and over and over again. Her hunger for more of Conrad and the pure ecstasy of doing it all in front of a woman she envied were only now perceived as wrong in her mind. Still, she refrained from saying anything more—determined to save herself, even if it was just long enough to ask Conrad for the truth about his feelings for her.

The detective gave a bit of a grunt, which signified a lack of belief on his part. But, being an expert, he moved on to the next question. "And you never tried to stop Conrad?"

"Oh, I did! *I did*! I said already that we argued. He got really scary when we argued."

"How so?"

"By raising his voice and sometimes he grabbed me..."

"So now you are saying that he *was* violent with you?"

Here was her chance to get out early. Here the path was laid plainly out for her. As a woman, after all, she was considered the victim before the man. She knew it. Everyone knew it. "I suppose I did not think that that was abuse...he was just mad. Maybe I'm still in shock. I don't know all the forms of abuse there are. Can grabbing be considered abuse?" Elizabeth lifted her eyes up softly underneath her long eyelashes and gave the most *innocent* look to the detective that she could muster.

It seemed to be working, according to her view. He took down another note on his waterproof notepad before looking back up, seemingly kinder in his facial expression. More softly, he asked, "We will let the legal system determine what was considered abusive behavior, but I am going to put down that he grabbed you and yelled. Did you yell or act aggressively back?"

"*No*," said Elizabeth emphatically, shaking her head from side to side. But what she did not tell the officer was that it was simply not in her nature. In fact, she enjoyed how physical he was with her. Elizabeth praised Conrad's dominance.

Briefly glancing up at the ceiling, she was afraid of pansies falling down like rain since they would clearly point to her thinking about Conrad and her love for him. Their violet faces would stare up at her from the floor of the interrogation room, forcing her to open up about how she felt. Meanwhile, a sea of peonies would burst through the door and squash the pansies with their symbolic presence of bashfulness. Their large pink petals curling inward to protect her mouth from speaking about him. And then she would pull out a single petunia from her bosom and hand it to the detective to express her anger in a fuchsia-colored rage. The black eye of the center sucking him into its black-holed void. The other men would run out of the room screaming, leaving the door open, allowing her to run to save her Conrad.

Elizabeth still loved him so. Conrad was her soul mate. She squirmed in her plastic chair just thinking about how he touched her, how he grabbed her with such vigor, understanding that she was alive and here in reality, on earth. She loved his emphasis added to his words when he became rough. Feeling his calloused hands on her arms, no matter how scared she felt, gave her weak knees and a fluttering heart. He was in charge; he was her very foundation. When Conrad held her, it was as if he was shouting to the world that what he wanted was real and physical—not hollow and mystical. He wanted me to be present in that moment of time alongside him, she thought. I followed, and I would follow him again. *I love him.*

"Why didn't you fight back?"

"...fear." That was the easiest way to escape from answering with the truth. Elizabeth knew that deep inside, what made her move was her masochism answering the call of his sadism. Her lust for pain and his for giving it. They were like magnets, and she had to escape prison now in order to reconnect with Conrad. That was her *only* goal.

"Okay, ma'am, I think those are all the questions I am going to ask you for today. Thank you for your time. It is now two o'clock and we will conclude this section of the interview. Off the record."

Once more, the detective turned off the recorder and placed it in its own box with the label everyone signed. The main officer took the box out, most likely to lay right on top of Conrad's, as if they were buried together there, or, at least, their crimes were.

No one said anything else either to Elizabeth once the recording was shut off, and she was left alone, much like Conrad. New tears flowed down her cheeks as complex emotions boiled up in her chest. She had to betray Conrad over and over again to have any chance of seeing him again. She felt like a lost puppy.

CHAPTER V

After the interview with Conrad, a couple of new officers took him to a jail cell. He let them put the handcuffs back on him and walk him toward his new home for the foreseeable future. Conrad remained unafraid. This was all a mistake, he thought. They will let me go once they realize their error.

Everything was bathed in sterile white, with only mustard-colored doors marking out any difference to the brick walls. He walked down a long corridor, the handles all made of stainless steel and enormous locks. It smelled of cleaning supplies, vaguely masking the scent of sweat. The faint bleach smell reminded Conrad of his home when Elizabeth had drenched the entire place in its horrid smell.

She had damaged his possibly last memory of their Queen Anne-styled house with her cleaning. A new sense of regret and fury filled his internal well. He wished their house was draped in curtains of Queen Anne's lace to provide protection from the outside. If only the white bundle of flowers could fold over the entire house, rendering it invisible to the human eye. They would have never been caught then.

Elizabeth could cover the inside with dark red roses to symbolize their love and maintain it within the walls of the manor. While Conrad could use poppies rather than chloroform to put his jobs to sleep. They would enter their secret hell and leave again without remembering a thing. But they would no longer be criminals because a lingering fear of what hell was like would follow them for the rest of their mortal lives.

Conrad did not want his jobs to remember him, but he did want them to remember the pain. If only there was a way for him to touch a button that would elicit excruciating pain to any person who committed a crime against another, then his job would be made much easier. But for now, men had to deal with Man. Men had to get dirty themselves in order to extract justice from those wrongdoers. It was a dirty job still, much like the gong farmer of medieval Europe who would collect all the excrement from within the castle and bury them outside somewhere.

This is the story that Conrad told before the judge a couple of weeks later in a brief statement. The judge sat high up in his seat, looking down at Conrad. His brows lifted when he heard Conrad compare his job to that of a medieval gong farmer, but the effect did not seem to do anything more than amuse.

Conrad was in shock now that weeks had passed and the mistake had not been realized yet. He was actually standing before a judge representing the state and judging his actions. The main point of his brief statement was that he was not guilty of any of the charges.

"Your Honor, I am *not* guilty. I was doing the law's work, only better by teaching these criminals a lesson that they actually would remember. I have thoughts, Your Honor...whether they are a gift or a curse, I've lived long enough to feel both... but I used my thoughts of killing for good, see? My perhaps sadistic tendencies were quieted by doing good with force. I cannot live in a world where criminals get off easy. They get three square meals a day in their cells and a bed to sleep in at night, usually until the end of their natural lives. What kind of punishment is that? Some people, do you not agree, do not deserve another chance to feel the joy of their next breath. A man who robs another of life should not get to watch another sunset or feel the grass on their toes. That's why I am there, making sure the laws are upheld."

The judge merely shook his head, like an old, doddering fool, Conrad thought. Within the next nod, he said, "Conrad, you cannot take the law into your own hands. You seem like an educated man. You should know better. The law has evolved from medieval times into what it is today precisely because of men like you, men who think they know everything about the conflict when they do not. Perhaps you have made an educated guess and are correct, but what about those you may have hurt that are, in fact, innocent? Would you not then become no more than a criminal yourself? It becomes too messy and unwieldy when individual people go out on revenge killing missions."

"But, Your Honor—"

The judge raised his hand suddenly, cutting Conrad off. "You have made your brief statement. I remain unconvinced. You are not leaving here without a trial and twelve jurors there to show you the error of your ways. I'm afraid you need more people to tell you that what you have done is illegal. You cannot take another person's life. True, you can legally make a citizen's arrest under certain terms, which then requires you to hand the accused over to the police. But then that person goes through the legal system. That is completely legal. You also have the right to self-defense. But you cannot go into another person's home, kidnap them, and torture them in your basement before personally executing them, sir. That is not legal and the fact that you still believe you are innocent, frankly, frightens me. I will see you again with your attorney for the pretrial phase before it goes to trial. Good day to you all."

With that, Conrad was led back to his jail cell, back to the smell of disinfectant and body odor, back to the tiny room with the bars and the bed and the steel toilet. His mind racing as he walked at the pace of the officers, unable to understand really what made their steps different from his. Fear cut his throat now, and he stayed silent in his cell for the rest of the night.

***

The next morning, Conrad lay in his cell with no will to open his eyes ever again. The scene before him was nothing but the white ceiling. Turning on his side revealed white bricks, and laying on his stomach was nothing more than a face full of white sheets. An endless sea of white followed him, which he strangely thought would be black. Nothingness to him was black, but here nothingness was white...which was worse was difficult to tell at the moment.

Either way, the smell of frozen, packaged food wafted up to Conrad's cell. The days were always the same: breakfast at six thirty, lunch at eleven thirty, and dinner at six thirty. The darkness began at ten until the morning started all over again. As long as he followed this regime of being fed, then he could pass the time.

But, again, this morning he could not eat. He could not rise. There was no Elizabeth to get up for, no manor to take care of, no job to keep his thoughts stable and well-fed. His purpose for living had been stripped from him at the door, all of his belongings taken, everything he called home. This cell was no home. This cell was not meant for a good man like himself.

Closing his eyes once more, he hoped to shut out the world and cover his eyelids with a snowdrop for hope, rue for regret, and rosemary for remembrance. The mixes of yellows and whites and purples would sink into his eyes and the fragrance fill his lungs with something other than the sterile white that surrounded him now.

The dead of winter dragged on. Everything was cold and white. From the few windows he passed, Conrad could see the snow falling on the jail and he knew now that time was passing without him. All of those plants he wanted were dead. Nothing could make the smell of jail go away.

In his cynicism, Conrad thought that perhaps the entire world would continue without him forever. He would die in this whitewashed cell and the world would have already forgotten him forty years ago. Children would have become adults without knowing of his existence. Never before had he felt so hollow as right now, laying in the bed, surrounded by nothingness.

But his body began to retaliate against his thoughts of a hunger strike. His stomach began bubbling, its form of protesting, he supposed. Then came the rumbling and afterward a feeling of acute pain. He felt like a bloated corpse, lying there with a stomach filling itself up with air. But he just kept ignoring it, hoping that it would deflate on its own. But the cold came and the shivers. His lips went blue on him and there was nothing but a thin, sterile sheet to cover his rebelling body.

In his pain, he fought harder and harder against the hunger. He knew his system would switch into survival mode sooner or later and then he could feed on himself for weeks before finally expiring in his own juices. But there was no water in his cell and water was necessary before three days' time when death would follow.

He knew that dehydration would happen quickly, causing him to feel extremely thirsty and tired before his organs failed and he expired. The toxins inside his body would accumulate without being removed through his urine and excrement; he would stop being able to sweat and grow hotter; the oxygen he breathed in would not be able to travel throughout the body; there was an endless list of cogs and wheels that would begin to deteriorate without water. Like a rusty wheel, his body would dry up and he would become a fine dust in his cell after all the juices running it were gone.

In a way, that kind of death felt cleaner than overindulging oneself to death, not that he could in jail, but withering seemed less messy. He would rather dehydrate like a pressed petal and stand on someone's mantelpiece, like Elizabeth's, for years to come. Of course, if he ever made it back to Elizabeth, he would be sure to haunt her for her crimes against him.

She told the officers on the porch, when they were still *free*, about the ax slicing through the man's neck. She told them the grand finale without even being stuck in a cell like this. How weak…*how weak*…was all Conrad could think, as if his cognitive wheel were already growing parched and sticking in place.

Elizabeth should have never become involved with him, thought Conrad. He should have never offered her dinner at his previous place. Instead, they should have walked right past each other on the sidewalk each day and kept to themselves. That way, no one would have been hurt or imprisoned and justice would have prevailed. Conrad would have never told them about the finale without them first knowing that he was the good guy. He would have made it clear to them before dooming himself to the white rooms and having to bear being next to the *real* criminals.

He *hated* it. He could not stand being placed on the same footing as those men who actually committed crimes and harmed other people. They were the first users of coercion, the first perpetrators—not him. I am good, he thought. I am a good man. *I am good.* The wheel stuck and spluttered, his stomach ached, filled with gas, he shivered there on the bed with the single sheet and flat pillow and smelled nothing but stale air.

If hell was truly cold in the center, then he was in the center. If hell was fiery hot around the middle, then he longed to be further out, closer toward the sun. This hell was freezing and stilted, as if everything was frozen in place. After all, the toilet was welded to the floor and so was the bed. Everything in jail was stuck in its place and forced to feel the endless cold for eternity.

***

Elizabeth, like Conrad, was taken to her own jail cell after her interview with the detective. She quaked with fear as the handcuffs went on her afresh and she walked along with the officers she had never seen before in a building she had not been in before. It felt like her first day of kindergarten all over again. Her heart raced as her parents left her there among all the other children and the teachers. She had never felt more small.

CHAPTER V

The hallway was white with mustard-colored doors that led to each person's cell. Elizabeth's cell was one among many, and she broke into freshly shed tears before the doors were even locked. She made herself sit on the floor as if one of her parents were watching and feeling sorry for her. She whimpered and whined loudly in her own way by sitting on the hard, cold floor rather than on the bed.

Elizabeth stayed sitting there until her eyelids grew heavy and the excitement of the day wore off and she fell asleep right on the floor, sans blanket or pillow. She awoke to the smell of microwave breakfast on a tray. Her stomach served as her alarm clock at six thirty, followed by lunch at eleven thirty, and dinner at six thirty in the evening. She did not know that Conrad was mirroring her habits in his own section of the jail, though she still felt connected to him in a spiritual way.

He was *always* on her mind, reminding her of how much she wanted to run to him. Even when she fell asleep on the floor of her jail cell last night, she still dreamed about him...though it was more of a nightmare than a pleasant dream.

She dreamed Conrad was behind her backside and pressed himself into her. His member was that of a thistle that went from the back of her all the way through to the front and out of her mouth. All she remembered experiencing was this choking sensation. She was suffocating on his prickly member that represented his hatred for people—all people—including her. Yet, in her sick, twisted way, she felt honored that he chose to penetrate her to express his hatred. She was still chosen out of all the other pretty little women in the world.

She choked and suffocated, remembering that thistles were used in the story of Adam and Eve. They were thrown onto earth with thorns and thistles on the land as punishment.

Elizabeth was clearly being punished by Conrad for betraying him. She never meant to confess so quickly, so easily, but he should have known that she was a terrible liar, a terrible keeper of secrets for her soul was pure, her heart full, and her sensibilities fragile, especially in the face of such tragedy.

In the final moment of her dream, before she woke up to realize herself on the hard floor, she watched in horror as Conrad pulled out and then poured mashed-up tansy liquid down her throat. The yellow flower bits bruised from being crushed and mixed into an elixir that would induce abortion so that nothing could grow inside of her after he relieved himself. As a form of hostility, Conrad emptied out her womb without asking her first. It was an act of war.

Elizabeth woke up on the floor feeling vengeful. Several mornings passed like this, with a sense of unfulfilled resentment growing in her heart. After a couple of weeks, she too was called in to see the judge for her arraignment.

Her brief statement comprised all the things she wanted Conrad to pay for. She talked about his strength and his grabbing of her. She spoke of his job and being dragged into it as a way of proving her love for him. She told the judge that nothing was initiated by her—it was all Conrad. Conrad was the criminal. She was merely the unwilling follower.

The judge, aged and covered with brown spots on his face, furrowed his brows as he listened closely to her pleas. What frightened her the most, though, was his seeming lack of emotion on his face as he was listening. His face showed nothing by way of sympathy for her.

"So, you see, Your Honor, I was merely a victim in this case. I mean, perhaps I would have even been Conrad's next victim," said Elizabeth. Squeezing her fingernails into her palms to stop her trembling, however, the shakes just moved up her arms regardless of her efforts to stop them. "Conrad used his power over me to use me, like a pawn, in his 'job.' I argued with him that this was criminal behavior, but he kept on telling me he was on the good guys' side and that the police always looked the other way before. Well, not this time. This time he was caught, and the law has clearly sent a message that what he did was not okay."

The judge nodded finally when she condemned the actions of her soul mate. That was the only acknowledgment he made toward any of her statements. He adjusted his position to the microphone and said: "Yes, Ms. Fleischer, I agree with you that the law does not permit acts of revenge or retaliation committed by one citizen against another. I have already seen and spoken with Mr. Fleischer and said as much. He still does not seem to comprehend that he cannot take the law into his own hands, for the safety of our whole community and the integrity of our entire legal system. You can make a citizen's arrest under certain circumstances, but that then involves handing the criminals over to law enforcement and allowing the legal system to do its job. He has heard that from me and now so have you. However, ma'am, it appears that we will have to go through pretrial and then trial with you too. We will need to look at the evidence presented as to how much you helped Conrad commit his crimes. That is the only way to sentence you properly. So, I will see you again with your attorney for the next phase of this long process. Good day to you."

A couple of officers took Elizabeth back to her cell, but she made a point to curtsy like a lowly servant to the judge before leaving. The only thing she knew in this life was how to serve. Perhaps it was her womanly pride that kept her servile. She wanted to be under some man's thumb—whether that was Conrad's or the judge's or even the officers'. Someone, somewhere, had to serve as her foundation.

***

The morning after her arraignment, Elizabeth lay on her flimsy bed with a single sheet over her body. She imagined she was dead and covered over with the pure white sheet. She flipped the top over her head, obscuring her vision.

Imagining the officers carrying her out carefully like a crushed flower, Conrad would be allowed to see her one last time and place a single red tulip on her chest, declaring his love for her once more. The precious tulip petals caressing her warmly as she is buried beneath the dirt under a willow tree. The tree would be out just beyond the jail gates and would remind Conrad forever to mourn the loss of his true lover.

Elizabeth imagined him watching the tree droop far downward with its branches, enough to caress gently the ground beneath it and sorrowfully embrace the tombstone carved above Elizabeth's head. Conrad would chew on the bitterest of wormwood to rival his unending pain at seeing that tree. He would wish that he was the tree, so at least he could forever be near Elizabeth's grave.

Yes, it was a vision that kept her going day after day, waiting for her pretrial followed by the trial with the twelve jurors who were expected to judge her character and her ultimate fate. But she knew somewhere deep down in her guts that she would never see Conrad alive again.

She was already in mourning, sitting there in her cell, just waiting. Elizabeth wished that she had worn all black when she entered the jail for the first time that day. It would have been more fitting for a grieving woman. But alas, she followed along with the routines of the day and looked somber enough to mask herself in an aura of darkness anyway.

Elizabeth stared deeply into the floors, as if there would be an answer to her end, her suffering etched there. She paid attention to the walls for the same reason. Maybe someone before her had written an enlightening word on the cell wall before being hauled away to prison. But there seemed to be nothing.

She did notice, though, that there was layer upon layer of white paint used throughout the jail. Maybe her answer lay beneath the paint. One day, which was indistinguishable from the rest, Elizabeth saved one of the plastic forks from breakfast. She used the cheap tines to scratch away at the uppermost layer of paint. After a while, the paint started to chip, but nothing was underneath that spot in her cell. So, she moved on to another spot and another and another until one side of the wall was completely chipped.

I have not gone far enough, thought Elizabeth. And so she dug deeper and deeper until the red brick beneath was exposed. However, by the end of the week, an officer caught her and moved her to another cell, a dirtier one, until they repainted over all the work she had done.

She passed the weeks by looking for an answer, even as the longest stretch of winter approached. The land beyond, when she got glimpses of it, was covered over with a blinding white. Often when catching such a sight, she wondered if the world mocked her from outside the jail, mimicking its interior white hellscape.

Wondering if whiteness represented nothingness or darkness, Elizabeth kept staring at the walls containing her. At night, when the lights went out by ten, she often considered what she had learned in a science class she once took where the professor filled her mind with fears about the death of the sun, this planet, and eventually all the stars to be sucked into a void by black holes and wondering if another big bang would start the universe all over again. Were there beings who erred as we did before? she wondered. According to her professor, darkness, an utterly dark universe, was nothingness.

Her teeth clicked together as she shivered at the thought. The hair on her arms stood tall with the running tingle of goosebumps. Elizabeth did not want the world to end. She wanted to *live*. She wanted to snuggle up to Conrad, even after all of this happened.

Thinking about what she told the judge, about Conrad using her merely as a pawn and how he may very well have killed her too, she still could not fully believe it. And even if he did end up killing her, then she felt willing to take that risk. For even after death, she thought, I will still haunt him. I will still be on his mind. He would never forget me then if he replayed every bit of my death in his mind. I would become a poignant staple to his subconscious and conscious mind. If he murdered me with his own bare hands, then we would never *truly* be apart.

This awful thought brought some amount of peace to Elizabeth when she lay there in her cell at night, when the dark nothingness frightened her. She thought about Conrad and how his fickle love was enough for her to survive on. Even the tiniest drop, an accidental drop, from her Adam was enough to quench her thirst for him. She still would do *anything* for him, no matter how much she wanted her freedom.

With each day that passed, she confirmed her feelings more to herself that Conrad would always be her foundation, and she was irrevocably tied to him already through the bonds of another man's death. They were inseparable. She could not thrive without her other half. In fact, Elizabeth worried she may cease to exist without him. If only she could have one more kiss to savor, one more hug…

CHAPTER VI

Conrad grew unrecognizably thin. His skeletal frame forced him to move more slowly, which, to him, was a gift. For with the slower physical movement, came slower thoughts. There was no more rushing and time hovered. He stayed stuck in jail, like the welded-down toilet and the bed, with no will left to move.

His attorney, with his neat suit and slick watch, rallied behind Conrad and asked him a million questions and threw all sorts of documents in front of his sallow face before the pretrial. Well, the pretrial came and went with no dismissal or offer from the court. Then along came the jury trial—the final sentencing for Conrad.

He was charged with first-degree murder of the man found in the cemetery. None of his previous jobs could be traced back to him with enough evidence to convict. But he was given life in prison without the possibility of parole for at least fifteen years.

Meanwhile, Elizabeth went through a similar process of the pretrial and then the trial. Her attorney advocated for her by painting a picture of abuse and utter power under Conrad's direction. Elizabeth was simply a quiet bookworm who got caught in a spider's web one day.

Her pleas of "Conrad made me do it" and "I just wanted to please Conrad" made the jury split—some believed her to be a true victim of Conrad's, while others found her to be just as guilty. They argued even longer over her situation than Conrad's jury did about his. But after two full days of deliberation, the jury decided to sentence her to manslaughter with a prison sentence of only five years. She won. She would be free in no time.

When she heard the final verdict, her soul snapped, and Elizabeth felt surprisingly pulled in two directions. She had already heard about Conrad's conviction and she felt dirty for portraying herself as so innocent. Was she not as guilty as him for feeling jealous and having sex in front of his victims? she wondered. But the jury did not know that and now they never would. She was a victim. She *played* the victim very well. Her tears in front of the judge and jury were proof of her sorrow and repentance and not for herself and Conrad.

Someday when she got out in five years, she would visit Conrad, if the officers even let her. Whatever prison system he would be hauled off to, she would follow. Her soul was tied to his. Elizabeth went to sleep that night hoping that he would never know how much she betrayed him on the stand—blaming him, accusing him, throwing his name down into the dirt all for her own freedom.

Now, more than ever, Elizabeth felt she deserved nothing more than the bottom of his foot. When she moved into her new, more permanent, prison cell, she would place her head on the cold floor for hours, imaging Conrad there stepping on it, squeezing the lifeblood out of her brain.

Her sense of self in prison was utterly demolished. Elizabeth felt unhappy and alone. The only thing that made her get up off her bed in the morning was being able to crawl right back to Conrad when she was set free. Her desire for freedom was not truly free since it all balanced on Conrad being there afterward.

She spent many a night imagining herself bringing him a bundle of yarrow to use as a salve, as Achilles did on the battlefield to heal his men's wounds. Crushing their little white heads to a pulp, much like her own deserved to be, she would offer it to him as a sign of curing his broken heart. The salve would be slathered on his chest, he would breathe in the fumes, and suddenly he would forgive her for her ultimate betrayal of her god.

Yes, she thought, I want his forgiveness…I *need* his forgiveness. I wish we could go back, but we cannot. Instead, I would simply ask for his forgiveness and offer to heal the wounds I opened in any way possible. My reward would be for him to just be with me, sit with him while I visit, acknowledge me. I suppose a proper husband and wife future together is over now, but we can still sit by each other and waste away together.

Clinging to this notion of aging together, she threw away any thoughts of children or a nice house or anything that resembled a normal life. Human beings were amazing, she thought, for they can adapt to situations so effortlessly. And she did adapt. There was no feeling of loss after she made up her mind that this was her new vision—to be as near to Conrad for as long as she could.

He dominated her thoughts, her very soul, even when he was not physically near her. Thoughts of Conrad carried her through her five-year sentence. No matter how many therapists she saw or classes she took on being independent and responsible in the outside world, her only goal was to serve him.

Never having been religious or devoted to Christ, Elizabeth could feel the power a man could have over a woman. She worshiped Conrad in more of an abstract sense the longer she was away from him. Perhaps by the time she got out of prison, her image of him was so far removed from the real man that Conrad would no longer serve her ideal form.

Still, that did not stop her from having faith that he would be there for her when she got out. He would always be there for her in any scenario that played out in her head. She kept seeing him cooped up in his cell, wide-eyed with tears. Maybe, as he got up to meet her at last, all things in the past were forgotten. Her heart beat joyously at the thought of seeing him again in the flesh.

***

As the first few years ticked by ever so slowly, Conrad remained incredibly thin. He continued to stay inside, avoiding the prison's hour of recreation outside. Any time that his attorney came in to update him on anything, he still accused the officers of making a mistake.

"I don't belong in here…with criminals," he would say to his attorney. But the flashing smile would come out and the agreeable, empty head nod and nothing more of substance.

"Yeah, I know. We fought hard for you, bud. And when you are eligible for parole, then we will certainly fight for a shorter sentence. Life without parole for fifteen years is really much too long for a man who was dealing with criminals and had good intentions," said the attorney.

"Did you hear about Elizabeth?" asked Conrad.

"Yes, yes, that sentence was much more lenient than yours."

"And how do you think she got her little five-year deal, huh? By blaming it all on me. That's how. I bet she said *I* did everything and made her do all the rest. But we all know that she wasn't forced. That's ridiculous! She loved me. She would do anything to keep me. You and I both know that, so how come the jury could not see that? What I wouldn't give to have been there at her trial…the lying whore."

"Conrad," said the attorney, "I know, I know. I need you to calm down, though, or I will have to talk to you from behind bars. She went through the legal system just as you did, and that is what the jury determined."

"That is why I *hate* it! This legal system is backward. It puts good men behind bars and lets mealymouthed women out in an instant!"

"Please, stop yelling, Conrad, or I will have to leave," said the attorney.

Conrad drew in a sharp breath before exhaling loudly. His nostrils flared as he sat there on his hard bed, thinking about the injustice and pain the courts caused him. "I'm afraid. I don't think I can make it for fifteen years. You cannot cut a good man off from society like this and expect him to thrive. Look at me." He hung out his wrist, which looked as delicate as a woman's. His flesh clung closely to his bones beneath. There was no muscle left.

"Conrad, hang in there, buddy," said the attorney, giving him a pat on the back. "I know this is hard, but think about the man you killed who has no hope of ever being free again. He is under the ground. You still have the ability to see and speak and hear and taste and smell. Think about how many things you do have. Just don't give up. Okay? I'll be back in with any updates as soon as I hear anything new from the judge."

Conrad only nodded. He knew he could still breathe and move of his own volition, but that almost made being alive even worse. For there was no *point* in his movements anymore. He had no purpose. He was a man stripped of everything that made him human, and now he was nothing more than an animal—an eating, sleeping, pissing animal.

Losing his purpose meant no more self-esteem about himself and his work and, therefore, there was no way to use his reason or his mind. Instead, he began focusing on thoughts of killing again, but this time, it was without a filter. Images of the officer providing him his meal flashed before him, all bloody and gory. Thoughts of stabbing the closest inmate with a plastic knife crossed his mind. Reels of pictures of the last job he did and the ax's whooshing through the air hit him over and over again. Soon he replaced the image of the man with another officer or inmate or even Elizabeth. Off with her head! he often thought to himself in his anger.

After all, he thought, she put him in here for the rest of his life. She deserves every bit of my anger, and he remained angry at her for days on end. Occasionally, though, he remembered her warmth and felt such a powerful urge to protect her pretty little head. He still had dreams about waking up with her in his arms like they used to together in bed. When he felt the urge, his fantasies were always about that day they rolled around covered in the blood of another woman. She had such a tight, fresh, youthful body.

But then a fresh wave of anger beat the dream from his head and he felt like being violent with her in retaliation. Sometimes his dreams went from sex and love to rape and the murder of Elizabeth within seconds. She deserved his wraith but, perhaps, after his anger subsided, he could go back to loving her. This cyclical thought process occupied much of Conrad's time in prison.

In fact, the idea of seeing Elizabeth once more kept him eating. But the scales of love continued oscillating between his hatred and love for Elizabeth. He never could seem to find the right balance. The scales kept teeter-tottering back and forth. Until he faced the reality that he would never leave this prison cell. He was devoid of purpose and skill and any meaning in his life now, so much so that he might as well have died after his sentencing. For he could not love Elizabeth in the way he wanted to anymore. He could not hold her or touch her, and touch for a man was essential. Without touch, he could never feel close to her again. He could never feel her warm, soft skin or kiss her full lips or cup her breasts in his hands. She was nothing more than a dream to Conrad. Elizabeth was gone, unable to be loved by him anymore, and he knew it was time to let her go...

***

On the day Elizabeth got out, five years later, she was hidden under a blanket, the press team snapping pictures and making what could have been a relatively quiet release a much louder one. They followed her—hounded Elizabeth—like wolves to fresh blood. She hid under the blanket and behind her attorney. Her day of freedom was finally here.

She spent her first hour on the outside breathing in the fresh air and walking around on the sidewalk of her attorney's house. He was allowing her to stay until she found work and then, hopefully, her own apartment. It was strange to walk around outside without the feeling of cold metal against her skin or a fence with spikes on it being an ever-present reminder of her captivity.

After a month or so, she had gotten a job as a waitress at some local, unknown restaurant and managed to get an apartment as close to Conrad's prison as possible. Elizabeth bought hair dye and clothes that hid her identity since she presumed she would not be allowed to see Conrad ever again, even as a visitor. At least, the judge said as much with his "you two are a danger to society when together." This was her first real chance to see him again. Even if the officers found out, maybe they would feel sorry for her and let her in. All Elizabeth knew was that she had to try because her life depended on being able to see her soul mate.

On that fateful morning, Elizabeth lived so close to the prison that she could walk to it. She had not asked for a preapproval to visit. She simply crossed her fingers and was willing to beg to get in. Arriving at the front desk, Elizabeth gave a different name from her own and claimed that she was a close friend of Conrad's.

The officer sitting there had no way to prove that she was a friend. Although once she heard the name of the prisoner, her face grew dark and sad. "Ma'am, I'm sorry to tell you this, but your friend died last night in his cell."

If the officer had said anything else, Elizabeth did not catch it, for she was seeing stars as soon as her mouth formed the shape of that final *d*. She fainted away from the shock. And the next time she woke up, she was lying on a bed in one of the cells.

"Are you okay? Do you need an ambulance?" the officer asked her once she came to.

"No, no…no, *no*!" Elizabeth grew frantic. "Say it again! Tell me I misheard. Say it again!" she screamed.

The officer told her again that Conrad had died.

"How? *How* did he die?"

"He starved himself, ma'am."

"Why? *Why* did he die?"

"I don't know, but perhaps the Lord knows."

"Forget what your god knows!" she screamed, bitter tears streaming down her red face. She clearly appeared as more than just a friend, and the officer presumed correctly that it was his closest accomplice and lover despite the different hair color, clothes, and makeup.

More officers swarmed around Elizabeth now as she was riling up the inmates, all peeping through their bars at her. Some mimicked her screams, others mocked them as if she had no right to be so upset. She let the officers carry her out, leaning on them for support as far outside as they would let her.

She needed to hold on to something before the world split in two and swallowed her whole. Elizabeth wished it would fall apart—everything—the apocalypse was upon her and it should be for everyone else too, she thought. Life was, indeed, over. Her own purpose in life had been taken from her. Her highest values were snuffed out. How dare he! she raged inside, boiling over in the form of froth around her mouth.

She could visualize Conrad laying in his cell bed last night, committing himself to make a point, like being on some kind of hunger strike for his own innocence. He was the good guy—he had always declared himself as such. He must have been starving for *weeks* beforehand…

Elizabeth could see Conrad's body thinning, his body feeding on itself through the breakdown of proteins to glycogen and fats. Then, his whole body survived off of his small amount of fat until proteins were used, dehydrating him further down to a raisin of a man. In the final days, he must have faded away from fatigue and succumbed to heart failure, brought on by the severe degradation of tissue. His insides must have looked barren.

Her heart ached at the thought of Conrad succumbing to anything, let alone his own body. If only, she thought, I could have been there to feed him and fill him up with my love. I adored him. But perhaps he figured he would never see me again or worse…he no longer loved me. There was no point in breathing again.

In some ways, Elizabeth understood his lack of purpose, forced to spend eternity in a small cell without love. But only now that he was gone could she understand what it meant to be without a base, without a home, without your soul mate. Fresh tears streaked down her cheeks as she crumpled onto the ground—a tiny insect turning over to die soon.

She could not start over again. It was simply not possible when she had committed such horrible crimes. The *only* one who could understand her soul now was dead. The prison she was in for five years did not kill her, Conrad did. By ending his life, he chose to take hers as well. But did he know that? she wondered. Could he understand what a woman truly desired in order to be happy? Did he know she needed him to be happy? And a life without happiness in it was no life at all.

***

Life was over for Elizabeth. She remained a hollow person, framed around the edges with hate and anger and resentment. How could Conrad leave her behind? Why could not he have waited until they were old and gray? she wondered.

The day that she discovered his death and lay in ruins on the ground outside of the prison, she stayed there until dark, only to drag herself back to the darkness of her apartment later.

Conrad had never touched the inside of those walls before, yet Elizabeth saw him everywhere. He was in her shower, in her bed, in her kitchen every morning.

By the end of that month, she no longer saw her reflection in the mirror but his. And she only left her apartment for food or other necessities, although even doing that became nearly impossible. Even though Conrad left her still a young woman, he made Elizabeth feel like an old widow. For she had always felt like they had known each other since birth, and then they had killed together and were punished for their crimes, and now life was over.

With each passing day, Elizabeth mimicked Conrad's final path. She grew thinner and stayed awake many nights in terror. Like a film rolling without a beginning or end, she was forced to see images of the ax, meeting Conrad for the first time, the blood everywhere, the bleach bottle, the abominable chair placed in the center of that back room. She could do nothing to stop the constant stream nor, in a way, did she desire to shut it all off, succumbing to the belief that this is how she would hold on to what she had left of Conrad.

If he wanted to haunt her, then so be it. Just as long as she could recall his voice and see his face and imagine what his arms felt like around her, then he could keep appearing in whatever form. In prison, she had kept fantasizing about their afternoon together covered in the blood of another, picking the fruits from the highest echelons of pleasure. If her life was over, then she could objectively declare that her highest ecstasy was in that moment and would never be felt again.

Elizabeth spent more and more time in her bed and less and less time leaving the apartment. She had missed work for three days without calling in and was presumably fired by now. No one came to check on her, and no one needed to, she thought. Everything was wrapping up nicely.

Elizabeth promised herself to never outlive the memories she had of Conrad. The most terrible part of surviving another is forgetting them entirely. With the passing time, people told her her wounds would heal, but they forgot to mention that they only healed due to her forgetful, truly horrible memory and fallible skill at retaining everything.

Of course, nowadays, there were photographs and videos made of Conrad, but *nothing* could contain his spirit and his touch—nothing but the memories she still held, both the good and the bad. And so, she stayed awake with her mind fully open to *all* the thoughts she had about Conrad. After a while, she feared that filling her time with new things would push out the old, so much so that she feared to move.

At first, each step was measured and only the most efficient steps were taken to feed herself. Elizabeth used to bathe before this ultimate fear overtook her and then bathing became optional before it was cut out altogether. She got up to use the restroom, but even then, it was only when she thought she might explode. She even managed to find a bowl large enough to use to cut down on any unnecessary bathroom trips. There she lay, often in the dark with the shades drawn, dreaming of Conrad.

Conrad was good, she thought over and over again. He only wanted to help keep society safe. He was a man of action. Evil was done intentionally by a person who wanted to harm the innocent. That was not Conrad...nor is it me. I am *not* evil. We were both sane and followed through on what we thought was best. She caught herself nodding as if seconding herself, though it may have been her muscles trembling.

She lifted her thin arm and let it drop on her chest. The bones were poking through the layers of sunken flesh.

Closing her eyes for a moment, she thought about Conrad actually choosing to kill her, as if what her attorney said was true. He was using her as a pawn who would just become another of his victims, eventually. But she just could not believe it. She could not reconcile his warm hold with the cold blade of an ax. Perhaps, if she had some food to fuel her weary mind…

She rolled over on her bed before unwinding, too exhausted to rise. Conrad was her god. Even if he had decided to kill her, at least she would be touched by him once more before the world ended. She would have preferred death at his hands than to lie here now, too weak to rise, too beaten down by the outside to stand.

Elizabeth lingered around like the dust falling around her, lightly coating the room with her final breaths. They were slow in coming and going in and out of the hollow cave made of ribs. She lay there, stuck in between images of Conrad and the weakness of her body. It was a torturous division. But the wisps of breath ceased with the setting of the sun and the world ended for Elizabeth.

She had placed so much stress on her heart that it grew weak and failed her one evening. On that evening, she was watching Conrad, once again, tie up the man found in the cemetery to a chair and lift the ax high above his head and bring it down with all of his weight. The awful cracking sound was the last sensory apparition she took in, and without enough water to produce tears, Elizabeth dryly wept to death.

CHAPTER VI

THE END

About the Author

Kaitlyn Bankson (born Kaitlyn Marie Quis in New York, January 3, 1994), better known by her pen name Kaitlyn Lansing, is an American writer. She studied literature and philosophy throughout her education, which shaped her creative voice. She is the author of the novels *The Paper Pusher, The Dormant Age,* and *A Man of Silence.* Kaitlyn's unique perspective and raw prose bring light to matters that are often left untouched. She lives in Dubuque, Iowa, with her husband. Readers can see more of Kaitlyn's work at www.kaitlynlansing.com.

You can connect with me on:

- https://kaitlynlansing.com
- https://twitter.com/kaitlyn_lansing
- https://linkedin.com/in/kaitlynbankson

Subscribe to my newsletter:

✉ http://eepurl.com/glJhKf